The Torso in the Town

By the same author

A Shock to the System
Dead Romantic
Singled Out

The Fethering mysteries
The Body on the Beach
Death on the Downs

Mrs Pargeter novels
A Nice Class of Corpse
Mrs, Presumed Dead
Mrs Pargeter's Package
Mrs Pargeter's Pound of Flesh
Mrs Pargeter's Plot
Mrs Pargeter's Point of Honour

Short Stories
A Box of Tricks
Crime Writers and Other Animals

Charles Paris novels
Cast, In Order of Disappearance
So Much Blood
Star Trap
An Amateur Corpse
A Comedian Dies
The Dead Side of the Mike
Situation Tragedy
Murder Unprompted
Murder in the Title
Not Dead, Only Resting
Dead Giveaway
What Bloody Man Is That?
A Series of Murders
Corporate Bodies
A Reconstructed Corpse
Sicken and So Die
Dead Room Farce

Simon Brett

The Torso in the Town

A Fethering Mystery

MACMILLAN

First published 2002 by Macmillan
an imprint of Pan Macmillan Ltd
Pan Macmillan, 20 New Wharf Road, London N1 9RR
Basingstoke and Oxford
Associated companies throughout the world
www.panmacmillan.com

ISBN 0 333 90530 X

3 5 7 9 8 6 4

A CIP catalogue record for this book is available
from the British Library.

Phototypeset by Intype London Ltd
Printed and bound in Great Britain by
Mackays of Chatham plc, Chatham, Kent

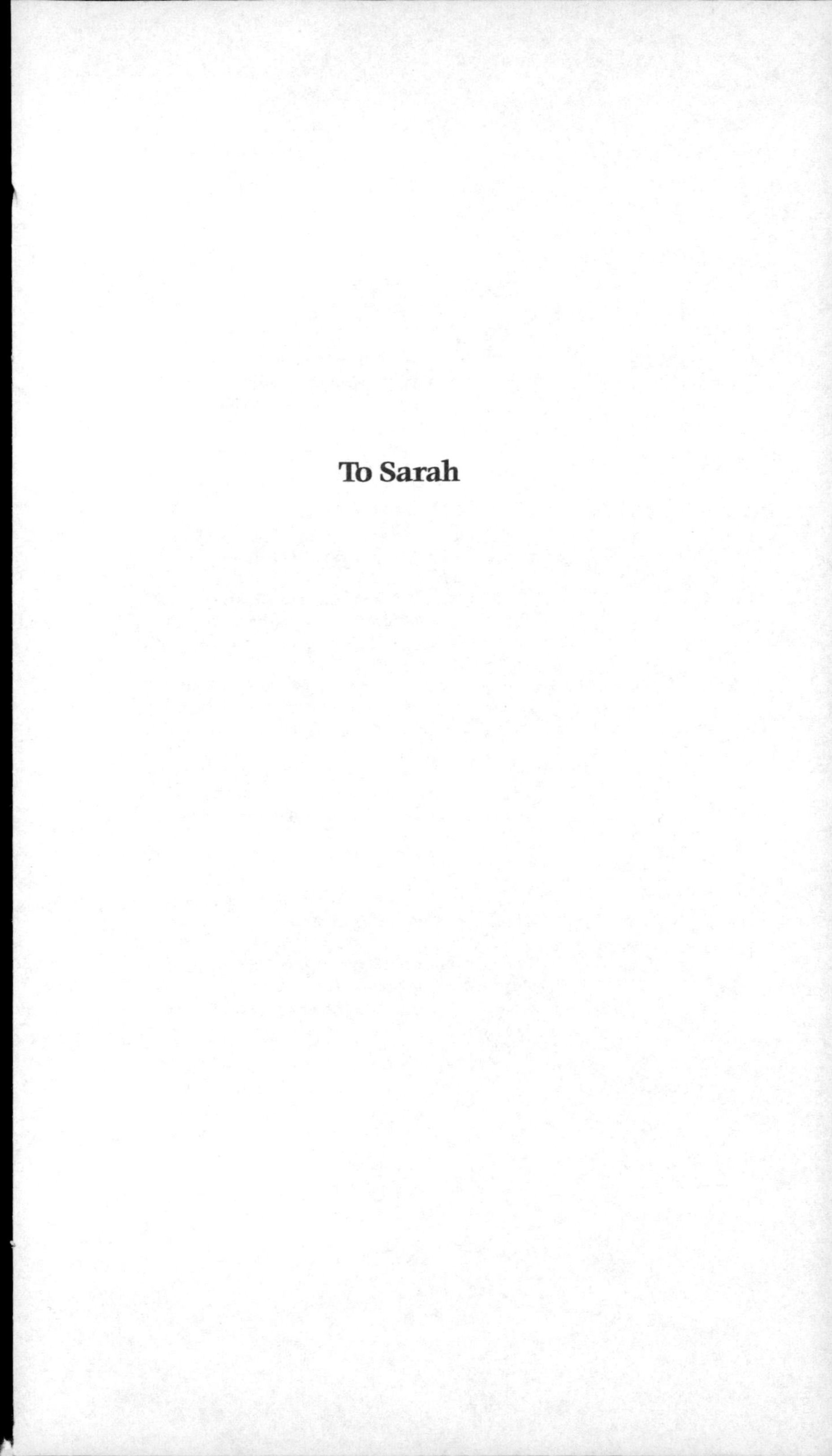

To Sarah

'God made the country;
Man made the town;
and the Devil made the little country town.'

Old Proverb

Chapter One

'The other thing about Fedborough,' said Grant Roxby that evening before the torso was discovered, 'is that everybody mixes together. There are no social divisions.'

What? thought Jude. He's got to be talking about somewhere else.

Fedborough was a country town some eight miles inland from where the River Fether reached the sea at Fethering. The town's considerable architectural splendours attracted tourists throughout the year; in the summer its streets were clotted with the elderly contents of coaches and adolescent foreign language students, wandering around looking for something to do. Most ended up in the antique dealers, tearooms and gift shops. Fedborough was the perfect venue for someone trying to buy an antique brass bedpan, a cream tea or a china figurine of a ballet dancer; less suitable perhaps for those in search of basic groceries.

The assertion by her host that the town had no social divisions suggested to Jude the truth – that Grant Roxby hadn't lived in Fedborough very long. Her own life had more important priorities than where she stood in any social hierarchy – she judged people by their inner qualities rather than their backgrounds – but she could still recognize that Fedborough was riddled with class-consciousness.

The town's inhabitants, mostly well-heeled, cosseted by sensible pension arrangements and private health insurance, knew to a nicety where they stood in the middle-class pecking order. The people up the road had public school education and inherited money, so they were upper-middle-class. The people opposite had money from retail trade and no taste, so they were lower-middle-class. The couple in the next road, who seemed to have no money, but dressed in worn well-cut tweeds and spoke in patrician accents of relatives in the House of Lords, must be lower-upper-middle-class. And the people on the council estate were common.

What made these rules of Fedborough society even more complicated was that no two residents of the town saw them in exactly the same way. People whom the neighbours on one side would condemn as lower-upper-middle-class might be seen by their neighbours on the other side as upper-lower-middle-class. In England at the beginning of the twenty-first century the much-vaunted ideal of a classless society remained as far off as ever.

The permutations became more intricate still if you factored in the self-images of the individuals involved. As always in life, how the individual people of Fedborough saw themselves and how the world saw them were very different. The void between those two views led to much of the town's humour (from the viewpoint of an outside observer). And also to much of its tragedy.

Jude had often found herself in the role of an outside observer, particularly since she had moved to Fethering. A comfortably rounded woman in her fifties, she had blonde hair piled up in a random coil on her head, and a predilection for layers of floaty garments in a haphazard mix of colours and patterns. The resulting image should have been a mess, but somehow contrived to be stylish.

Jude had done many things in her life, but in conversation didn't volunteer much detail about any of them. She rarely got the chance. People found her easy to talk to, there was a warmth about her that invited confidences; on very brief acquaintance, total strangers frequently found themselves telling her their life stories. So they never got round to asking about hers. Which suited Jude very well.

She had met Grant Roxby and his wife Kim on a holistic holiday in Spain. He had made an indecent amount of money in computers, and the Roxbys had at the time been 'looking for some dimension in our lives beyond the material'. The couple – particularly Grant – had embraced the various therapies, counselling and soul journeys available on the holiday with enormous butterfly enthusiasm. He had the ability – which must have been invaluable in his business career – to get completely caught up in the moment. His self-belief was total, and so was his belief in a new idea. The fact that the next day he could believe in an opposing idea with equal conviction never dented the self-belief. He liked to think that he went as deeply into everything as the very soul of his being; in fact, he went as deeply into everything as the sole of his shoe.

Grant Roxby's enthusiasms were infectious. His past was scattered with the husks of lifestyle options he had snatched up and discarded without recrimination or rancour. Jude wondered whether moving out of London to the country was just the latest in this series.

Certainly their relocation had had nothing to do with her. She hadn't even lived in Fethering when she'd met Grant and Kim, but they'd quickly followed up on her change of address card when they moved into the area.

The Roxbys had, as ever, done the thing in style. Pelling House, the Fedborough mansion they had instantly settled on after one viewing, was a tall, late Georgian oblong, red-brick in the best sense, with three storeys and a cellar. The frontage boasted a classical white portico, and stone steps led down to Pelling Street, one of the town's most exclusive residential addresses. The rooms were high, with tall windows, which had folding shutters on the inside. There were two staircases, a rather grand one in the hall, and another at the back of the house, used in the past for invisible domestic stage management by the servants. The previous owners of Pelling House had made a start on renovating the property, but there was no doubt that Grant Roxby's computer-generated millions would soon be employed to complete the job to an even more exacting standard.

On the evening of the dinner party, any suggestion that moving to Fedborough had been a mere whim would have been condemned as sacrilege. Grant and his wife were totally caught up in their new dream. 'It's going to be so great for the children,' Kim enthused. She was a thin, blonde woman in her early forties, dressed down in designer-hippy, expensively cut jeans and mock-snakeskin cowboy boots. Grant, sleek with success, his hair an unlikely chestnut, wore Levi's, a blue fleece and leather moccasins. Their clothes struck a more casual note than those of their guests, except for Jude.

The two couples who'd been invited demonstrated the extremes of Fedborough fashions, and the resolution of the dilemma which must have faced them earlier in the evening: what level of dress do you think these new people expect? Donald and Joan Durrington had opted for the traditional. It wasn't difficult for him. As one of the local doctors he wore the uniform of a double-breasted pin-striped suit. If his bleeper summoned him he would look appropriate at a patient's bedside – or even deathbed. Because he was potentially on duty, Donald Durrington was drinking only mineral water, but his wistful air as he watched others' wine glasses being filled suggested he'd rather not be on duty.

His wife, who was also on the mineral water, had perhaps overdressed for the occasion, but only by comparison with the host and hostess's jeans. She was wearing a little black cocktail number, decorated round the top with spangly black beads. The chest revealed by the décolletage was freckled and slack; its depth suggested greater confidence than did her uneasy blue eyes. Her hair had been recently and neatly cut; also recently blonded. Given the thinness of her frame, her face was surprisingly broad, puffy under heavy make-up. Though she hadn't contributed much to the general conversation, earlier in the evening Joan Durrington had spoken with trepidation of her approaching sixtieth birthday. Trepidation, indeed, seemed to be her dominant emotion. She kept looking nervously at her husband, as though fearful she might in some way let him down.

The Burnethorpes, Alan and Joke, were at the more casual end of the clothes spectrum. He, trying to look younger than his late forties, wore a collarless black shirt and black jeans, with a rough-knit grey sloppy cardigan on top. She, fabulously toned and twenty-eight, wore what looked like a track suit in burgundy crushed velvet. Her

English was excellent, her Dutch origins betrayed only by a tendency to say 'dat' and 'dere' for 'that' and 'there'. On introduction, Jude had been told that the name was pronounced 'Yo-kah', though, as Alan said with practised ease, 'the spelling's a joke'. Then, in case she hadn't got it, he'd spelt out, 'J-O-K-E.'

It had been established early in the evening that he was an architect whose office was a converted houseboat near Fedborough Bridge, and that this was his second marriage. Joke had been working in Fedborough, they had met and fallen in love, so the first Mrs Burnethorpe and two children had been put out to grass. Joke, in her turn, had quickly produced two children; her conversation was dominated by their skills and charms. Alan, having been through the process before, seemed less ecstatic about their growing family. But he was clearly still obsessed by his young wife. His eyes hardly left her during the evening. He looked capable of deep jealousy.

On the other hand, he still had an eye for other women. On being introduced to Jude, he had repeated her name and looked deeply into her brown eyes. His hand had held hers that moment too long and too tightly, immediately identifying him as one of those men who believe themselves to be irresistible to the opposite sex.

The eighth member of the party, matching Jude's single state, was the local vicar, the Rev Philip Trigwell. Of thinning hair and blotchy complexion, he'd reached the stage of unattractiveness that comes with age, and gave the impression that he'd never gone through the stage of attractiveness that can come with youth. Being of the school of clergy that doesn't believe in thrusting religion down people's throats, he wore an ordinary collar and tie, and spent the entire evening avoiding mention of his profession. He also seemed deeply aware of potential flashpoints in Fedborough society, and on any subject expressed no opinion which was not immediately counterbalanced by the opposite opinion. If the Roxbys are matchmaking and have lined up the Rev Philip Trigwell for me, thought Jude, they have seriously wasted their time.

The dinner party could not have been described as 'sticky', but then again nor was it particularly relaxed. Dinner parties were not Jude's favourite social events under any circumstances and, with the Roxbys having only just moved, they had assembled an *ad hoc* guest list for the occasion.

The mix was, she reflected, pretty standard for newcomers to a town. She was the one old – though not close – friend, met somewhere else. The Roxbys would have encountered the local vicar and the local doctor in the natural course of events – being visited by the one as part of his parochial duties, registering with the other. And she'd put money on the fact that Alan Burnethorpe was the architect Grant and Kim had consulted about the extensive alteration plans they had for the old house that was new to them.

So the Roxbys had made their first social foray in Fedborough predictable enough, while the long-established principle of reciprocal entertainment would ensure that they soon met other locals and, presumably in time, came across some they got on really well with.

The established Fedborough residents – the Durringtons, the Burnethorpes and the Rev Trigwell – all knew each other, and most of their conversation revolved around mutual acquaintances whose foibles and background they kept having to explain to the newcomers.

For the Roxbys, characteristically enthusiastic to immerse themselves in the new community, presumably these explanations were relevant, but they failed to hold Jude's attention. There is something stultifying in being constantly told 'he's a character' about people one is unlikely ever to meet, particularly when the accompanying illustrative anecdote suggests that the person in question has very little character at all. Jude was beginning to get the impression that not a lot happened in Fedborough.

'Yes,' Kim Roxby was saying now, 'kids can breathe when they get out into the country.'

'I'd hardly call Fedborough "country",' objected Alan Burnethorpe. 'I was brought up here and it's very definitely a town.' Lacking the professional restraint imposed on Donald Durrington, he was letting himself go with Grant Roxby's excellent choice of Chilean and New Zealand wines.

'But country's so readily accessible from here. All of the South Downs to walk on, and you can follow the Fether for miles, you know. And then all those beaches to wander over Still, I don't know why I'm telling you all this. You know. You must spend all your spare time taking walks like that.'

Kim's pronouncement prompted a slightly embarrassed concert of throat-clearing. It had marked her out irredeemably as a 'townie'. Few people who actually live in the country ever walk further than they have to, and then only if they've got dogs.

'But also the health factors,' she persevered. 'London – all big cities – are so choked with pollution these days. I feel happier knowing my children will be out breathing healthy country air. There are so many less allergies in the country.'

'I wish that were true,' said Donald Durrington with professional gloom. 'The number of kids I see through my surgery with asthma and similar complaints . . . you wouldn't believe. It's partly the pesticides and other pollutants out in the country. Then, of course, living in centrally heated houses and being ferried around in cars all the time doesn't help. Compared to ours, the next generation are incredibly vulnerable to infections.'

'Oh.'

Kim was cast down for a moment, and Joke Burnethorpe muscled in to shift the conversation. 'How many children do you have, Kim?'

'Three.'

'For our sins,' Grant threw in meaninglessly.

'What ages?'

'Harry's fifteen . . .'

'With all that that entails,' Grant added darkly.

'Tina's thirteen . . .'

'Going on twenty-five.'

'And Grace is eleven . . .'

'And she can twist all of us round her little finger.' Grant chuckled.

Joke Burnethorpe looked across at the empty laid-up place at the dinner table. 'I thought you said Harry was going to join us.'

'Ye-es.' Grant Roxby looked flustered.

Kim came to his rescue. 'You've just got the two kids?' Her question was completely gratuitous. Since she'd arrived, Joke Burnethorpe had talked about nothing else.

'That's right. Caspar and Linus.'

'Ah.'

Donald Durrington cleared his throat. His wife

watched him nervously, as if afraid he was about to reveal some deeply protected secret.

But he didn't. All he said was, 'Have you thought about schools at all yet?'

Oh dear, thought Jude, is it going to be one of *those* dinner parties?

But it didn't develop that way. Joke Burnethorpe, who Jude had already assessed as a very strong-willed young woman, persisted with her line of questioning. 'So where *is* Harry?'

Grant again seemed embarrassed by the question, and a moment of marital semaphore passed between husband and wife. 'He must've got caught up in . . . you know what they're like at that age . . . some computer game . . . something on the internet—'

'Or just exploring the house,' Kim cut in; and then, as though such a pursuit were somehow more respectable than computer games or the internet, she went on, 'All the children are fascinated by history, you know, and this house is full of history.'

'So's all of Fedborough,' said the Rev Trigwell, pausing for a moment to check that this statement had not been controversial. Reassured, he continued, 'You must get James Lister to take you on one of his Town Walks. He's a real character, James . . . though of course in the nicest possible way,' he concluded weakly.

'Oh yes, a great character,' Donald Durrington agreed. 'I tell you, it was very amusing during the Fedborough Festival a couple of years back when . . . well, let's say the drink had flowed liberally in the Sponsors' Tent and Jimmy had indulged rather more than his wife Fiona would have approved of and—'

But the anecdote which was to detail James Lister's

qualification as 'a character' would have to be wheeled out some other time. A child's scream was heard from downstairs. Seconds later, Harry Roxby burst in through the dining-room door. He carried a large rubber-covered torch, which was switched on. His face was so red Jude could hardly see the spots which had been prominent earlier, and his eyes were staring.

'Dad!' he shouted in sheer childish terror. 'We've found a dead body in the cellar!'

Chapter Two

Professional priorities might have dictated that Dr Durrington would be first to the body, but he showed a marked reluctance to move from the dinner table. It was Kim Roxby who led the way into the hall, where she immediately stopped to comfort her hysterical daughters.

Her husband took the torch from his son and set off through the door that led down to the cellar. He was grim-faced, determined not to appear panicked. If the commotion turned out to be a practical joke perpetrated by his children, they were about to be severely reprimanded. Disrupting their parents' social life, they would learn, was not funny.

It seemed natural for Jude to follow Grant down the stairs into the darkness. Harry, half-fascinated, half-repelled, trailed after them.

The beam of the torch waved around in the gloom. Jude had difficulty judging the precise dimensions of the space, but it felt low-ceilinged and smelt of mildew.

'Where is it, Harry – this thing you claim you've seen?' The father's voice was taut with contained emotion.

'I didn't *claim* to see it, Dad,' the boy protested weakly. 'It's there – over through that partition.'

The torch beam landed on a discoloured sheet of

chipboard, bloated with damp, which had been nailed across one end of the cellar space. The top corner had been pulled away and flapped down like a piece of torn paper.

'Did you do that, Harry?' asked Grant sharply. 'Pull it down?'

'Yes,' came the grudging admission from behind Jude.

'Why?'

'Just to see what space there was down here – see if we can turn this into something.'

'Into what, Harry?'

'I don't know. Computer room . . . ? Den . . . ? Some place where I can go, somewhere I can be on my own . . .'

Jude was struck, given the situation, by the incongruity of the father questioning his son in this way. For a moment she wondered if Grant was just delaying the sight of the horror that lay ahead, but then she decided the exchange was simply a reflection of their relationship. Grant Roxby still wanted to know about – possibly even control – everything his son did. And Harry resented this constant monitoring of his life.

Grant raised the torch through the exposed triangle to illuminate the void beyond. From behind her, Jude heard a sudden dry retching sound.

'I think I'm going to be—'

'It's all right, Harry! Let's get you out of here!' Grant put his arm around the boy's shoulders and hurried him towards the light at the top of the stairs. The father seemed empowered by his son's weakness, more confident when he could treat Harry as a child. Passing her, he thrust the torch into Jude's hands.

Some people would not have wanted to look, but squeamishness had no part in Jude's nature. She redirected the torch to where Grant had been pointing, and peered over the broken chipboard partition.

Any notion that the children's hysteria might have been prompted by an anthropomorphic dummy was quickly dispelled. What the torchlight revealed was very definitely human.

The body lay horizontally at the foot of the wall, dark, almost black, with leathery skin tight over the bones. Beaky, reminiscent of an unwrapped mummy whose photograph Jude had once seen in a *National Geographical Magazine*, the face was still topped by a straggle of mud-coloured hair.

Rotted round about on the floor were the remains of the box in which the corpse must have lain hidden. From the soggy corrugated debris, this appeared to have been made of no more than stout cardboard. The angled plastic strips which had reinforced its corners lay splayed out on the floor.

There was no evidence of clothes. The object's shrivelled breasts and pudenda showed that what Jude was looking at had once been a woman.

The body had no limbs. The arms had been neatly removed at the shoulders, and the legs at the hip joint.

Chapter Three

When Carole Seddon opened her front door the next morning, the Sunday, she looked frosty. Her pale, thin face did frosty rather well. The sensibly cut steel-grey hair offered no concessions, and when she wanted them to, her light blue eyes could look as dead as the glass in her rimless spectacles. The fact that it was a fine June day, that seagulls were doing exploratory aerobatics across the Fethering sky, did not penetrate her gloom.

'Hello,' she said, without enthusiasm.

There was a momentary impasse before Jude asked, 'Aren't you going to invite me in?'

'Oh, very well.' Carole drew back, still making no pretence at a welcome. That someone normally so punctilious in her social usages should behave like this indicated she was in the grip of some powerful emotion.

Jude knew that. She also knew what the emotion was, and what had caused it. For the last few weeks she had been aware of Carole retreating into her shell and, from the experience of luring her friend out of it once before, Jude knew how tough and impregnable that shell could be. She herself had been away and busy and hadn't had time to concentrate on fence-mending with her neighbour. But now she was back, determined that a rapprochement should be effected. And she had a feeling that the news of the torso in Fedborough might, perversely, be just the thing to restore the health of their relationship.

Carole closed the door behind them. 'Would you like coffee?' She was aware of how boorish she was being, and that knowledge compounded the darkness of her mood.

'Listen,' said Jude. 'Forget coffee. Let's get things sorted. I know exactly why you're behaving like this with me, and I promise you – you don't have to.'

'Would you like to sit down?' asked Carole with icy politeness, gesturing towards the sitting room.

'No, I bloody wouldn't like to sit down! I'd like to take hold of you, shake all this nonsense out of you, then give you a big hug.'

'Oh.' Carole almost visibly shuddered. Every disciplined middle-class fibre of her being recoiled at the concept of big hugs.

They stood facing each other, Jude poised for a hug, Carole prepared to repel any such approach.

'You're just making things worse by cutting yourself off.'

'I would have thought that was my business,' came the tart reply.

'Oh, come on . . .' Jude took her neighbour's hand. Carole, on hug alert, was unprepared for this, and did not immediately snatch the hand away. 'Let's go into your kitchen, make some coffee, and get this sorted.'

Carole felt another twinge of middle-class resistance. She was the hostess. She should serve coffee in her sitting room. Women huddling cosily in the kitchen had overtones of northern soap operas. Which reminded her, she never had found out where her neighbour came from. In fact, given how close at times they had been, she knew remarkably little about Jude's past.

Carole switched on an electric kettle. She had decided it was now warm enough to turn the Aga off for the summer. It wasn't, quite, and the kitchen felt chill, a deserved reflection of Carole's mood. Gulliver, her Labrador, rose from his stupor in front of the regrettably cold stove to greet their guest with bleary delight. Whatever may have happened to the mistress, the dog hadn't lost his social graces.

Gulliver had a bandage round the thick end of his tail, but Jude knew this wasn't the moment to enquire what had happened to him. There was another, more demanding, priority.

'I know it's because of Ted,' she announced. 'That didn't work out, and you feel really low as a result. We've all been there.'

'I haven't been there as many times maybe as you have.'

It was a sharp line, which might have offended someone less easy-going. But Jude just gave a warm chuckle. 'Fair criticism. Carole, I know you think everyone in Fethering's laughing behind their hands at you, but they're not. Only about half a dozen people knew there was anything between you and Ted, and none of the ones who did are the sort to gloat over someone else's misfortune.'

'I just feel I've made a fool of myself,' said Carole, and turned pointedly away to make the coffee.

But Jude recognized it as a start, the first hint of thaw in the frost.

'I know you don't commit yourself easily, and I know

how much your husband walking out hit your confidence.'

'You don't know that. We hadn't even met at the time it happened. Anyway, so far as I'm concerned, I'm well shot of him.'

'I don't doubt that's true, but I'm sure his leaving you made you withdrawn, unwilling to engage with other human beings.'

'David said I had always been like that. He said it was one of the reasons why he did leave me.'

Slowly, the thaw was continuing. Very slowly, but then a quick thaw was not in Carole's nature. With an easy laugh, Jude took her coffee cup and sat down at the kitchen table. Gulliver, besotted, nuzzled into the back of her knee.

For a moment Carole was tempted to insist they take their coffee through to the sitting room, but instead she sat edgily on a chair opposite Jude.

'Ted just wasn't the right person for you, Carole. God, people spend their whole lives searching for the right person, it's no surprise the process can take a long time.'

'It's a process I've never completed. David turned out to be a complete disaster. Then Ted . . .' The pale blue eyes focused on Jude's brown ones. 'Has it ever happened to you?'

'Hm?'

'Have you ever found the right person?'

'I've thought I have a few times . . .' Carole wanted more detail, but before she had a chance to put a supplementary question, Jude went on, 'Ted's a nice guy. Not an evil bone in his body.'

'I know that, but . . .'

'But?'

'He's terribly . . . scruffy. He really doesn't care what he looks like . . . or what kind of conditions he lives in. He doesn't have any standards. He actually doesn't seem to notice things like that.'

'Ah.' Jude pictured Ted Crisp, landlord of Fethering's only pub, the Crown and Anchor. He was a large man with straggling hair and beard, whose idea of a fashion statement was a clean sweatshirt. Though his pub was not dirty, it did express a raffish untidiness which Jude found rather comforting, but Carole apparently didn't.

Jude looked round the antiseptically gleaming surfaces of the kitchen, and could not even imagine Ted Crisp in such an environment.

The relationship had always been an unlikely one, a surprise to both participants when it started, and for the two months of its duration. What effect the affair's ending had had on Ted was hard to estimate. Never one to wear his heart on his sleeve, he remained the same bear-like presence behind the bar of the Crown and Anchor, ready with an endless supply of jokes remembered from his days working the stand-up circuit. Whether he was putting on the brave face of the suffering clown, who could tell?

The effect on Carole was much more overt, at least to the eyes of her neighbour. It was entirely in character for Carole Seddon, as a civil servant retired from the Home Office, to withdraw into what she thought of as anonymity; though, perversely, such behaviour had the effect of drawing attention to what she was doing. Carole had taken to shopping at times when she was unlikely to meet anyone she knew, even avoiding Fethering's Allinstore and driving in her trim Renault to distant supermarkets. With the light mornings, Gulliver's compulsory walks on the beach had been getting earlier and earlier.

At that moment Jude resolved to get Carole functioning properly again. Though the two women were polar opposites, there was potentially a strong affection between them. Jude even made a resolution to get Carole back into the Crown and Anchor.

But any realization of her ambitions would be a long way ahead. With Carole, she knew, she'd have to proceed with caution and circumspection.

'But you already knew Ted well enough,' said Jude gently, 'to *know* he was scruffy. Or did you fall into that old female error of thinking you can change a man?'

'No, I fell into that even older female error of having a template for what a man should be and trying to fit one into it.'

'Ah.' Jude shook her head sagely. 'We've all been guilty of that.' Then, with a toss of the blonde bird's nest on top of her head, she moved the conversation on. 'I didn't just come here, however, to commiserate with you about the end of your affair . . .'

Even in her current mood, Carole couldn't suppress a little glow from Jude's use of the word. Although it had ended in disaster, the fact that she was a woman who had had an 'affair' seemed to her slightly daring, even rather grown-up. Which, she knew, was a ridiculous thought to be entertained by a woman in her fifties.

'I came because last night I saw a dead body.'

Jude didn't get the reaction she'd been hoping for. On two previous occasions she and Carole had got caught up in solving murders and their enthusiasm for the challenge had been mutually infectious. This time all she got was a glassy stare from the pale eyes.

'What, was this a road accident or something?'

'No, Carole. The dead body had been hidden in the cellar of a friend's house. It must have been a murder.'

'Not necessarily,' said Carole, doggedly contrary. 'Could have been an accident.'

'I think it's quite difficult to have an accident in the course of which both your arms and legs get cut off.'

Carole was silent, unequipped with a riposte to this argument. Then she said lightly, as if nothing in the world could have mattered less to her, 'Well, I'm sure the police will sort it out.'

'I'm sure they will, but you can't deny it's intriguing, can you?'

Carole shrugged, and reached down to ruffle Gulliver's ears. Her body language was trying to say, Yes, I can see it might be mildly intriguing to some people – not to me, though. But Jude was heartened to see a new alertness in her neighbour's eyes.

This was confirmed when, for the first time that morning, Carole – albeit grudgingly – asked for further information. 'Where did you see this body then?'

'In a house in Fedborough.'

'Oh.' There was a wealth of nuance in the monosyllable. At one level it said, Oh yes, well, that's what you'd expect from people in Fedborough. At another level it said, If the body's in Fedborough, then that's none of our business. And, encapsulated in 'Oh' too, was the conviction that, though only eight miles up the River Fether from Fethering, Fedborough was another – and undoubtedly alien – country.

'I didn't know you knew any people in Fedborough.' There was almost a hint of affront in Carole's voice. She was constantly reminded how little she really knew about Jude's life and background. But the longer their friendship continued, the more difficult became asking the basic questions that should have been settled on first introduction.

'Not many. These are some not-very-close acquaintances who've just moved down from London.' This reply seemed subtly to reassure Carole, so Jude, still working to thaw the frostiness, went on with humility, 'You know a lot of people up there, though, don't you?'

'I wouldn't say a lot. And none of them are that close.'

'No, but you said you've often been to see shows and concerts in the Fedborough Festival.'

'I may have done in the past.' The implication was that Carole never intended to have any kind of social life, ever again. Then she softened. 'But yes, I do know some people up there. Very full of themselves, the residents of Fedborough, I must say. Just because they live in a town that's very beautiful and has a certain amount of history attached to it, they seem to imagine that makes them superior to everyone else.'

'Lots of people think like that about where they live. Good thing too, saves a great deal of disappointment and envy.' Jude giggled. 'Mind you, I can't imagine many people feel that way about Fethering.'

This had been a foolish thing to say, and nearly undid all the morning's good work. The frost glazed over again. Carole herself may have said many harsh things about Fethering, but the village she had made her home was like a child. A parent could criticize it, but woe betide any outsider who did so. And in many ways, Jude still was an outsider. Though she'd lived more than a year in Woodside Cottage, she'd made very little attempt to take on the values of Fethering or to fit into Fethering society.

In the stratified middle-class world of the village, Jude remained a potential loose cannon.

She moved on quickly to cover her lapse. 'Anyway, the police interviewed me last night. Because I was one of the first people to see the body . . .'

Carole tried hard, but couldn't stop herself from asking, 'Did they mention the word "murder"?'

'Not as such. But you don't need to be Sherlock Holmes to deduce that a limbless body has had, at the very least . . . some outside interference.'

'No . . .' Once again reticence lost the battle with curiosity. 'Had the mur—' Carole corrected herself. 'Had the killing taken place recently?'

'No, the body was dried up, almost like a mummy.'

'So if your friends have only just moved, it can't have anything to do with them . . .'

'Wouldn't have thought so, no . . .'

In spite of herself, Carole found her mind making connections. 'Though suspicion would inevitably turn to the previous owners . . .'

'Yes.'

'You don't know who they were? Your friends didn't mention the name?'

'No. All I know is that the house belonged to a couple who were splitting up, which made the customary agony of British house-purchase even more prolonged.'

'Hm . . . If I knew their name, I might recognize it, or know someone I could ask about the former owners . . .'

Jude shrugged apology.

'What's the address? Fedborough's not that big. I might know it.'

'Pelling House.'

A huge beam broke out like sunshine, finally thawing Carole Seddon's face. 'Ah. Now I do know who used to live there.'

Chapter Four

Fortunately, Carole did have a reason to get in touch with Debbie Carlton. During the brief glow of confidence she had felt while things were working out between her and Ted Crisp, she had decided to do something to her house. Just as her wardrobe had blossomed with new colours to edge out her customary pale greens, greys and beiges, so she started to think of changing the safe magnolia walls and white gloss which characterized – or perhaps bleached character from – her home. She even – momentarily – contemplated changing its name from High Tor. Such a move would have been unthinkable for her in any other mood. Names of houses – even names as inappropriate as 'High Tor' in the totally flat coastal plain of West Sussex – were among the many things that were never changed in Fethering.

But in that mood of heady insouciance, Carole Seddon reckoned she could change anything she wanted to. Even her customary financial caution started to dissolve. She was, after all, very comfortable on her Civil Service pension. The mortgage on High Tor was paid off; if she wanted to spend money on the house, there was nothing to stop her.

Having consulted the local directory for interior designers, Carole had selected Debbie Carlton because of her local telephone number and on the – frequently fallacious – assumption that someone operating on their own might be cheaper than a large company. Debbie had paid one visit to High Tor to assess what was needed, and breathed all kinds of fresh ideas into the functionality of the house. Despite finding some of the suggestions a bit extreme, Carole had still felt sufficiently daring to say she would mull over what Debbie had said and get back to her.

Though the interior designer had not imposed any of her personal history on her client, Carole had still pieced together that Debbie Carlton had recently moved from the splendour of Pelling House to a small flat in Fedborough. The reason had been a common one – divorce. The subject once broached, Debbie had been very upfront about the details. 'Francis fell in love with someone else, and that was it, really. She's very wealthy and they divide their time between London and Florida. Just one of those things that didn't work out. Thank goodness we hadn't got any children, and it happened while I was still young enough to pick up the threads of my career.'

The matter-of-fact stoicism had not disguised the hurt, at least from Carole, who knew how much she had suffered when her husband David had left her. The common experience, she felt, forged an unspoken bond between them, and she was determined that, if she did go ahead with the transformation of High Tor, Debbie Carlton would get the job.

But just around that time things had started to get sticky with Ted and, preoccupied with the collapse of their relationship – or non-relationship, as with increasing hindsight she thought of it – she had never made the follow-up call.

So common courtesy – not to mention an interest in

the torso found in the basement of Pelling House – dictated that she should phone Debbie Carlton.

'It's Carole Seddon.'

'Oh, hello.'

There was no resentment or recrimination in the greeting, but Carole still felt obliged to say, 'You've been on my conscience. I promised I'd call you back . . . what, three months ago . . . and I'm sorry, I never did.'

'Don't worry. Happens a lot in my sort of business. People watch some television programme, suddenly get caught up in the idea that they're going to "make over" their house, then lose interest, or decide they're going to buy a new car instead. It's not a big deal.'

'No, but I still feel I should have got back to you, so . . . I apologize.'

'Well, thank you. You're in the minority who would think that was necessary.'

There was a silence, and Carole realized that Debbie was waiting for a decision. Interior design was, after all, the woman's business. She would assume that this was a call to say whether Carole wanted to proceed with the job.

'Um . . . I was actually ringing to say that . . . though I was terrifically impressed by the ideas that you put forward . . .'

'Don't worry, it's fine,' said Debbie Carlton, too quickly. There was a slight disappointment in her voice. To have got the job at High Tor would have meant a lot to her.

'The thing is, you see, my circumstances have changed somewhat . . .'

A cynical 'Huh. Tell me about it, Mrs Seddon.'

Carole realized, with some dismay, that Debbie thought she was referring to her financial circumstances.

Normally, she would have hastened to correct this embarrassing misunderstanding, but on this occasion, having a rather different agenda, she let it go.

'Anyway, I do hope you'll understand.'

'Of course. And maybe, if things pick up for you, you'll get back to me.'

It hurt to have the misunderstanding compounded, but Carole still didn't make any correction. 'Yes, yes, that'll be fine.' She paused for a moment. Unless she changed its direction quickly, the conversation was about to come to a natural end. 'I bet you're glad to be out of Pelling House,' she said abruptly.

'What? No, as it happens, I still miss the place dreadfully. Feel a great pang every time I walk past.'

'I didn't mean that. I meant you must be glad to be out of it . . . given what was found in the cellar there . . .'

'I'm sorry? I've been away for a few days. I don't know what you're talking about.'

'The body. The torso. Didn't you hear about it on the local news? On the national news, come to that.'

'What? Well, I . . . Was that in Pelling House?' The voice was quiet with shock.

'Yes. I'm surprised the police haven't been in touch with you yet.'

'As I say, I've been away. Literally just walked in when you rang. Haven't even checked the answering machine yet.'

'Perhaps it's as well I warned you, then. Because I'm sure the police will be in touch.'

'Yes, I'm sure they will.' There was a shudder in her voice as Debbie Carlton went on, 'So that . . . what they found in the cellar . . . may have actually been there while Francis and I were living in the house?'

'I've no idea, but a friend of mine was having dinner with the new owners when the body . . . torso . . . was found. She said it looked as if it had been dead a long while.'

'Oh. Well, thank you for warning me, Mrs Seddon. I'll . . . Look, if you . . . if you hear any more details from your friend . . . I'd be most grateful if you could let me know. Or, if you happen to be in Fedborough at some point, give me a call and come round for a coffee.'

'I'd like that very much.' Carole hesitated, then decided to be bold. 'In fact, have to bring my dog in to the vet's tomorrow. Round ten-thirty. I don't suppose you'd be in . . . elevenish . . .?'

'Couldn't be better. You have my address on the card I left with you. I'll look forward to seeing you at eleven tomorrow, Mrs Seddon.'

Goodness, thought Carole, with a little spark of excitement as she put the phone down, that was easier than I expected.

Chapter Five

She knew Fedborough well enough to find one of the few free parking spaces. Because of the constant invasion of tourists, the town boasted many double yellow lines and, since residents made it a point of honour not to succumb to the 'Pay and Display' car parks, the unrestricted roadsides were quickly filled. Still, ten-fifteen was too early for the daily summer influx of bewildered pensioners and spotty French students, so Carole managed to squeeze the Renault into a narrow space outside one of the many antique shops at the top of the town.

Gulliver was disappointed. He had got into the car with high expectations of being taken for a walk, possibly up on the Downs near Weldisham, but getting out in the middle of a town dashed those hopes. Also Fedborough had connotations for him of the vet's, and distant unhappy memories of being unnecessarily pricked and probed. His woebegone head drooped and his bandaged tail hung between his legs as Carole attached the lead.

She knew he didn't like what was about to happen, but she had little sympathy. He had brought it on himself. Gulliver had taken the decision to chase that Yorkshire terrier on Fethering Beach, although he knew Yorkshire terriers are notorious for misinterpreting the playful advances of larger dogs. So he'd really asked for the bite on his tail. And the fact that the wound had become infected was ultimately his fault too. So Carole ignored the pitiful whining as she dragged Gulliver down Fedborough High Street towards the veterinary surgery.

In the early June sunlight the town was looking its best. Set where the undulations of the South Downs met the flatness that led to the sea, Fedborough had once been a notable port. Ocean-going vessels had plied up the River Fether from Fethering to deposit their goods from far away – wines from France, coals from Newcastle – and this trade had been the foundation of the town's prosperity. Now the only vestiges of seafaring were a few privately owned launches, moored with great care to accommodate the considerable tidal rise and fall of the Fether, and a string of some half-dozen houseboats to the north of Fedborough Bridge. The nearest of these had been punctiliously refurbished to its former Edwardian splendour, but the old hulks beyond appeared to be sinking into the river in progressive stages of decrepitude. Few of them looked as if they could still be inhabited.

On the opposite side from the houseboats, a small quay had been dredged out of the riverbank. This was surrounded by a collection of wooden huts, on which faded notices advertised ice creams and pleasure-boat trips on the Fether. But there was an air of dilapidation and business failure about the silted-up inlet, no sign of any ice creams or pleasure boats.

The bridge was at the bottom of the High Street, down whose steep incline Carole pulled the reluctant Gulliver. At the top of what was uncontroversially called Castle Hill, stood the remains of Fedborough Castle. On the site of an old fort, from which Saxons had resisted Vikings marauding up the Fether, a nobleman, rewarded by

William the Conqueror with the lands around the town, had built a massive keep to dominate the river valley. Over the following centuries the fabric had been strengthened and the ground plan extended, until Fedborough Castle could withstand the worst that mediaeval armaments could hurl against its walls.

But it could not withstand the cannons of Cromwell's New Model Army during the Civil War. At the end of a short but brutal siege, the people of Fedborough paid the price of their loyalty to King Charles. Their town was sacked and most of their precious castle reduced to rubble. The ruin was left as a warning to future aspiring rebels.

With the restoration of the monarchy, its symbolism changed but there seemed no purpose in rebuilding the structure. Gradually, surreptitiously, over the years the loose stones were appropriated by local builders and incorporated into the fabric of the growing town.

And the familiar silhouette of the remains, like the irregular teeth of an old man, continued to dominate Fedborough from Castle Hill. With the advent of the Romantic Movement, when ruins suddenly took on fashionably Gothic qualities, the outline became the subject of many paintings, etchings and prints. Then, through the twentieth century, as the heritage industry developed, the Castle ruins were translated into a symbol of West Sussex, a logo for the town of Fedborough, and an essential part of any tourist itinerary.

The major expansion of the town had occurred during the late Georgian and Victorian periods. Fedborough's market attracted produce from the riches of surrounding agricultural estates, while improvements in communications by road, rail and water made the town a centre for trade. With only a few flint-faced cottages surviving from earlier times, newly enriched entrepreneurs built substantial brick houses to demonstrate their unassailable social position. Large, elegant shops were erected to supply their growing consumerism, and Fedborough found itself in the genteel stranglehold of the middle classes – from which it has never escaped.

Though a certain amount of building occurred during the twentieth century, most of the construction work was new houses being put up on the sites of old ones. There was also a lot of conversion work, as buildings changed usage. Former shops, warehouses, workshops and even chapels were transformed into tasteful flats and houses for the newly wealthy or the wealthy retired. Fedborough's geographical position gave little opportunity for the outward sprawl which has affected so many towns. Trapped in a triangle, bounded on one side by the Downs, on another by the River Fether, and on the third by Sussex's main east–west arterial road, the A27, there was no direction in which Fedborough could expand further.

So the vista down which Carole Seddon and Gulliver walked was predominantly Victorian. Tall, graceful buildings with multi-paned windows lined the High Street. A few were residential, though most of the town centre population lived in the equally elegant side roads. An old coaching inn, the Pelling Arms, offered tourists the charms of anachronistic authenticity. The logos of a chemist chain, three estate agents and two of the major banks distinguished other buildings. There were a couple of teashops and four pubs (from which Carole, after her recent involvement with the landlord of Fethering's Crown and Anchor, found herself instinctively shrinking).

But, except for those listed above, every other building in Fedborough High Street was an antique shop.

Carole hauled Gulliver, whimpering with unwillingness, into the vet's reception area. He continued to whimper while they waited their turn, while the vet cleaned his wound, gave him an injection and prescribed further antibiotics. He was still whimpering when Carole took him back up the High Street and locked him in the Renault to await her return.

As she set off towards the address Debbie Carlton had given her, Carole deliberately turned her back on the look of reproach that followed her through the partly opened car window. That look summed up all the perfidy of humankind. To put a dog in a car as if taking him out for a walk, then to trick him into a visit to the vet's, and finally to lock him back up in the car . . . Gulliver was having a seriously bad day, and it was all Carole's fault.

Debbie Carlton was thin, but the thinness implied toned muscle rather than frailty. She had naturally blonde – almost white – hair and surprisingly dark blue eyes. Carole always found it difficult to judge the ages of those younger than herself, but reckoned mid-thirties must be about the right mark.

Debbie was wearing a large sloppy red jumper, in which – as intended – she looked waif-like. Deceptively simple black trousers and frivolously large red trainers. For make-up only a hint of blue on her upper eyelids and red lipstick the exact colour of her shoes. She knew precisely the effect of the ensemble.

Her designing skills were also evident in the small sitting room into which she ushered Carole, but for someone working from home, that made good business sense. Her domestic décor had to be an advertisement for the skills she hoped to sell.

The flat was pleasant enough. On the first floor, above a hairdresser's in Harbidge Street, it was not what the finely tuned local snobs would call one of the best addresses in Fedborough. Perfectly acceptable, though, for anyone who hadn't once enjoyed the lavish expanses and magnificent proportions of Pelling House.

The décor demonstrated Debbie Carlton's ability to do the best she could with the space she had. On walls and ceiling the predominant colour was terracotta; furniture had been stripped down and stained the colour of pumice stone. Dusty green in the curtains and cunningly faded red on the upholstery gave an impression of a sleepy Italian town, which was intensified by robust morning sunlight streaming through the small panes of the windows.

The Mediterranean theme was maintained by the rows of framed paintings on the walls. Delicate water-colours picked out the apricot honey of tiled roofs, the hazy green of cypresses, the silver shimmer of olive leaves and the soft grey of ancient statuary. The style was so uniform that they had all to be the work of the same artist. Carole wondered whether it was Debbie herself.

Time enough to find that out. Her hostess, gesturing her guest to an armchair which was bleached to a rose colour, sat herself down in front of a table with a waiting cafetière. 'Thank you very much for warning me about the police. Theirs was the first message on the answering machine. Might've given me a nasty shock if you hadn't said anything.'

Carole shrugged that it had been no problem.

'Now, how do you like your coffee?'

'Just a dash of milk. No sugar.' As Debbie busied herself pouring, Carole asked, 'Have the police talked to you then?'

'And how! Had about three hours with them yesterday afternoon.'

'Here?'

'Yes.' Debbie smiled. 'They didn't take me down to the station. So far as I can gather, I'm not their number one suspect.'

'No, of course not. I don't suppose they have any idea who the body – the torso – was.'

'If they have, they didn't confide it in me. There you are.'

'Thanks.'

'Would you like a biscuit?'

There were none on display, but Carole would have refused the offer, anyway. Though there had been a strong biscuit culture in the Home Office, she had always borne in mind her mother's proscription of eating between meals.

'So what did the police ask you about?'

'Oh, purely factual stuff. When we moved into the house . . .'

'When was that, actually?'

'Two . . . no, I suppose two and a half years ago.' The recollection threatened her poise for a moment, so she moved quickly on. 'And of course the police wanted to know who we'd bought Pelling House from . . .'

'Which was?'

'Man called Roddy Hargreaves. I doubt if you've met him. A Fedborough "character". Bought up the place where the pleasure boats used to run down on the Fether, but the business didn't work out. He had to sell up.'

'Did he move away?'

'No, no one ever moves away from Fedborough. They just move into smaller premises,' she added ruefully. 'Not sure where Roddy's place is currently. He's moved around the town a bit in the last couple of years. His permanent address seems to be the Coach and Horses in Pelling Street.'

'Hm. What else did the police ask you?'

Though Carole's questions were already tantamount to an interrogation, Debbie Carlton seemed either not to notice or not to mind. 'They wanted to know when we sold Pelling House, all that sort of detail. And, needless to say, whether we often went down to the cellar.'

'And the answer to that was . . . ?' This time Carole realized that her instinctive curiosity was becoming a bit too avid for a Fedborough coffee morning, and back-tracked. 'That is, if you don't mind my asking . . . ?'

'I don't mind at all . . . Mrs Seddon.'

'Please call me Carole.'

'All right, Carole. And call me Debbie. Well, in answer to your question – and indeed the police's question, I very rarely did go down to the cellar in Pelling House. We had so much space there that we reckoned we'd colonize it slowly. Did our bedroom first, then the sitting room, then the kitchen and . . .' The sentence, like the relationship it referred to, was left in mid-air.

'But the cellar must've been inspected when you bought the house, you know, when it was surveyed?'

Debbie Carlton shook her head. 'We actually didn't have it surveyed. Mad, I know, but I'd have still bought Pelling House if a survey had said the whole of Dauncey

Street was about to fall into the Fether. And Francis saw the economic sense of it. He resented the idea of paying the money to some surveyor who'd just spend ten minutes in the place and send in a whacking great bill. You see, my husband was – well, is – an architect, so he checked the basics.'

'Seem to be a lot of architects in Fedborough.'

'Certainly are. Architects, antique dealers, and the retired. Anyway, Francis had always been careful with his money, and he came into some when his parents died, so we didn't need a mortgage. Which meant we didn't need a survey for the building society. And I'd dreamed of living in Pelling House since I was a little girl. Dreamed of bringing up a family there, but . . .'

Carole began to realize the depth of the pain moving out must have caused. But there had been another implication in Debbie's words. 'You were brought up round here, were you?'

'Yes. Fedborough born and bred. I'm a genuine Chub.'

'Chub?'

Debbie grinned at her bewilderment. 'People who're actually born in Fedborough are nicknamed "Chubs". After the fish. Chub still get caught off the bridge sometimes.'

'Ah.'

'My parents used to run the local grocery – in the days when there *was* a grocery in Fedborough. So I was brought up and went to school round here. Then obviously moved away when I went to St Martin's College of Art. After that Francis and I moved back down here and . . .' She grimaced wryly. 'Here I am again, as Debbie Carlton.' A frown. 'I should really have changed back to my maiden name after the divorce, but I'd got the design stationery printed before I thought of it.'

'What was your maiden name?'

'Franks. Debbie Franks.'

'Either of them sounds all right for an interior designer.'

'Yes.' A light chuckle. 'At least I had a maiden name I *could* go back to. Unlike my poor mother.'

Carole waited for a gloss on this, but it didn't come. So she smiled briefly, then asked, 'Didn't you want to move after the divorce?' She remembered after David's departure how frantic she had been to get out of the marital home as soon as possible and make her permanent base in their country cottage in Fethering.

'I desperately wanted to move,' said Debbie with feeling. 'But my parents are still down here. Dad's in a home, which means Mum's virtually on her own. She sold the big house, to pay for Dad's hospital expenses and lives in a houseboat on the Fether. I can't really leave her, so . . .' The shrug this time encompassed all the hopeless inevitability of life.

'Mm. You say you were at art college . . .' Carole gestured to the walls. 'Are those yours?' Debbie nodded. 'They're lovely.'

'Thanks. I'm hoping to start selling a few, you know, bolster the old income a bit. This flat's actually going to be part of the Art Crawl.' In response to Carole's puzzled expression, she explained, 'In the Fedborough Festival in July. Only a couple of weeks away now. You've heard of the Festival, haven't you?'

'Oh yes.' Carole thought of the programme book that had come through the letter-box a month before, and which this year had remained unopened. 'I've been to the odd play or concert in the past. But I haven't been aware of the . . . what did you call it?'

' "Art Crawl". So called because it's kind of modelled on a pub crawl, I suppose. You move from venue to venue. Artists display their work in various houses round the town, and people get maps showing where the stuff is and walk round looking at it. Very popular. Possibly brings more people to the Festival than the theatre and the concerts do.'

'Does a lot of art get sold?'

'Some artists do quite well, yes. Some less so.' Her face twisted with the effort of saying what she was about to say with the maximum of diplomacy. 'The fact is, in a place like Fedborough you get a lot of *self-appointed* artists.'

'Whose talent isn't up to that of professional artists?'

'I didn't say that. You did. I'd hoped to show my stuff in Pelling House during the Festival, but . . .' Debbie briskly shook off maudlin thoughts. 'So I'm going to turn this room into a bit of a gallery for the Crawl and see what happens. Which reminds me, I've still got a lot of framing to do.'

'Do you do your own framing?'

'Yes. Saves money.' She sighed. 'At least I can guarantee to get a lot of people through the flat, even if they don't buy anything.' She provided another explanation. 'For most people in Fedborough, the Art Crawl is just a Snoopers' Charter – chance to have a crafty look round other people's houses.'

'Ah.' Carole grinned.

So did Debbie. But her mood swiftly changed, as an unwelcome thought returned to her. 'The really horrid thing about this whole business . . . you know, what I've been talking to the police about . . . is that that . . .

thing . . . the torso . . . must've been there all the time we lived in Pelling House . . .' She shuddered. 'A kind of malign presence. A curse on the house . . . and on those inside it.' She let out a short, bitter laugh. 'People of a superstitious nature might imagine that that's what cast a blight on Francis and my marriage.'

'And are you of a superstitious nature, Debbie?'

'No. I'm of a very realistic nature. And I'm fully aware that the only malign presence which cast a blight on our marriage was a younger, richer American woman called Jonelle. Francis was always very interested in money. He was almost obsessively . . .' She swallowed back the bile in her voice. 'Sorry. I shouldn't burden you with my troubles.'

'It's all right. I've been there.' As she said the words, Carole realized that she was being sympathetic, showing people skills of the kind that came so effortlessly to Jude. For the first time in months, she felt a tiny flicker of returning confidence. Emboldened, she moved the conversation back to what in her mind was starting to be called 'the investigation'.

'The police didn't say anything else of interest about the torso, did they?'

Debbie Carlton, relieved by the change of subject, firmly shook her head. 'No. Presumably they're doing all the forensic tests, going through Missing Persons files and what-have-you, but they were hardly likely to share anything they knew with me, were they?'

'Hardly. So, Debbie, you weren't even aware of the boarded-up bit in the cellar in Pelling House, were you?'

'No. I may have glanced down there when we were looking round with the estate agent, but that's it. There wasn't a light fixed up, so, as I say, I never went down to the cellar.'

'Surely you must've been glad of the space for storage?'

'No. We moved from a tiny flat just along the road here, so we didn't have nearly enough furniture for somewhere like that. And you've no idea how much cupboard space there is in Pelling House,' she added wistfully.

'What about Francis?'

'Sorry?'

'You've said you didn't, but did Francis often go down to the cellar?'

There was a distinct beat of silence before Debbie Carlton replied, 'No. Hardly ever.'

Chapter Six

There was a click of the downstairs door being unlocked, and someone called up, 'Are you there, Debbie love?' The voice was elderly, but strong, with the hint of a Sussex accent.

'Yes, Mum, come on up. I've got someone here.'

The woman who appeared at the sitting-room door was stout with a tight grey perm and a bulging raffia-covered shopping basket. She looked infinitely reliable. Carole had no difficulty picturing her behind an old-fashioned grocer's counter, able instantly to put her hand on all her stock, ready to take and pass on confidences. The grocery would have been a sub-station in the network of Fedborough's communications, the kind of essential information source which has disappeared in the days of out-of-town superstores.

Debbie's mother looked like a character from a bygone age, a card from a game of 'Happy Families'. Mr Bun the Baker. Mrs Franks the Grocer. Comparing Debbie's elegance, Carole reflected on the unlikeliness of Miss Franks the Grocer's Daughter ever being part of the same set. But seeing the two of them together did help to put Debbie Carlton into context. Her rise to art school, wealthy marriage and interior design consultancy had been from comparatively humble origins.

'This is my mother, Billie Franks. Carole Seddon.'

The old woman's brow wrinkled. 'I don't think we've met, have we?' There was no criticism in her words, only puzzlement. It was unusual for Mrs Franks to meet anyone in Fedborough whom she didn't know.

'I live in Fethering.'

'Ah. That would explain it.' If Carole had said Reykjavik or Valparaiso, she would have got the same reaction. Billie Franks reached into her basket. 'Reg got me a couple of lettuces out of his allotment, and I thought you could probably do with one, love.'

'Thanks, Mum.'

'I'll put it through in the kitchen.' Billie Franks bustled off. She treated the flat as if it were her own, and her daughter showed no signs of resenting the assumption.

'I'd better be off, if your mother's . . .'

'Don't worry. She won't be staying. She's just on her way to visit Dad.'

'Oh?'

'He's in a nursing home down at Rustington. The Elms.'

'Yes, you said. I'm sorry.'

'Completely gone. Alzheimer's, I'm afraid. He hasn't a clue what's going on, but Mum still goes and sees him every day.' Debbie looked up as her mother came back from the kitchen. 'Just telling Carole about Dad.'

'Ah.' Billie Franks held the basket comfortably against her stomach. 'I thought he seemed a lot brighter yesterday. Really taking things in. He recognized me. Called me "nurse", but he did definitely recognize me. I think he's on the mend, you know.'

There was a plea in Debbie Carlton's eyes, begging Carole not to say anything about the unlikelihood of anyone making a recovery from Alzheimer's Disease. Let my mother keep her fantasies, however unrealistic they may be. Carole smiled acknowledgment. She wouldn't have said anything, anyway.

'Won't you stay and have some tea, Mum?'

'No, thank you, love. I'll go straight down to Rustington. You know your Dad frets if I'm late.' This, Carole felt sure, was another of the illusions that sustained Billie Franks in her hopeless predicament. 'I'll give you a call later and let you know how he is.' She paused, for the first time ill at ease. 'You haven't, er . . .'

Mother and daughter had an almost telepathic understanding. 'Heard any more from the police? No, Mum, not since yesterday. I was just talking about it,' she went on, with what sounded to Carole like deliberation.

'Terrible business.' Billie Franks shook her head. Not a hair of her tight perm shifted. 'You'd heard presumably, Carole . . .?'

'Hard to escape. It's been all over the media.'

'Yes. People are disgusting. You know, when I walked past Pelling House coming up here, there was a big crowd outside. Ghouls, I call them. Why can't they go and look at the Castle instead? I don't think murder should be a tourist attraction, do you?'

Carole dutifully shook her head.

'It's the single, solitary reason, Debbie love, I'm glad you're no longer in that house. To think that thing was probably down there in the cellar all the time that you . . . Ugh, it makes me shiver to think about it.'

Carole decided to risk a little investigation. 'Mrs Franks . . .'

'Billie, please. Everyone calls me Billie.'

'All right, Billie. It sounds to me that there's not a lot

goes on in Fedborough you don't know about . . .' The old woman smiled complacent acceptance of this truth. 'So what's the talk on the street? Does anyone have any idea who the torso may have been?'

Billie Franks gave a contemptuous 'Huh. There are as many theories as I've had hot dinners, and I'm seventy-four, so that's a good few. No, the gossip-mills have been churning around like nobody's business. Virtually everyone who's left Fedborough in the last twenty years has been suggested, not to mention drug dealers, prostitutes and unacknowledged members of the Royal Family. Reg even reckons it's the work of a serial killer.'

'But surely this is only one case. There haven't been any others, have there?'

'Exactly, Carole. Which may give you some idea of the level of Reg's intellectual achievement. He was a dunce from the day he was born, always being kept in after school.'

Carole grinned, then, casually, asked, 'And do you have any theory as to who the dead woman might be, Billie?'

Was she being oversensitive to detect an almost imperceptible hesitation, before Billie Franks said, 'No. No idea at all'?

Chapter Seven

'There was nothing on the local news,' said Jude. They were in Carole's sitting room, in front of the log-effect gas fire, which looked even less welcoming when switched off. Every surface in the room gleamed from punctilious polishing. The décor was unimpeachable, but anonymous. Like its owner, the room resisted intimacy.

Jude had tried to get Carole to come to her house for coffee – or even, as it was already late afternoon, a glass of wine – but her neighbour had opposed the suggestion. The process of rapprochement between them might have started, but any further progress would be at the pace Carole dictated. So Jude had acceded to the request to talk in High Tor rather than Woodside Cottage, and Carole had filled her in on the morning's visit to Debbie Carlton.

'So the police have no idea who the torso belonged to?'

Jude shrugged. 'No idea they're yet ready to make public, anyway.'

'It is frustrating,' Carole observed, not for the first time, 'knowing they have all kinds of information at their fingertips, and we don't have access to it.'

'Murder is their job,' Jude pointed out. 'With us it's only really a casual interest.'

'Like bridge and line-dancing and amateur dramatics and all those other things recommended for the retired to fill their lives with.' The bitterness in her voice showed how much Carole still resented her enforced early departure from the Home Office. Jude was sometimes disturbed by the depths of varied resentments that lay within her neighbour, and wondered whether they could ever fully be eased away. Carole did seem to make life unnecessarily difficult for herself. Prickliness was not part of Jude's emotional vocabulary, and she had had long-term plans to humanize Carole. The plans had even been making some progress, until the split-up with Ted Crisp had moved everything back to square one.

Still, not the moment to pursue that. Jude moved the conversation on. 'I had a call from Kim Roxby this morning. I'd left a message, thanking them for the dinner party. A bit late, but quite honestly, given the way Saturday evening ended, social niceties got rather forgotten.'

'Did she talk about the torso?'

Jude was encouraged by the eagerness in her friend's voice. She'd been right. Investigating a murder might be just the thing to jolt Carole out of her cycle of self-recrimination.

'Yes. She hadn't got much to add to the little we already know. Needless to say, the Roxbys have had a lot more to do with the police than I did. Pelling House is still sealed off. Kim's sent the kids to her mother's. That's in Angmering. Kim and Grant have booked into a plush hotel up on the Downs for the duration.'

'Will the police pay for that?'

'No idea. With the money Grant's got, I'm sure he'll never even bother to ask.' Jude looked thoughtful. 'I hope Harry's all right . . .'

'Hm?'

'Grant and Kim's oldest. The one who found the thing.

He's at a very tricky stage of his life, and it was a ghastly shock for him.'

'Oh, he'll get over it.' Carole hated sentimentality about the young. Her attitude to children had always been brusque and practical. She sometimes worried that she had taken that approach too far with her own son. Maybe that was why Stephen didn't come and see her very often, a symptom of the coldness of which David had always accused her.

And maybe that coldness was also what had made her relationship with Ted Crisp come to grief. She felt herself sinking into the familiar spiral of self-hatred, and with an effort brought her mind back to the torso in Fed-borough. 'So Kim Roxby hasn't got any sidelights from the police about anything . . . how long the body had been in the cellar, for example?'

'She did overhear one of the forensic people saying he reckoned it was at least three years old.'

'Which would mean the death happened before Francis and Debbie Carlton bought Pelling House.'

'Hm. I wonder who owned the place before them . . .?'

Carole smiled smugly. 'I can, in fact, give you that information. It was owned by a man called Roddy Har-greaves. According to Debbie, he now virtually lives in the Coach and Horses pub in Fed. He had something to do with the pleasure boats down near Fed Bridge.'

'Presumably the police will have talked to him?'

'I imagine so. Again, it's so frustrating not knowing what they're up to.'

Jude smiled. 'Unless we can find someone who'll hack into their computers, I'm afraid we're stuck with that.' She pushed a hand thoughtfully through the twists of her blonde hair. 'There was something about the body that was funny, you know . . .'

'Having no limbs is pretty funny. Funny peculiar, that is, not funny ha ha.'

'Something else. I don't know anything about forensics or pathology, but I'd have thought a body that'd been dead three years would have lost most of its skin and flesh.'

'Depends entirely on where it's been kept for those three years.' Here was a subject Carole did know a bit about. Her work in the Home Office had occasionally involved talking to policemen on related subjects. 'Bodies buried in peat or in glaciers have been preserved virtually intact for centuries.'

'Not a lot of peat or glaciers round Fedborough, are there?'

'No, but there are other things that can have a kind of mummifying effect. Being in a very smoky environment, for one. Or in some cases, bodies have been preserved by wind, draughts even . . . I think I'm right. Hang on, I've got a book on the subject.'

Carole knew exactly where on her shelves the required volume was, and quickly found the relevant page. 'It can be in a draught. Or in the sun and air. The tissues don't putrefy, but just slowly dry up.'

'Like dried meat or fish.'

'I suppose so, yes.' Carole grimaced.

'Well, if that's the case,' Jude went on, 'then I don't think the torso could've been in Pelling House for very long.'

'Why not?'

'The cellar was terribly damp. It smelt musty and mildewy. And Grant was saying earlier in the evening that he'd heard it actually fills up with water when the Fether gets really high.'

'Maybe the body had been moved then . . .' Carole's eyes were still scanning the page as she spoke. 'Ah, no, that may not be it, though . . . Book also says a body can become petrified . . .'

'I'd be petrified if someone was cutting off my arms and legs.'

'Very funny, Jude,' Carole responded primly, and went on, 'Adipocere – that's a sort of waxy stuff – forms on the external parts of the body and it can end up looking like a marble statue. Trouble is, that only happens in very damp, airless conditions. So . . . did the torso you saw look more mummified or petrified?'

Jude shook her head glumly. 'I don't have the expert knowledge to answer that, I'm afraid.'

'Well, all right, did it look more dried-up or waxen?'

'Dried-up, I'd say.'

'That would mean it'd been mummified, which would certainly be unlikely in a damp cellar.' Carole closed the book with annoyance. 'There's so much we just don't know.'

'Like, for instance, where are the two arms and legs that were once part of the torso?'

'Good point.' Carole returned the reference book to its allotted place. 'Mind you, if for the moment we put on one side the more extreme explanations, like a psychopath getting his kicks, a religious ritual . . . or cannibalism . . . there's only one sensible reason why someone would cut up a body.'

'What?'

'Ease of disposal. It's a cliché of criminality that murder's easy enough to commit; the difficult bit is getting rid of the body. Much less difficult, though, if you scatter limbs round the country and then get rid of the torso separately. You could even carve the torso up too. And doing that could also help to make identification more difficult.'

'So,' Jude started slowly, 'we might be looking at a scenario where our murderer . . .' Carole didn't pick up her use of the word. Both of them were now convinced that they were dealing with a murder. ' . . . our murderer was in the process of disposing of the body, had got rid of the arms and legs, and then had to stop for some reason . . .'

'For some reason.' Carole sounded testy with frustration. 'And what chance do we have of finding out that reason? Very little, I would think. We seem to be up against a brick wall. There's no other avenue of investigation we can follow.'

'Oh, I wouldn't say that.'

'What do you mean?'

'We know the name of the person who owned Pelling House before the Carltons.'

'Yes, but we don't know him. We don't know where he lives.'

'Debbie said he's always in the Coach and Horses in Fedborough.'

'But we still don't know him,' Carole wailed. 'We haven't been introduced.'

'Oh, for heaven's sake! Come on, get your coat. I'm going to treat you to supper in the Coach and Horses.'

As recollection of her recent shame encompassed her, Carole froze. 'Jude,' she whispered, appalled, 'I can't go into a pub.'

Chapter Eight

There were no rough pubs in Fedborough – there was nothing rough in Fedborough – so the town's drinking-holes had to be graded upwards by degrees of gentility rather than downwards by loucheness. On this scale the Coach and Horses in Pelling Street was just over halfway up, not aspiring to the manicured hotel splendour of the Pelling Arms, nor yet as ordinary as the Home Hostelries chain predictability of the Black Horse.

The Coach and Horses had been built as a pub in the early nineteenth century, and sympathetically restored at the end of the twentieth. The new owners were a shrewd couple, skilful managers who recognized the appeal of old beams and large fireplaces in a tourist trap like Fedborough. The stripped-down brick walls were decorated with old photographs of the town – horse-drawn carriages labouring up the High Street, a long-aproned poulterer with a display of Christmas turkeys hanging from his shop front, an Edwardian pageant amid the ruins of Fedborough Castle, a flag-waving crowd celebrating VE Day. The bar was lit by discreet coach-lamps, whose reflections sparkled on polished tables, on the handles of beer pumps and on the display of bottles behind the counter. Elegantly done, but a little impersonal in its efficiency. As they entered the pub, Carole couldn't help thinking of the scruffier welcome of the Crown and Anchor, and once again tried to force her mind away from corrosive thoughts.

The evening was warm enough for people still to be sitting in the back courtyard, but Jude and Carole decided they would stay inside. A man, in Debbie Carlton's words, whose 'permanent address seems to be the Coach and Horses', was more likely to be found propping up the bar than enjoying the evening sunshine.

The well-trained young barman offered a good choice of white wines and they settled on a Chilean Chardonnay. Carole's instinctive demurral about having any alcohol was swept aside. 'One glass isn't going to affect your driving. And it's bound to end up as two, which won't affect your driving either.'

Carole didn't raise objections, but it wasn't the thought of the car that had prompted her reaction. Much of the time she'd spent with Ted Crisp had been in a pleasant vinous haze, and to resist alcohol now seemed a necessary deprivation – or even punishment.

They found a table and consulted the menu, whose offerings were carefully themed to the locality: 'Steak and Sussex Ale Pie', 'Cod in Batter, fresh every day from LA (Little 'Ampton)', 'Fedborough Fishcakes', 'Castle Quiche'.

'I think I might go for the South Downs Sausages and Mash . . .' said Jude.

' . . . served with Sussex Onion Gravy. Mm, sounds good. What does that mean, though? Does it mean the onions come from Sussex? Or the gravy's made to an old Sussex recipe?'

'It means they get a lot of Americans in here.'

'Yes, you're probably right.' Carole looked around the bar. There were a few men in suits, possibly estate agents having a drink after a heavy day's mortgage-recommending; some fairly obvious tourists in bright T-shirts and unaccustomed shorts; and, at the bar, a knot of four older men whose exclusive, introverted body language showed that they were regulars, and wanted to be recognized as regulars.

'If Roddy Hargreaves is here,' Carole murmured, 'he must be one of those.'

Jude nodded thoughtful agreement. Then abruptly she stood up. 'I'll order the food. You still going for the South Downs Sausages . . . ?'

Carole watched the ensuing scene with amazement, not untinged by envy. Jude had a quality that Carole knew she never had possessed, and never would possess. Jude could talk to people, talk to anyone, and her intrusion was never resented.

It was an alchemy that Carole could not fathom. Partly, she knew, Jude was attractive; men responded to something welcoming in her cuddly body and her large brown eyes. But the technique worked equally well with women. Even as she had the thought, Carole knew that 'technique' was too calculating a word for what Jude did. Casualness, artlessness were the keys to her success.

What Carole witnessed at the bar of the Coach and Horses that evening was a perfect demonstration of the magic. Jude saw the young barman moving towards the group of four regulars and somehow timed her approach to get to the bar at the same moment he reached them. He registered her arrival and for a moment looked uncertain. The regulars knew they'd be served in time; his bosses had instructed him not to keep new business waiting. He turned towards Jude.

'No, please.' She gestured to the four men and grinned. 'Wouldn't want to keep a man from his pint.'

One of the regulars, a red-faced man in his seventies with a luxuriant white moustache, guffawed. 'Now there's a woman who's been well trained. Wouldn't like to give a few lessons to my wife, would you?'

Carole was once again struck by the effortlessness of it all. Jude didn't appear to be trying, nor was she demeaning herself by going along with this sexist nonsense; she was simply indulging in small talk at the bar of a pub. Having never in her life been able to produce the smallest syllable of small talk, Carole felt very envious.

While the barman filled two empty pint glasses and topped up the other two with generous 'Sussex halves', Jude chuckled at what had been said and, holding out the menu, continued, 'Now, you gentlemen look as if you know your way around this area . . .'

'You can say that again,' agreed the man with the moustache and the disapproving wife.

' . . . so perhaps you can tell me what a "South Downs Sausage" is . . .?'

'You've got one of those, haven't you, Roddy?' the moustached man chortled. 'Big one and all, if the town rumours are anything to go by.'

'Very funny,' said the man who had been addressed. His voice was surprisingly upper-class, at odds with his discoloured jeans, broken-down trainers, and a faded Guernsey sweater, which Jude thought must be very hot on a day like that. The voice also contained a hint of reproof, a suggestion that the remark might have been unnecessarily crude. He turned his face to Jude, and she saw that he had a real drinker's nose, a sad purple cluster of broken veins. He was probably only in his early fifties, but looked older.

'I must apologize for my friend. I would imagine that a South Downs Sausage is extraordinarily like any other kind of sausage, but that Keith and Janet, mine host and hostess, reckon they'll sell a few more if they give them some spurious local connection.'

He was extremely polite, but spoke with the punctilious concentration of the regularly drunk.

'Oh, well then, I think I'll go for them.' Having given her order to the barman, Jude took a risk. Turning to the purple nose, she said, 'Your friend called you "Roddy". You're not, by any chance, Roddy Hargreaves, are you?'

'At your service.' He made a little half-bow, which threatened his stability on the bar stool. The friend who'd made the crude remark reached out automatically to steady him.

Having identified her quarry, Jude was faced with a problem. How on earth was she meant to know him? What possible connection could there be between them? What could she say that didn't sound like blatant interrogation?

As ever, she took the direct route. 'Somebody was saying you used to live in Pelling House . . . you know, where the body was found . . .'

This was greeted by a guffaw of recognition from the group. 'Becoming quite the local celebrity, Roddy,' said the red-faced man, wiping his moustache. 'You may not be able to pull the birds by your looks, but they're still fatally attracted to your Jack the Ripper side.'

'Very witty, Jimmy.' Roddy turned to look at Jude. His scrutiny was not openly suspicious, but it was searching.

'The gossip's been spreading then. You don't live in Fedborough, do you?'

'Fethering.'

'Ah.'

'Different kind of folk in Fethering. Very odd people. Low aspirations – that's because so many of them live in bungalows,' observed the one called Jimmy in a jocular tone. Clearly he was the self-appointed wit of the group.

Automatic male laughter followed the sally, but Roddy didn't join in. He appeared to make the decision that he could trust Jude. 'So what are they saying about the torso in Fethering?'

'Everything and nothing. A lot of ill-informed gossip.'

'Much the same as Fedborough, then. By the way, I see you are drinkless. That's a real damsel-in-distress situation. Allow me to remedy it for you.'

'I've got a drink over there with my friend.'

Roddy Hargreaves looked towards their table. 'Why doesn't she come and join us?'

Carole ignored the perfectly clear invitation in Jude's eyes, and looked away. There were some instinctive reactions she could not avoid. From school dances onward, she had resisted the social embarrassment of being dragged across to men with the line, 'Oh, and this is my friend Carole.' She knew she was being stupid, she knew in this particular instance she was losing the chance to be part of the investigation, but there were certain spots which, even after half a century, this particular leopard could not change.

Immediately understanding, Jude said lightly, 'Oh, she hasn't noticed. Well, I will have a Chilean Chardonnay with you then. Thank you very much.'

'Large Chilean Chardonnay, Lee. Sorry, I didn't get your name . . . ?'

'Jude.'

'Good evening, Jude. I, as you pieced together, am Roddy Hargreaves. This is Jimmy Lister, and . . .' As he identified the other two, Jude realized that the man with the moustache must be James Lister, the conductor of Town Walks, he whom the Rev Trigwell had hailed as 'a real character'. Might be a useful source of Fedborough history, Jude filed away – if I could put up with his jokes.

'I suppose, Roddy,' she went on, direct as ever, as he passed her the wine, 'the police have talked to you about what was found in Pelling House?'

'Exhaustively. I was with them for . . . what, four, five hours? Five hours without a drink, imagine that.' There was more knee-jerk laughter. Jude had often thought there was an academic thesis to be written about male laughter in pubs. The words that prompted it didn't need to be funny – indeed, they very rarely were. The important thing was that the cue should be unmistakable and delivered in the right nudging tone; then laughter would inevitably ensue.

'But presumably they didn't confide in you the current state of their investigations?'

'Sadly, no. Didn't give me any pointers to the identity of the corpse, nothing intriguing like that. Just lots of questions about precise dates, when I bought Pelling House, when I sold it, how often I went down to the cellar, all that kind of stuff.'

'Five hours seems quite a long time for just that.'

'Ah,' chipped in James Lister, who felt he had been silent too long, 'that's because Roddy's their number one suspect. The police'd heard some of the things he'd got up to with his South Downs Sausage, you see, so they reckoned the torso was the result of a sex game that went wrong.'

This tastelessness triggered another bark of male laughter. Roddy, to give him his due, did not participate. Despite his drunkenness, he seemed to have slightly more sensitivity than his companions.

'No,' he said quietly, 'they didn't question me as if I was a suspect. The reason that it took so long is that I have a terrible memory for dates. Just about tell you when my own birthday is, but that's it. So all these "when exactly did you take possession of Pelling House, and when exactly did you sell it?" questions got me rather confused. Because I'm afraid the whole period while I was selling up is a bit of a blur.'

'Like every day for you, eh?' guffawed James Lister.

In a practised way, Roddy again ignored this, and amplified his comments. His friends knew the story, had heard it many times, but he needed to tell the newcomer what had happened to him. There was a note of self-justification in his voice. 'I went through a bad patch round then. I'd invested a lot in the pleasure-boat franchise down by Fedborough Bridge . . . do you know where I mean?' Jude nodded. Ruefully he continued, 'Bit of a mess down there now, I know, but I did have big plans for it. Bought the site from Bob Bracken, old bloke who was retiring . . .'

'Still lives in Fedborough, though.' James Lister was ready with the information. As Debbie Carlton had said to Carole, nobody ever left Fedborough. Or perhaps the memory of those who did was immediately erased from the collective consciousness.

'Yes, and Bob'd run it as a nice simple business, selling

ice creams and teas, taking tourists on his motor boat up and down the Fether.' Roddy Hargreaves sighed. 'But of course that wasn't good enough for me. I had much bigger ambitions. I was going to have rowing boats, motor launches, trips down to the sea at Fethering, even hoped to build a small marina. But the Town Committee were against it . . . or against me, I'll never know . . . so they got the planners to back-pedal – never a difficult thing to achieve round here and . . . well . . . My money was trickling away as fast as the little harbour I'd dredged out was silting up again. And it was round that time the marriage was breaking up, so . . .'

The gesture which faded away with his words seemed to express the futility of all ambitions.

'I'm sorry,' said Jude.

'Very nice of you, but you don't need to be. My own fault. What, when I was in the Navy, they would have called "a self-inflicted wound" . . . like getting an infection from a tattooist's dirty needle. Fact is, I've always been crap with money. Lost a packet in the Lloyd's crash and . . .' a shrug ' . . . so it goes on. Money and me can't wait to be parted. Just seems to trickle away.'

'Mostly down the urinal here.' James Lister was inevitably ready with his quip. And, equally inevitably, the laugh followed.

'Did the police ask you if you had any idea who the torso might have been?'

'Oh yes, Jude, they did. And I'm afraid I couldn't give any very helpful answers. As I said, that whole period's a bit of a blur. Mind you,' he continued, as if suddenly thinking of the idea, 'I don't know what other answer they were expecting me to give. "Oh yes, officer, of course I knew there was a dismembered corpse down in the cellar all the time I lived there. I just didn't mention it because I didn't want to cause any trouble."'

This too got a laugh from the other three men, but Jude was not certain Roddy had delivered it as a joke. There was a pain behind his words, perhaps an awareness of what he had become. Roddy Hargreaves had once had higher ambitions than ending up as a barfly in a Fedborough pub, recycling stale conversation and jokes with three old bores.

'Good Lord, my glass is empty! That's a nasty shock for a chap! Emergency – pint transfusion, please!' James Lister got his grunt of laughter. 'Your shout, I think, Roddy.'

The ordering of another round coincided with the appearance from the kitchen of a waitress bearing heaped plates of food. 'Two South Downs Sausages!' she called out.

'Two?' James Lister winked at Jude. 'Sure you can manage two at the same time?'

At other times she might have given the innuendo a sharp answer, but on this occasion she just smiled and turned to Roddy Hargreaves, who was having trouble getting his wallet out of his jeans' back pocket. Once again he swayed perilously on the bar stool.

Just before moving across to join Carole with their South Downs Sausages, she looked straight into Roddy Hargreaves's eyes, her brown ones probing the bloodshot blue of his.

'So you really have no idea who the torso might be?'

The bleary eyes became focused in a moment of intelligence and caution.

'No,' he said. 'No idea at all.'

Chapter Nine

Their meal was slightly awkward. They could not be unaware of Roddy Hargreaves and his chortling coterie at the bar, and Jude was not offended but rather puzzled by Carole's standoffishness when she'd been invited to join them. Carole herself was painfully aware of yet another example of the spikiness in her character. Just being in a pub had started up again the cycle of recrimination about having made a fool of herself with Ted Crisp.

And it wasn't the moment for Jude to give a resumé of the little information she had got from Roddy Hargreaves.

So they didn't talk much as they waded through their plates of South Downs Sausages. Jude had two large Chilean Chardonnays to drink, but Carole refused the offer of a second for herself. She didn't even finish her first, feeling that the punishment she deserved was not yet complete. Jude, not usually bothered about waste, still didn't like to see alcohol going undrunk, so she downed the remains of Carole's glass as they rose from the table.

'Oh, just a minute,' she said.

Carole hovered by the pub door, feeling more than ever a social outcast, as Jude went back to the group of men.

'Pleasure to meet you all,' she said. 'And it's suddenly

struck me . . . are you the James Lister who I've heard does Town Walks round Fedborough . . .?'

He beamed. 'The very same, at your service. Always at the service of the ladies,' he smirked.

'When do they happen?'

'Sunday morning at eleven. I always service the ladies at eleven o'clock on a Sunday morning.' He winked in a manner which was intended to be roguish rather than repellent, but failed to achieve its object. 'Allow me to present my card.'

'Thank you very much,' said Jude. 'I'd really like to find out more about Fedborough.'

'Let's go the long way round,' she said when they got outside the pub. The June day was dwindling to twilight, but the tall frontages of Fedborough's houses still looked unimpeachably respectable.

'Did you find out much?'

'Not a lot. You could have heard anything I did find out.'

'Yes.' A blush suffused Carole's pale cheeks. 'I'm sorry. There are certain situations when . . .'

'It's all right,' said Jude easily. 'Don't worry. Roddy Hargreaves denied knowing the torso was there while he owned the house.'

'Presumably he would have made that denial, whether it was true or even if he had killed and dismembered the body himself.'

'Exactly. Still, we've made contact. If we need to follow up—' Jude looked at the card in her hand. 'Do you fancy doing a guided walk round Fedborough on Sunday morning?'

'Well, I . . . What would be achieved by that?'

Jude shrugged. 'Bit of background. Get to know the place. Find out perhaps what horrors lurk behind all this middle-class respectability.'

'All right. I'm game for it. Why're we going this way?'

'This is Pelling Street, which in the perverse way of English country towns is not where one will find the Pelling Arms, that being in the High Street, but is, however, where one will find Pelling House.'

'Ah. We're joining the ghouls, are we?'

'If you want to put it that way, Carole, yes. Though I doubt if there'll be many of those around now. Unless the police release more information soon, I think this murder will be very much less than a nine days' wonder.'

'The gossip won't stop.'

'Not in Fedborough, no. But I don't think many more out-of-towners will bother to come down here in search of cheap thrills.'

They were now within sight of the house. A Land Rover Discovery was parked opposite. 'Ah, they're back,' said Jude.

'Mm?'

'Kim and Grant. That's their car. They must have been allowed back into the house.'

They walked past the red-brick façade and the fine white portico without breaking step. No bloodthirsty onlookers stood drooling outside. There was no police tape, no notices visible. Pelling House had lost all signs of its recent notoriety and reverted to being just an expensive, respectable dwelling in Fedborough.

'Police didn't really stay long,' Carole observed thoughtfully. 'Body discovered on Saturday night and by Tuesday the house is no longer sealed up. Well, maybe the cellar's still closed, but otherwise the police would appear to have finished their on-site investigations.'

'So, from the knowledge of their ways you gleaned in the Home Office, what would you say that indicated?'

'One of two things,' Carole replied. 'Perhaps they've found no signs of anything untoward in the rest of the house and therefore concluded that the body was either killed in the cellar or moved to the cellar post mortem. So the cellar is the only part of the house they're continuing to examine . . .'

'Or?'

'Or the police have already reached their conclusions as to who the torso belonged to, and how she was killed. Which would mean that their investigation is at an end.'

Chapter Ten

The beach was the only place in Fethering where Carole Seddon felt secure. Ted Crisp never went on the beach. Indeed, he managed to conduct his whole life as if ignorant of the fact that Fethering was on the coast. His base was inside the Crown and Anchor, and for all the difference its location made to his lifestyle, the pub could have been in any part of the British Isles.

To get to the beach, though, now involved a detour for Carole. The direct route from High Tor went too close for comfort to the Crown and Anchor, so, resisting Gulliver's pulling the other way in his enthusiasm to be amongst the delectable smells of the shoreline, she walked determinedly along to the banks of the Fether, and followed the river to the shingle by Fethering Yacht Club.

Carole's spirits were low again that Wednesday morning. The detour made her feel foolish, bringing back the bilious taste of all her other foolishness. And the revival of excitement brought on by thinking about the Fedborough torso now seemed another example of over-reaction. She and Jude had so little to go on, so little information, there was no point in even thinking about the mystery. The fact that the Roxbys had been allowed back into Pelling House probably meant that the police already had the investigation neatly tied up with a bow on top.

And now she couldn't even discuss it. With characteristic casualness, as they parted the evening before, Jude had said, 'I'm going to be away for a few days. Back Saturday, I should think. So hope we're on for the Town Walk on Sunday.'

It was typical. Jude was always making remarks like that, and never backing them up with any detail. Where was she going to be 'away for a few days'? Was it work or pleasure? Who was she going to be with? Would that be work or pleasure? But, as ever, before these supplementary questions could be posed, the moment had passed.

What increased Carole's frustration was the knowledge that if she had managed to ask any of them, Jude would have given straight, truthful answers. The lack of precision which surrounded her life was not a result of deliberate concealment; but opportunities to ask about its basics were rare and, when they arose, seemed to flash by. After many months of what, by Carole's standards, was close friendship, the sum total of the facts she knew about her neighbour was distressingly small.

Jude had done a lot of varied things in her life. She had almost certainly been married at some point, and had had a lot of lovers. She might still have a lot of lovers, for all Carole knew. Jude had possibly once been an actress, she may have worked in catering, she'd certainly lived abroad for a while. She showed sympathy for New Age ideas, and may have done some work as an alternative therapist. She was fifty-five years old.

And that was it. A pathetically meagre haul of information. Carole didn't know where Jude had been brought up, where she had gone to school, whether she'd had further education of any kind. She didn't even know her neighbour's surname, for God's sake. Or what Jude lived on. Though her home, Woodside Cottage, was filled with second-hand furniture and gave the impression that money was tight, she was still capable of sudden generosity and extravagance.

For Carole, who liked everything in her life defined by detail, this ignorance was extremely galling. Jude's personal history was like the horizon; all the time you felt you were getting closer, it remained exactly the same distance away.

Carole let Gulliver off his lead, and he dashed off over the heaped pebbles to the flat sand, kicking up little flurries in his excitement. The tide was receding, exposing expanses of deep grey which in the June sunlight gradually turned lighter and crustier. Maybe there would be a good summer this year . . . Maybe not . . . Global warming had recently made such changes to the climate that even the weather-wise fishermen of Fethering no longer trusted their own predictions.

Carole found herself looking up towards the Yacht Club and the adjacent seawall that protected the beach against the fast tidal flow of the Fether. From what seemed like another life, her mind instantly pictured Ted Crisp helping in the rescue of a teenage boy from the river mud. Resolutely, she turned her back on the scene and strode across the crunchy sand, searching for new thoughts to drive out the unwelcome image.

The only subject that would engage her mind was the limbless body in Fedborough. If the police had reached a solution, then there would be something about it on the news. But if they hadn't . . . maybe continuing her investigation would be worthwhile after all . . .

But how? Because of her standoffishness in the Coach and Horses the previous evening, Carole still had only one contact with any connection to the case. Debbie Carlton. But the interior designer seemed to have told her everything she knew that might be relevant. How could Carole justify further questioning, and indeed what further questions could she ask?

Behind her glasses the pale blue eyes scrunched up with the effort of concentration as she tried to get her thoughts in order and to draw a line of logic through them.

Jude's description of the state of the body made Carole increasingly sure that it had not been killed in the cellar of Pelling House. The crime – or accident, it could still just be an accident – had happened elsewhere and the body had then been moved. If she'd seen the torso herself, Carole might have been able to judge whether the dismemberment had also taken place elsewhere. Her ex-Home Office reference library contained some pretty gruesome photographs of pre-mortem and post-mortem injuries. But the description relayed by Jude hadn't been detailed enough for her to form a reliable opinion. All she knew was that the removal of the limbs had been a neat job.

Another argument for the death taking place elsewhere was the collapse of the cardboard box which had contained the remains. The damp, or rising water, in the Pelling House cellar had got to that, but had little effect on the torso, suggesting that mummification had taken place before the body was put in the box. Carole wished she could have seen that box. Once again she felt unreasoning resentment against the advantages the police force have over the enthusiastic amateur.

The movement of the body to Pelling House could have happened during the ownership of the Roxbys (which was very unlikely), the Carltons, or of Roddy Hargreaves . . . and maybe of his wife. He'd talked about a marriage breaking up, which might well have coincided with his moving from the marital home . . . She must try to find out something about Mrs Hargreaves.

Carole strained for other connections, for other pointers, other clues. All she could come up with was the moment of hesitation before Debbie Carlton had said her husband rarely went down to the cellar, and the flash of caution exchanged between Debbie and her mother when Carole had asked if they knew who the dead woman might be.

Not much, but it was all she had. Carole called to a reluctant Gulliver and set off back up the beach to make a phone call.

'Debbie, I just wanted to say thank you so much for coffee yesterday . . .'

'My pleasure. It was nice to see you.'

'And I also wanted to apologize . . .'

'I told you there's no need. In my line of business people are always blowing hot and cold. Don't worry about it.'

'That wasn't what I wanted to apologize for. I'm sorry that I went on so much about the . . . you know, the discovery in Pelling House.'

'If I hadn't wanted to talk about it, I wouldn't have done.'

'No, but I'm sorry. I got a bit carried away,' said Carole, who had spent her entire life in avoidance of getting carried away. And, she thought bitterly, regretting it on the rare occasions when I do.

'You're not the only one. Nobody in Fedborough seems to be talking about anything else. And everyone's got their own pet theories about who the body is, and who killed her. All kinds of dreadful old prejudices are rising to the surface. Sometimes it's hard to believe the depths of resentment you get in a place like this.'

'In small country towns everyone has always known everyone else's business.'

'Yes. Or thought they did. And in many cases been one hundred per cent wrong.' Debbie Carlton spoke as if she was referring to some unpleasant experience of her own. 'Not, of course, that that stops the gossip-mills from churning round.'

'I gather the Roxbys have been allowed to move back into Pelling House,' said Carole tentatively.

Debbie seemed to have no curiosity about her source of information. 'Yes, they have.'

'Mightn't that suggest that the police have finished their investigations there?'

'Who knows? They haven't said anything about it to me.'

'But they have spoken to you again?'

'Oh yes. They wanted Francis's address. He's in Florida. With Jonelle.' She tried to say the name with no intonation, but failed. 'Seems in the future he'll be spending a lot of time out in Florida.'

'Ah. The police didn't say why they wanted to talk to him?'

'Presumably the same reason they wanted to talk to me. Check dates, when we bought Pelling House and so on.'

'And how often Francis used to go down to the cellar there?'

'Yes,' said Debbie Carlton shortly.

'You implied yesterday that Francis went down there more often than you did . . .'

'Well, obviously, men spend more time doing DIY and . . . He kept some tools down there . . . He—' She was flustered. 'But I'm sure he didn't know about the torso.'

'You can't be positive about that.'

'No, I can't be positive, but . . . Look, I know we ended on bad terms, but I was with Francis for more than five years. I was in love with him, and I can still recognize the good qualities in his character. OK, he wasn't that reliable and he was a bit tight-fisted and, yes, I know he had other affairs before Jonelle . . . but there is no way my husband – my ex-husband – is a murderer!'

Funny, thought Carole, I didn't mention the word 'murder'. At the end of their conversation, she put the phone down with some satisfaction. She knew what she had just heard: the sound of a woman protesting too much. Debbie Carlton was suspicious that her ex-husband might have some connection with the torso.

Chapter Eleven

Jude got back late on the Friday night. It had been an emotionally draining trip and she slept in on the Saturday morning. When she got up, the garage door of High Tor was hooked open, and there was no sign of the immaculate Renault. Carole was probably off doing a big Sainsbury's shop.

Jude knew she should really do the same. She was out of virtually everything. Not even enough in the freezer to make herself lunch. For Carole, that would have been a definite argument to go shopping. For Jude, it was an argument to go and have lunch at the Crown and Anchor.

The bar looked welcoming and relaxed, but even scruffier than before. The same could be said for its owner. Ted Crisp's hair and beard were shaggier, and it was a few days since their last encounter with shampoo. His uniform T-shirt and tracksuit trousers also looked as though they had been on for a while. Perhaps, Jude thought, like Carole, he was reacting to the end of their relationship by becoming more intensely himself. She had become more uptight than ever, he more sloppy. As if to say: This is what I'm really like. You'd hate me if you saw me now. It could never have worked.

Jude hadn't had any breakfast and was hungry, so arrived at the pub soon after twelve. There were a couple of weekending families squabbling over crisps and Coke at the open-air tables, but she was the only customer inside the bar. Ted Crisp looked up lugubriously, took her in slowly, and said, 'Hello, stranger.'

'Yes, sorry I haven't been in much recently. I've had to—'

'No need to apologize. Still a large white wine, is it?'

'Please. And are you taking food orders yet?'

'Sure. Recommend the Fisherman's Pie today. Got a bit of everything in it, that has, and all fresh from the quay. Cheesy potato on top, and it's served with chips the size of logs. Get outside of that and you won't hurt.'

'Your silver-tongued sales talk has persuaded me. I'll go for it. God, I'm starving.'

Ted called the order through to an unseen presence in the kitchen, then turned back to her. 'What you been up to, then?'

When asked direct questions, Jude always answered. Carole was the only one whose gentility made her think she'd gone too far into their friendship to start asking.

'I've been with a friend who's just lost her husband. Very cut-up, needless to say. I've been hand-holding to get her through the funeral.'

'Ah. I see. There you are.' Ted pushed across her glass of wine. There was a silence. The ghost of Carole seemed to hover between them, and could only be exorcized by the mention of her name.

Ted took a clumsy run at it. 'Thought I might have lost *your* custom too.'

'Hm?'

'You know, when I put your friend's back up. Thought I might get the old sisterly solidarity reaction.'

Jude shook her head and sighed in exasperation. 'No,

I wouldn't behave like that. And you haven't exactly put Carole's back up. She just feels embarrassed, that's all. Oh come on, Ted, it's not as if you treated her badly.'

'Didn't I?'

'No. It just didn't work out between you, that's all. You were looking for different things.'

'You can say that again.' Ted Crisp wearily ran a hand through the foliage of his beard. 'Carole . . .' There, he'd managed to say it. 'Carole kept wanting to define everything. Where were we going? What was the nature of our relationship?' He let out a defeated sigh. 'Why is it that men think in terms of enjoying things right now and are never in any hurry to see what happens next, whereas women are always thinking in terms of bloody *relationships*?'

'That's been one of the great gender issues since time began,' said Jude.

'Yes, in the bloody garden of Eden I bet Adam was just thinking "This is all very nice", while Eve was working out how many fig-leaves it'd take to make the curtains. Well, I'm afraid, in terms of what me and Carole were thinking, we could have been on two different planets.'

Jude grinned. 'Might be a good idea for a book in that.' She went on, 'You have to remember, of course, Ted, that I don't think Carole's ever before been in a casual relationship.'

'You're right. Seems like the marriage was about it for her. Funny, 'cause she's a bloody attractive woman.'

'I'm not sure that she thinks that.'

'No. The husband – bloody David – when he left her, he drained away any little bit of confidence she might have had. Really knocked her sideways, that. She never opened up to me much, you know, like emotionally, but she said something once that indicated just how much he'd hurt her.'

'Anyway, I'm sure soon you and Carole'll be able to . . . you know . . . see each other without any pressure or recrimination.'

' "Just be friends"?' He grimaced cynically. 'Yeah. Sounds simple. Trouble is, it never turns out like that, does it?' Having performed the ceremony of exorcism, he now wanted to put it behind him. 'Anyway, what you been up to? Apart from comforting the bereaved?'

'Been having some thoughts about that business up in Fedborough . . .'

' "The Torso in the Town". Yeah, lot of the old codgers in here been maundering on about that. Heard every kind of theory about who the body might've been – names ranging from Eva Braun, who somehow survived the bunker in Berlin, to Lord Lucan after a sex change. One old geezer even reckoned she was a serial killer . . . who got into a feud with another serial killer. Mind you, I don't believe that.'

'Why not?' asked Jude, stepping straight into the trap he had prepared for her.

'Because I know she was totally 'armless.'

She groaned. 'God, I do set them up for you, don't I, Ted?'

'Sorry. Old habits die hard. When you done the stand-up circuit as long as I did, you're always looking for the comic angle.'

'And the tasteless angle?'

'Oh, got to be tasteless in comedy these days. If you don't offend a few people, then you're not cutting-edge.'

Jude took a long swallow from her glass. Isn't wine

wonderful, she thought. And now doctors are even saying it's good for us. Maybe there is a God, after all.

'So, Ted, apart from the speculations of the Fethering old fogeys, have you heard any intelligent ideas about what might have happened in Fedborough? I'm sure you've been keeping your ears open.'

'You bet I have. And I dare say you have too . . . you and . . .' Unable to say Carole's name again, he moved swiftly on. 'Even got a theory of my own, and all . . .'

'What's that?'

He made a self-deprecating shrug. 'Well, not so much a theory, more an idea of where I might start investigating if I was in charge of the case.'

'Really? I didn't know you knew anyone in Fedborough.'

'A few people. In this business you tend to know who runs the local boozers. Meet them from time to time, chat on the phone, keep tabs on dangerous elements, you know.'

'I didn't think there were any dangerous elements in Fethering.'

'Don't believe everything you read in the brochure, darling. They're not all old farts come in here, you know. And even the old ones can be troublemakers. Be amazed how much carnage you can cause with a Zimmer frame.'

Jude chuckled. 'So . . . who? Where would you start your investigations, Superintendent Crisp?'

'Two or three years back,' said Ted, scratching at his beard, 'just after I took over this place, geezer came to see me. Wanted to organize pleasure trips down the Fether from Fedborough, and was trying to get some deal to include lunch in the pub here. He'd just bought up the old boatsheds and café from an old geezer called Bob

Bracken, who I know from way back. And he was working on the project with an architect who sometimes comes in here, so I'd heard a bit about what was going on. Anyway, the new owner's figures didn't work out, the discount he was asking would have eaten up any profit so far as I was concerned, so the idea's a complete non-starter . . . but he was a nice bloke. Bit of a boozer, but, you know, very well-spoken, real gentleman of the old school.'

'Roddy Hargreaves,' Jude murmured.

'You know him?'

'Met him earlier in the week.'

'Right. Anyway, we had a few drinks together and he started pouring his troubles out, way people do. Occupational hazard in my line of business. And he tells me the lot, how his parents left him with a load of Catholic guilt and a load of money, but how he's never had much of a business brain. Got stung badly when Lloyd's crashed, and that seemed fairly typical of the level of his investment success. Sounded like his plans to set up this pleasure-boat deal was going the same way, and all. Just couldn't grasp the basics of running a business, no mind for detail.

'And the way these things happen, when everything financial's crashing round his ears, he's got problems with his marriage and all. He wasn't vindictive about the wife – quite nice about her, actually – but, reading between the lines of what he's saying, she – called Virginia, some bone-headed deb ten years younger than him – anyway, I got the pretty firm impression she liked him well enough while he'd got the dosh, but rapidly lost interest once that started trickling away.

'Next thing I hear, through Keith and Janet, the couple

who run the Coach and Horses in Pelling Street – that used to be our Roddy's favourite drinking-hole—'

'Still is.'

'Anyway, they tell me his wife's suddenly upped and left him.'

'Where did she go?'

'That's what nobody in Fedborough seems to know. And if I was in charge of the case,' said Ted Crisp, 'that's the first question I'd be asking now . . .'

Chapter Twelve

On the Sunday morning, before she went to Carole's for her lift into Fedborough, Jude had a phone call.

'It's Kim.' Her Pelling House hostess sounded uncharacteristically uptight.

'Anything the matter?'

'Harry.'

'What wrong with him?'

'Well, he's been quite difficult since we moved down here . . . you know, keeps going on about having left all his friends in London and having no one he can talk to. And he says he hates his new school. I keep telling him that he'll soon make friends down here, but . . . You know what they're like at that age. They think everything they feel at any given moment is going to last for ever.'

'Yes.'

'But the thing is, since . . . you know, what he found in the cellar . . . Harry's been much worse. Much more uptight and difficult. He's even been rude to Grant, which is most unlike him. And, well, I've got him an appointment with the local doctor down here, and maybe they can refer him somewhere. Or we've got friends in London who've used behavioural psychologists and could recommend—'

'Don't do that yet, Kim. I'm sure Harry doesn't need a psychologist.'

'No, well, I wasn't keen. But Grant's insisting. You know, Grant's always had that American philosophy that, whatever kind of problem you've got in your life, you simply need to find the right professional expert to cure it.'

'Which is fine for architecture and plumbing – and probably computers, but I'm not convinced it always works with human beings.'

'Nor am I. I tried to make that point to Grant, but . . .' A silent shrug came over the phone. 'You know what Grant's like.'

Jude was getting a much clearer picture of what Grant was like by the minute.

'Anyway, what I said was, before we resorted to doctors and psychologists, I'd ask you to have a word with Harry.'

'Ah.'

'When we first met you in Spain, you were doing that sort of healing stuff, developing a holistic approach to integrating the mind and body.' That wasn't exactly what Jude had been doing, but she didn't contest the description. 'And you seemed to have great sympathy – I mean, the people there got a great deal out of what you were doing – so I was wondering if you would mind talking to Harry . . . ?'

'Mm . . .'

'Obviously we'd pay your going rate for . . . you know, by the hour or a flat fee or—'

'There's no need for that. Yes, of course I'll see if I can help. When were you thinking of?'

'Soon as possible, really. I mean, we've got Sunday

lunch coming up, and Grant's a great traditionalist about liking to have all the family round the table for Sunday lunch, and Harry's going through a phase of not sitting down with us . . .'

'Like at your dinner party?'

'Yes. Yes, I suppose so.'

'Which suggests that it's not the shock of the body in the cellar that's made him like this. That it's just intensified something that was going on, anyway.'

'See, I knew you'd understand. Anyway, as I say, Sunday lunch is looming, and that's going to mean another row between Grant and Harry and—' Kim sounded already exhausted by the prospect, and pleaded, 'If you could come . . . ?'

'I can't do it before lunch, I'm afraid, but I do in fact have to be in Fedborough today. Suppose I dropped in round about three . . . ?'

'Oh, Jude. That would be wonderful.'

'I'll be with a friend, though. Carole Seddon. I'm dependent on her for a lift. Do you mind if I bring her too?'

'No, of course not.'

James Lister had clearly been doing his Town Walks for a long time. There was an automatic quality to his delivery of local history anecdotes which suggested they had been honed over many years. The same applied to his jokes, if that was the right word to describe them. They had the shape of jokes, but the level of wit shown in them was not much above Rotary Club level. And it is common knowledge that Rotary is the lowest form of wit.

Indeed, as James Lister gathered his walkers in the

courtyard of the Pelling Arms, he instantly made a reference to the Club. 'This coaching inn, which dates back to the early eighteenth century, is home to the meetings of the local Rotary, and should you pass by on a Wednesday evening and hear laughter coming from the dining room, that probably means I'm in there, telling one of my jokes.'

There was a tremor of slightly anxious laughter from the group, uncertain what the nature of his jokes might be. Jude, who had heard exactly what they were like, was silent. About a dozen people had assembled in the courtyard – a Japanese couple in designer leisurewear, four Scandinavians in bright colours, the remainder English, including a young couple with a whining toddler in a buggy who Carole thought would probably not last the distance.

'My name's James Lister – Jimmy to my friends – and, without false modesty, what I don't know about the town of Fedborough isn't worth knowing. I am a Chub, and for those of you who think there's something fishy about that . . .' He waited in vain for a laugh. 'Let me tell you that people who are actually born in Fedborough are called "Chubs" because . . .'

The explanation was duly given. 'Now what's going to happen this morning is we'll have a gentle walk round the town, and I will highlight various points of interest for you. The whole thing will take exactly an hour, which means that we will arrive back here where we started at the precise moment that the bar is opening, so those of you who want to can refresh yourselves with a pint of local Fedborough bitter. Don't worry, incidentally, the older ones amongst you . . .'

Carole looked round. She must be the oldest in the group. No, of course she wasn't, she reminded herself.

Jude was actually older than her. Why couldn't she get that idea into her head?

' . . . this walk is going to be taken at a very leisurely pace. I'm over seventy myself . . .' no reaction ' . . . which always surprises people . . .' no evidence of surprise ' . . . but I do keep very fit. Fedborough people, according to a survey, are amongst the fittest in the country. This is due partly to the particularly benign climate of the region, but also, I believe, to the number of hills there are in the town. If you've spent your entire working life climbing up and down the streets of Fedborough, I reckon you're as fit as an Olympic athlete . . . though I don't myself have any gold medals to show for it – yet.'

Again, this sally of Rotarian wit fell on deaf ears.

'What did you do?' The question was asked in good English, with only slight Scandinavian singsong intonation.

'I'm sorry?'

'What did you do for your working life here in Fedborough?'

'Oh.' James Lister seemed a little thrown by the question. 'I was the local butcher.'

They walked up to the Castle ruins, and James Lister gave them a potted history of the siege of Fedborough during the Civil War. 'I like to see myself as a Cavalier rather than a Roundhead – though, if you got my wife on to the subject, she'd say I was more of a bonehead!'

The Japanese couple, who didn't have much English, had by now caught on to the idea that their guide was telling jokes, and greeted each sally with disproportionate hilarity. The rest of the group, who understood exactly what he was saying, was silent. The couple with the toddler had melted away in the Castle grounds and weren't seen again.

From the Castle, James Lister led his party along Dauncey Street, at right angles to the High Street. 'This road, being at the top of the town with views down to the sea at Fethering, has always been one of the most exclusive residential areas of Fedborough. It was here, as you can see from all these fine façades, that the successful merchant traders of the early nineteenth century chose to build their mansions. And Dauncey Street is still a magnet for property buyers, commanding some of the highest prices in the area. Many of the leading lights of the town live here. And,' he concluded coyly, 'guess where I live?'

A Scandinavian voice, apparently not understanding the principle of the rhetorical question, asked, 'Where?'

'I actually live here. In fact, we are standing right outside my house.' He put his arm round Jude's ample waist and drew her face to his. Then, with elaborately manufactured anxiety, he sprang apart from her. 'Oops, better be careful! The wife might see!'

The Japanese couple laughed immoderately. The rest of the group shuffled their feet. Jude felt residual distaste from his beer-breath and the scratch of his white moustache.

'This is Pelling Street, which also, as you see, contains some fine examples of Georgian and Victorian architecture. Pelling Street has always had an inferior status to Dauncey Street . . . though some of the residents don't see it that way. They've even been heard to express the view that Pelling Street is better than Dauncey Street.' He chuckled conspiratorially, and added in an exaggerated whisper, 'They are of course wrong.

'Pelling Street has always had a slightly Bohemian reputation. The respectable people of Fedborough live in Dauncey Street. Down here you get more painters, photographers and people like that. At least two of the houses in Pelling Street were reported to be brothels during the early nineteenth century.' The way he juxtaposed the two ideas left no doubt about James Lister's views on artists.

'Some of you, of course, may have heard of Pelling Street recently on the television or radio, because of the macabre discovery that was made here a few days back. The house in question is Pelling House just along there on the left, with the big white pillars. I would ask you, as we go past, not to snoop too obviously. There is a family in residence at the moment, and of course we wish to preserve their privacy.'

Again the stage whisper was brought into play. 'On the other hand, I would point out that at the front of the house there are ventilation grilles from the cellar, so if you lean down and cop a look through there, you'll be able to see the actual place where the Fedborough torso was found.'

James Lister smacked his lips with relish. The Japanese couple nearly wet themselves.

'Down the bottom of the High Street here we have some fine old shops, of which this, in my view, is the finest. Had you been here five years ago – even three years ago, the sign outside would not have been advertising an estate agents. It would have said "John Lister & Sons, Purveyors of Fine Meat Since 1927". The John Lister in question was the father of yours truly, and very fine meat it was too . . . before any of this BSE nonsense put people off a nice bit of beef on the bone.

'Next door here, what is now rather quaintly called "Yesteryear Antiques" used to be the local grocer's. And behind the shop, if you look up the alley there, what has now been converted into a bijou artist's studio used to be the smokehouse for our shop, where we cured our own bacon and fish and all kinds of other produce.

'Right here we have what used to be the local bakery. Everything was home-made and fresh-baked every day. But now do I need tell you what we have there instead?'

'No,' replied the Scandinavian who didn't understand rhetorical questions.

'We have,' James Lister continued, ignoring him, 'another antique shop! "Bygones and Bric-à-Brac". Which is all very nice for the tourists, I dare say, but isn't so great for the people who live here. Because now, instead of walking down the road to get our meat and eggs and cheese and bread, we have to get into our cars and drive all the way to some out-of-town Sainsbury's or Tesco's and load up with exactly the same stuff as you could buy in any other supermarket in the country.

'Shopping's no longer a personal experience. You used to have businesses that passed from father to son, everyone in the family involved, real skills being developed actually on the job, without any of these meaningless college qualifications and . . .'

Realizing that he was well astride his hobby-horse, James Lister reined himself in, breathing heavily.

'Anyway, on we go. Down towards Fedborough Bridge.

The river – which is called the Fether – is still tidal for another four or five miles upstream. It reaches the sea at Fethering, and twice a day the tides wash up and down, so there's considerable variations in the water level. Which is why, as you see, the houseboats along there are moored with rings around those tall poles, so that they can ride up and down with the tide.

'Now, although some of the houseboats look as if they're about to sink into the river for ever, they are in fact all still inhabited by various Fedborough characters. The one nearest to us is, as you can see, the posh one. It's a very fine modernization of a purpose-built Edwardian houseboat – kind of place where King Edward VII himself might have sneaked off for a dirty weekend with Lillie Langtry. It's now the offices of a local architect. He's another Chub, like me, actually . . . though I don't know whether or not he uses his houseboat for dirty weekends.'

More merriment from the Japanese. And from the literal-minded Scandinavian, 'Is it because there is so much mud on the riverbank that you call the weekend dirty . . . ?'

The Pelling Arms had two bars, the back one refined and elegant for hotel residents and the front one, the Coachman's Bar, more functional for the townsfolk. Since people had drunk there since the eighteenth century, it might have been expected that as many old features as possible would have been preserved, but that wasn't the way the hotel's latest designers had seen things. They had panelled over the old brick walls and wooden beams, and superimposed on to this a structure of false beams. From a hatstand by the log-effect gas fire hung a highwayman's caped cloak and a few tricorn hats. On shelves were piled pieces of strapped leather luggage, dating from at least a hundred years later than the garments. Framed on the walls were ancient bills of fare and price lists for drinks, as well as prints of hunting scenes or of rubicund Dickensian coachmen cheerily flicking whips over their enthusiastic horses.

To Carole and Jude it all seemed a bit perverse, making so much effort to dress up a genuine eighteenth-century bar as a contemporary designer's idea of what an eighteenth-century bar should look like.

James Lister had insisted they have a drink with him. He'd said the same to all of the group, but did little to disguise the fact that Carole and Jude were the ones he wanted to stay. Just Jude really, was Carole's instinctive thought.

The offer of a drink had followed a little ritual, which again felt like a regular part of James Lister's Town Walk routine. He'd made the ending of the tour very precise, leading them all back into the Pelling Arms courtyard, and announcing, 'Well, that's it. As you've probably gathered, I'm extremely proud of this town, and I hope I've given you some interesting insights into its history. Do come and see us again – we're friendly folk in Fedborough – enjoy the rest of your day and remember: be good, and if you can't be good, be careful.'

The roar of uncomprehending laughter from the Japanese couple was followed by an awkward moment of silence. Then one of the Scandinavians reached into his pocket, prompting a bit of wallet-fumbling from the others. James Lister let the man come all the way up to him, proffering a fiver, before he said, 'No, thank you. I do these Town Walks for the pleasure, not the money. I won't accept your thanks in folding form, but if you were to suggest thanking me in liquid form, well, that's another matter altogether.'

His syntax, however, was too confusing for the Scandinavians. Not understanding that he was asking them to buy him a drink, they backed off in some confusion. Within seconds, the rest of the group seemed also to have vanished.

'Oh,' said James Lister, somewhat put down. 'Have to buy myself a drink then. Will you young ladies . . . ?'

'I'll get them,' said Jude, leading the way into the Coachman's Bar. 'What would you like, James?'

'Just say it's a pint of Jimmy's usual.'

Jude relayed the message. Unfortunately, there was a new barman on duty and James had to spell out that his usual was 'a pint of Fedborough, in a jug'. Without consulting Carole, Jude also ordered two large whites.

James Lister took a long swallow from his pint, then did an elaborate lip-licking and moustache-wiping routine, before saying, 'Ah, that hits the spot.' It was not spontaneous; it was learned behaviour. Both women felt pretty sure that, as a boy, James had watched his father John Lister go through exactly the same ritual.

He looked mischievously from side to side. 'Well, aren't I the lucky one – a thorn between two roses, eh? The old animal magnetism doesn't seem to have let me down, does it?'

The Japanese couple were no longer there to laugh at this sally, so he cleared his throat and went on, 'No, very nice to see you attractive young ladies.'

'Don't be ridiculous,' said Carole frostily. 'We're not young, James.'

'Jimmy, please. But let me tell you, when you get to

my age, every woman looks young. And attractive. Except the wife, of course,' he concluded with a predictable guffaw.

Jude cut through the flannel. 'Have you seen Roddy Hargreaves recently?'

'He was in the Coach and Horses lunchtime Friday. Didn't see him in the evening, because I was on duty. The wife was giving one of her Friday dinner parties. You haven't met Fiona, have you?' They shook their heads. 'A treat in store, I assure you. But Roddy, Roddy, let me think . . . Oh, yesterday I was off doing a Rotary fund-raiser, so I didn't see the old devil then either.'

'But he's quite likely to be in the Coach and Horses now, is he?'

'Imagine so. Virtually has his camp bed and sleeping bag behind the counter in there.' A chuckle. 'I might go along and join him for a pint later.' He consulted his watch and changed his mind. 'Or maybe not. Fiona does the full works for lunch on Sunday. More than my life's worth to be late for that, eh?' He followed this with another meaningless chuckle.

Jude drained her glass. 'Well, thank you so much, James, for—'

'Erm . . .' He seemed to want to detain them.

'Sorry?'

'I mentioned my wife gave a dinner party on Friday . . .'

'Yes?'

'It's something she does every Friday, you know.'

'Oh?'

'Roddy's coming to the next one. It's his birthday, so I actually persuaded Fiona to let me invite him.' The implication was that James Lister's wife didn't share his enthusiasm for Roddy Hargreaves. 'And the thing is . . .' He seemed to be having difficulty getting the words out. 'Fiona's always very interested in new people . . . I wondered whether you two would care to join us next Friday as well . . . ?'

Carole flushed. 'Oh, I don't think I could possibly—'

'Yes,' said Jude. 'We'd like that very much.'

Chapter Thirteen

'Odd, isn't it,' she said, as they walked from the Pelling Arms along Pelling Street, 'how helpful everyone in this town is. For our investigation.'

'What do you mean?' asked Carole. 'Are you worried about a conspiracy of helpfulness?'

'Well, think about it. We no sooner get a possible contact who may know something relevant about the mysterious torso than we get a chance to talk to them. You ring Debbie Carlton, she asks you round. We're told Roddy Hargreaves frequents the Coach and Horses; first time we go in there, we meet him.'

'*You* meet him.'

'All right. Doesn't change my point, though. Then for no apparent reason, James Lister, whom again we've hardly met, invites both of us round to dinner when we'll get another chance to see Roddy Hargreaves. To top it all, we're now going – by invitation – to Pelling House, the scene of the crime . . . or at least the scene of the body's discovery.'

'Yes, when you spell it all out, it does sound a bit coincidental, I agree. So is this a conspiracy theory you're putting forward?'

'I don't know. Fedborough's a small town. Everyone seems to know each other's business. Maybe they're all just curious. Maybe they think we have some information about the case they don't.'

'Mm.'

'Or maybe they're just trying to find out exactly how much we do know about the case.'

'That would imply they've got something to hide.'

Jude's lips pursed into a wry grin. 'Somebody's definitely got something to hide. Even if we're not talking about murder, the law still takes a pretty dim view of post-mortem mutilation of corpses.'

'So what do you think we should do about it?'

'Ooh, nothing. When you've got a favourable wind, you don't sail in the opposite direction.'

But inside the Coach and Horses, they found their favourable wind had dropped. Roddy Hargreaves wasn't there.

They walked further along Pelling Street to Pelling House. Jude stepped up the stone steps between the white pillars and raised the large brass doorknocker.

Grant and Kim Roxby didn't agree about Harry. That was clear as soon as Carole and Jude arrived. They were ushered into the room where the dinner party had taken place. The remains of a large Sunday lunch were on the table. There was no sign of any children.

'Jude you remember . . . ?' said Kim.

'Of course.'

'And this is her friend Carole.'

Grant reached across to shake her hand. He was polite, but there was a tension between husband and wife, as if they had been interrupted in the middle of a row.

Grant had just opened a second bottle of red wine. He

waved it as an offering to his guests. They both refused. He topped up his glass, and sat back in his fine old carving chair. He had the look of a man who intended to drink through the afternoon. His face looked tired, and the dyed chestnut hair accentuated its paleness.

'I know why you've come, Jude,' he said, 'and I can't pretend that I'm very much in favour of the idea. If Harry does need help, counselling, whatever – and I'm not sure that he does – I think it should come, with no disrespect to you, from a professional.'

'I'm just going to talk to him, Grant. It can't do any harm. And if it doesn't do him any good, then you still have the option of consulting a professional.'

He didn't look convinced. 'Oh, come on,' said his wife. 'Remember those group sessions Jude conducted out in Spain. You found those really helpful.'

'Yes, perhaps, at the time.' The way he spoke made it clear that, even though his wife was still intrigued by the idea. New Age consciousness-raising was another enthusiasm Grant Roxby had put behind him. 'But we are dealing with one of our children here. We want the best for him.'

'Are you suggesting Jude wouldn't provide the best?' Carole was no more an advocate of alternative therapies than Grant was, but she objected to what she felt was a slight to her friend.

Daunted by the sternness in her pale blue eyes, he backtracked. 'I'm sorry. Do what you think's right, Kim,' he said with a resigned shrug and a long swallow from his wine glass.

His wife took Jude off to find the troubled teenager. Grant still looked rather petulant, a spoilt child whose request had been refused, but he had sufficient manners to gesture Carole to a dining-room chair and wave the wine bottle again. 'Are you sure?'

'Quite sure, thank you. I'll be driving later.'

'Oh, right.'

There was a silence between them. Grant Roxby was having difficulty hiding displeasure at this interruption to his Sunday afternoon. But he managed to dredge up a bit more conversation. 'Are you a therapist like Jude then, Carole?'

'Good heavens, no.'

The vehemence with which she spoke gave him hope. Perhaps she was on his side after all. 'When I was growing up,' he said, 'the first port of call wasn't a therapist or a counsellor or a psychologist. If you'd got a problem, you sorted it out for yourself.'

'That's how I was brought up too,' Carole agreed.

'Built up self-reliance, that approach.' He gestured round the splendour of Pelling House. 'I wouldn't have all this if I'd gone running for help every time I hit a problem in my professional life – or in my private life, come to that. God helps those who help themselves.'

Carole nodded. She'd forgiven Grant his rudeness now. He was talking an awful lot of good sense.

'So I don't think God's likely to do a lot for my son.'

'Oh?'

'Harry couldn't help himself in an unmanned sweet shop.'

'Ah.'

Harry's bedroom contained everything thought essential by a privileged teenager in the early twenty-first century – television, CD and minidisk players, computer, DVD player, mobile phone. All the equipment looked brand-new, as though it had been bought at the time of the move to Pelling House – perhaps even as some kind of bribe or compensation for moving the boy away from his friends to Fedborough.

To Jude's mind the room looked distressingly tidy for a fifteen-year-old's. Not that Harry looked that old. 'He's rather a young fifteen,' Kim had confided as they went up the stairs.

He was hunched in front of a computer game, his whole body a stiff line of resentment. He didn't look round when his mother knocked and entered. Though he had been told Jude was coming and couldn't do anything to stop that happening, he was damned if he was going to be cooperative.

'Harry. Harry, don't be rude! You have a guest.'

'No, Mum. You have a guest. I wouldn't invite anyone down to this scummy place. Nobody I know'd want to come.'

'That is not the point, Harry. There is a guest in your room and I will not have you behaving—'

'It's all right, Kim.' Jude had been frequently struck by the way parents attracted to alternative lifestyles tended to be extremely traditional and proscriptive with their children. 'Harry,' she went on, 'I just wanted to talk to you about . . . you know, what you found in the cellar. It must have been a terrible shock for you.'

'I wouldn't have found it if we hadn't moved to this piss-awful place!'

'Harry! How dare you use language like that?'

'Why? Dad uses it all the time.'

'That is not the point.'

'I'd have thought it was exactly the point. When Dad

does something, it's all fine and wonderful. When I do exactly the same thing, it's crap.'

'Harry! You just—'

'Kim. If you don't mind, I'd like to talk to Harry on his own.'

'Well, I'm not sure if—'

'You asked me to do this. I think I should be allowed to choose the way I do it.'

The calmness with which the words were spoken did nothing to diminish their power. Kim Roxby's head bowed acceptance. 'I'll be downstairs if you . . .' She trailed out, closing the door behind her.

A long silence reigned in the room. The boy, determined to make no concession to Jude's presence, stabbed at the controls of his computer game.

'All right,' she said, 'so you hate Fedborough.'

'Wouldn't anyone? It's the arsehole of the world.'

'And you're just passing through?' The line was an old one, but he couldn't have given her a more perfect cue for it.

A moment was required for the joke to register, but then Harry couldn't help himself from giggling. He turned towards her. The spots on his face were new and shiny, the kind that would reappear almost immediately after being squeezed away.

Jude felt deep sympathy for the awfulness of adolescence, but that didn't stop her from pressing home her advantage. 'No surprise you hate being transplanted down here. No one likes being taken away from their friends.'

'No.' A moment of potential empathy came and went. 'If you're about to tell me all the benefits of living in Fedborough, forget it.'

'I'm not. I wouldn't like to live here.'

He was thrown. 'I thought you did live here.'

'No. I'm in Fethering. Down on the coast.'

'Oh. Well, it's not that different. Still not London.'

'True.'

'Anyway, I'm sure it's fine for old people, people who've retired down here, but I haven't got to that stage of my life.'

'No. At your age you should be having a good time.'

'What chance have I got of that in a dump like this?'

'Presumably your parents knew you weren't keen on the idea before you came?'

'I kept telling them. Whether they took it in or not is another matter. When Dad gets a bee in his bonnet about something, he does it, regardless of what anyone else thinks on the subject. And Mum . . . well, she just agrees with him all the time. Anything for a quiet life.'

Jude was impressed by how shrewdly the boy had assessed his parents' relationship. 'Putting the fact that you're stuck in Fedborough on one side for a moment . . .'

'How can I put it on one side? I'm aware of it every minute of the day. There's nowhere to go down here, nothing to do.'

'But—'

'Don't start talking to me about all the wonderful scenery around, and the walks I can go on, because who wants to go on a bloody walk? And I'm not into ponies like the girls are. Animals are just boring. And I don't care that Dad's buying a bloody sailing boat! You'll never catch me on that thing!'

'I wasn't going to say any of that, Harry. I was going to say that presumably you can still keep in touch with your London friends.'

'How?'

She pointed to his mobile phone. 'That. Or you can email them.'

'Yes,' he admitted truculently. 'I could.'

Suddenly Jude saw it all. Harry Roxby's problems didn't begin with the move to Fedborough. He hadn't had many friends in London either. He was suffering that terrible teenage sense of isolation. Geographical isolation only compounded a pain that was already there.

But she was too canny to say anything to him about her realization. Instead, she abruptly changed the subject.

'Let's talk about when we last met, Harry. When you found the torso in the cellar . . .'

All colour drained from the boy's face.

Chapter Fourteen

Downstairs, Grant Roxby and Carole Seddon were getting on much better than had initially seemed likely. Their mutual contempt for the excesses of healing and psychiatry had bonded them. She'd even, in spite of the car, accepted his second offer of a glass of wine.

Kim had cleared the lunch things around them. Grant made no offer to help, increasing the impression that he ruled his household in a rather traditional manner. The two girls were off having riding lessons. Being younger, they had been attracted more quickly than Harry to the charms of country life.

Carole had no difficulty in bringing the conversation round to the Pelling House torso. 'Must be a relief for you to be allowed back into your own house.'

'Yes. The police were surprisingly sensitive, caused as little disruption as they could, but even so . . .' He chuckled. 'Mind you, what happened may have speeded up our assimilation into Fedborough society. Everybody in the town knows exactly who we are now, and they all feel like they've got carte blanche to come up and talk to us in the street.'

'Giving their theories about what happened?'

'You betcha. God, the number of names that have

been whispered discreetly to me . . . You'd think Fedborough was entirely populated by serial killers.'

'And do you have any theories yourself, Grant?'

He made a negative grimace. 'I don't know enough of the personalities involved. I've a feeling whatever happened happened at least three years ago.'

'Do you base that on something the police have said?' asked Carole eagerly, as her mind matched his words with the date of Virginia Hargreaves's disappearance.

'No. While everyone else has been extremely generous to me with their theories, I'm afraid the police – the only people who might have anything vaguely authoritative to contribute – have said bugger all.'

'So where do you get your three years from?'

'Well, I met the Carltons . . . you know, while the house purchase was going through . . . and I just can't believe they had anything to do with it. Besides, the state of the body when I saw it in the cellar . . . it looked like it had been dead a long time.'

Carole shook her head wryly. 'Maybe. From the description Jude gave me, it sounded as if it had been sort of mummified, which would make precise dating a lot more difficult. Could be three years, could be a lot older . . . or indeed a lot more recent.'

'You know about these things?'

'I'm not an expert. But I used to work for the Home Office, and picked up some of the basics. The only thing that the state of the body does seem to indicate is that the woman was killed – or perhaps we should say, pending further information, met her end – somewhere else.'

'And was moved into the cellar here?'

'I should think that's almost definitely the case, yes.'

Grant Roxby looked thoughtful, and picked up the

wine bottle. Only about a third of its contents remained. He gestured towards Carole, who shook her head again, and he filled up his own glass.

'You sound as if that news has affected your thinking about the case, Grant.'

He shrugged. 'As I said, what do I know? On the other hand, it might make sense of something else . . .'

'Hm?'

'Well, because of what I'd assumed to be the age of the body, and because I hadn't considered the possibility it might have been moved here, I had rather ruled out as suspects the people we bought the house from.'

'Debbie Carlton and her husband?'

'Ex-husband, yes.' Grant Roxby tapped his chin thoughtfully. 'But maybe this explains it.'

'Explains what?'

'Apparently Francis Carlton has been summoned back from Florida.'

'Summoned?'

'Yes. The police want to talk to him.'

'I saw it,' said Harry truculently. 'Whatever they say doesn't change the fact that I saw it.'

' "They" being your parents?'

'Of course.' He looked at Jude with defiance. 'They like to control everything in my life, but they can't do that. They can't control my thoughts – or my memories.'

' "They" in this case being your dad.'

'Well, I suppose . . . Like about everything else, Mum just goes along with what he says.'

She was silent for a moment. 'Are you telling me your parents don't want you to think about what you saw?'

'Yes. "Don't dwell on it, Harry. Just forget it. Don't keep picking away at it, Harry."' Though the impersonation of Grant was not a good one, it caught some of his energy and bossiness.

'But putting that image out of your mind completely must be very hard.'

'Hard? It's impossible.' His bottom lip trembled and tears threatened. At that moment he looked nearer ten than fifteen. 'I'd never seen a dead body before. Any kind of dead body . . . let alone one in . . . in that condition.'

'Pretty ghastly, wasn't it?'

'So you can't just keep something like that out of your mind, shut the lid on it and never think about it again.'

'No, you can't. I don't think you should try to.'

The boy looked straight at Jude. For the first time, he seemed to believe she had something worth saying. 'You mean I *should* think about it?'

'Of course you should. You don't come to terms with something unpleasant by closing your mind. You have to go through the experience in detail, process it, reach some kind of conclusion about it.'

He was cynical again. 'Isn't that what a psychiatrist would say? *Are* you a psychiatrist?'

'No, I'm not.' She grinned. 'If I was, I'd just have used the word "closure", and I didn't, did I?'

'No,' he conceded. 'Then why did Dad ask you to talk to me?'

'Wasn't him, it was your mum. Your dad is extremely unkeen on my being here.'

'Oh.' Harry's reaction suggested Jude had gained credibility from his father's disapproval.

'I'm here,' she went on, 'because you and I have something in common.'

'What's that?'

'We've both seen the torso, haven't we? Apart from the police – and your dad – we're the only people who have. And since your dad doesn't want to talk to you on the subject . . .'

'Certainly not. He won't even allow me to mention it.'

'Then I'd say you and I really should talk about the torso . . .'

The boy nodded slowly. 'Yes, I think we should. Are you still, kind of . . . shocked by what you saw, Jude?'

The use of her name was very encouraging. 'A bit. More than shocked, though, I'm intrigued.'

'Oh?'

'Come on, Harry, the torso was a ghastly thing for us to have seen, but, in spite of that – or perhaps because of that – it does raise a lot of questions.'

'What kind of questions do you mean?'

'Who the torso belonged to when she was alive? How her remains came to end up in the cellar here? Who cut off her arms and legs? And was that the same person who caused her death in the first place?'

'You mean, like . . . a murderer?' There was horror as he spoke the word, but also fascination.

'Yes. You've been presented with a possible murder mystery right on your own doorstep. Harry. And I think the best way of working through the shock of what you saw would be to treat that as a challenge, try and find out for yourself what happened.'

'Sort of . . . do my own investigation?'

'Why not? Talk through all the information you have, try to work out the solution.'

For the first time there was a sparkle in the boy's eyes as he asked, 'Would you help me to do that, Jude?'

'No,' she replied. 'You'd help me, Harry.'

Chapter Fifteen

They tiptoed down the stairs. The door to the dining room was closed, with Grant and Carole presumably still behind it. There was no sign of Kim; no doubt in the kitchen, tidying up the lunch things.

Harry put his finger to his lips. He was enjoying the conspiratorial element in what they were doing. The torch was still in the large baggy pocket of his large baggy trousers. He wasn't going to produce it until they were past danger of being spotted.

'I sorted out how to break the police seals, Jude,' he confided proudly. 'Cut through with a metal saw and joined them together again with Blu-Tack.'

'Very James Bond,' she murmured. It was the right thing to say. The boy beamed. 'Must've taken a long time, though.'

'Did it yesterday. They were all out for *a walk on the Downs*.' He invested the words with all the contempt a disgruntled fifteen-year-old can muster. 'Took a while, but I made a neat job of it.'

As they reached the bottom of the stairs, a finger once again rose conspiratorially to his lips. Tentatively Harry reached a foot over the stripped floorboards of the hall. 'Have to go carefully here. Some of them creak.'

They successfully negotiated the route across to the

cellar door. Sure enough, it still had police tape and notices on it. The seals were threaded through rivets fixed into the walls. Proud of his handiwork, Harry pulled them gingerly apart.

'Why did you do it?' Jude whispered.

He shrugged. 'I was bored. Wanted to know what the police'd been up to,' he breathed back. 'Also . . .' He gulped, suddenly losing confidence. 'I wanted to go down there, to sort of, I don't know, look at . . .'

'Confront your fear?'

Harry nodded. Boldly taking hold of the handle, he opened the door down to the cellar. At the same moment, he produced the torch from his pocket, and pointed its beam down the stairs. 'Come on.'

He gently closed the door behind them, and they stepped into the void.

The cellar still contained police equipment, revealed by the sweeps of his torch. Lights on tripods, metal equipment boxes whose contents Jude could only guess at, unspecified objects binned in labelled polythene bags.

The effect was, if anything, antiseptic. The horror was gone. So was the chipboard partition which had screened the torso. The space where it had lain was clinically empty; every trace of body and box had been meticulously combed through, bagged up and removed for analysis.

'Was it just like this when you came down yesterday?'

Harry nodded.

'But you still needed to be here?'

'Yes. I pictured it again. I concentrated, and recreated the image of what I had seen.'

'How long were you down here?'

'Two, three hours.'

'Did it help?'

Another nod. 'As I said, nobody would talk to me about what I'd seen. But I needed to . . .' Though his words trailed away, they were very eloquent.

'Yes. I understand why you—'

There was a sudden clatter from above them. Light from the hall flooded the cellar.

Framed in the doorway stood the outline of Grant Roxby. 'What the hell're you doing down here?'

The beam of Harry's torch swung round to spotlight his father's face, which was contorted with rage. Not just rage, though. There was another emotion there, and it looked like guilt.

Chapter Sixteen

'It's all rather frustrating,' said Carole on the Monday. She'd proposed lunch, predictably rejected Jude's suggestion of going to the Crown and Anchor, and said she'd assemble something for them. But even the bottle of Sauvignon Blanc failed to make the chicken salad in her kitchen look convivial. The weather had changed too; it was dull and drizzly outside. Deprived of a long walk, Gulliver looked reproachfully mournful slumped against the cold Aga.

'I mean, we've got so little information,' she went on. 'And the vital question we haven't managed to answer yet is: who does the torso belong to? Until we know that, we haven't got proper motivation for anyone.'

'Doesn't stop us having suspects,' said Jude. She was, as ever, more philosophical about their lack of progress. 'And really those come down to the people who have at one time or another owned Pelling House.'

'Roddy Hargreaves . . .'

'Yes. Whose Sloane Rangerish wife Virginia disappeared, and thus becomes a potential candidate for the job of victim.'

'Debbie and Francis Carlton . . .'

'Who've suddenly moved up the suspect list, if the

police really have summoned him all the way from Florida.'

'That's what Grant Roxby told me. But we don't know the details. Francis Carlton may not be a suspect, they may just want to ask him some questions.'

'Couldn't they do that on the phone?'

'We have absolutely no idea, Jude. That's the trouble. We don't really know anything.'

'Stop sounding so miserable about it.' Jude smiled in a way that she knew to be potentially infuriating. 'Ignorance has certain advantages. Our minds are less cluttered by extraneous detail.'

Carole snorted. 'Thank you very much, Pollyanna. Our minds are less cluttered by *any* detail.'

'Which leaves them free and hair-trigger sensitive.' Jude wasn't going to be infected by her friend's gloom. 'OK, Roddy Hargreaves and Francis Carlton . . . I don't think we can rule out Debbie Carlton either. If her husband's a suspect, then so's she.'

'What do you base that on?'

Jude shrugged. 'As little logic as any other thoughts we've had about the case. But she does seem to have gone out of her way to be helpful to your investigation. Since the effect that's had has been to make you more suspicious of her ex-husband, maybe that's what she wanted to do in the first place. Divert suspicion away from herself?'

'Huh.'

'Just a thought. And then there's Grant. The way he reacted to seeing me and Harry in the cellar yesterday was very odd.'

'Anger at his son's behaviour, I would imagine. He must've realized Harry had cut through the police seals.'

'Don't know. There seemed to be more to it than that.'

Carole sniffed. 'Well, if you're going to have Grant as a suspect, we should have Kim too.'

'What makes you say that?'

'As little logic as any other thoughts we've had about the case,' she parroted.

'Touché.' Jude grinned. 'The trouble is, we don't seem to be being very proactive.'

'Sorry?'

'We aren't driving this investigation. People keep coming to us with ideas for moving it on.'

'Back to your conspiracy theory, are we?'

Jude shook her head ruefully. 'Maybe. There is something odd happening. As if someone is orchestrating the way we think about things.'

'So who is that someone? Or are we talking about all the residents of Fedborough?'

'At times it almost seems like that. Don't you find something spooky about the place, Carole?'

'Spooky?'

'Yes. As if everyone knows what everyone else is thinking. And as soon as anyone gets any information, it's immediately spread around the entire network.'

'That's how country towns work.'

'Hm. But it does somehow seem that the timing of things is arranged to—'

The telephone rang. Carole answered it. 'Oh, hello.' She mouthed to Jude, 'Debbie Carlton.'

'See what I mean,' Jude mouthed back.

They went into Fedborough again on the Thursday, the morning for which Debbie had issued another invitation to coffee. She'd got in some new curtain fabric samples which, while fully understanding that Carole wasn't committed to going ahead with any interior design work, she'd still like her to have a look at.

Carole had agreed, undecided whether what Debbie said was true, or was just an excuse to talk further about the discovery at her former home. Jude was convinced of the latter explanation. The timing of Debbie's phone call, apart from anything else, had to be significant. Jude believed in synchronicity and other mystical concepts which, in her neighbour's mind, were lumped together under the definition 'nonsense'.

In spite of herself, though, Carole still felt a little glow of excitement as she parked the Renault at the top of Fedborough High Street.

Jude had fixed to have another session with Harry Roxby. After his anger at finding them in the cellar on the Sunday, Grant had been very quickly calmed down by his wife, and agreed with surprising meekness that Jude's 'treatment' of their son should continue. He had even agreed that Harry should be allowed to take the Thursday morning off school, as if the boy's session with Jude was like a genuine medical appointment.

Grant's capitulation provided an interesting sidelight on his marriage. Like many egotists and control freaks, Grant Roxby could be cut down to size quite easily by the right person. The balance of power in the relationship between him and his wife was not as it appeared from the outside.

As Carole walked along to Debbie Carlton's flat, she felt the quality of Fedborough which Jude had described as 'spooky'. There was something about the picture-book prettiness of the town which contrived to be at the same time anonymous and watchful. Carole didn't know many of the residents, but got the feeling they were all aware of her. In that enclosed, incestuous atmosphere, she was an intruder. She'd made more appearances in the town during the last couple of weeks than normal expectations might justify. Her behaviour was suspicious. She was under surveillance.

Carole gave a curt shake of her shoulders to dismiss such stupid thoughts. She'd been listening to Jude too much. All that was happening was that she had been invited to coffee by someone who was hoping to secure a commission as an interior designer; there was nothing more sinister than that. The idea of a town having a personality or an attitude or – heaven forbid – an 'aura' was New Age self-indulgence and should be treated appropriately. She was Carole Seddon, for goodness' sake. Not prone to flights of fancy. 'Sensible' was her middle name.

And the attention with which Debbie Carlton showed her the new curtain fabrics suggested that the morning's was to be an entirely sensible encounter. The speed, however, with which her hostess put the sample books aside and started to talk about the torso would have added considerable fuel to Jude's conspiracy-theory fire – or would have done for anyone, unlike Carole, who was gullible enough to believe it in the first place.

'I'm sorry,' Debbie said, as she slopped coffee while refilling Carole's cup. 'I'm a bit jittery this morning. Francis is back.'

'Your husband?' asked Carole ingenuously, pretending she hadn't heard of his return. She noticed that Debbie Carlton was dressed more formally that morning, in a black trouser suit and high heels. Her make-up was again impeccable. She didn't want Francis to see her at anything less than her best.

'Ex-husband, yes. He flew in from Florida on Tuesday. I'm afraid knowing he's around makes me nervous.'

'But surely you don't have to see him if you don't want to?'

'He's staying here.'

'Oh?'

'He said it was daft to shell out for a hotel when I'd got an empty spare room. He . . .' Debbie was about to say more, but thought better of it. Carole felt sure there would have been a reference to Francis Carlton's meanness, which had been hinted at in their previous conversation.

'Why has he actually come back?' she asked, once again feigning ignorance.

'The police wanted to talk to him.'

'About what was found in Pelling House?'

'Yes. I mean, Francis isn't a suspect or anything like that.' Debbie Carlton didn't sound totally convinced by her words. 'But there were questions the police wanted to ask and he thought it'd be simpler to talk to them face to face . . . you know, to avoid any misunderstandings . . . That's all.'

Her conclusion sounded very inadequate. That couldn't be all. For someone as apparently mean as Francis Carlton to fly over the Atlantic to talk to the police suggested a degree of . . . perhaps not guilt . . . but at least anxiety to put his side of the story without risk of misunderstanding.

'And has he actually talked to them yet?' Carole was having difficulty sounding as uninvolved as she knew she must.

'He had one session with them yesterday.' Debbie

glanced apprehensively at her watch. 'And he's with them again now.'

'Going over the same sort of stuff as they asked you? Or hasn't he confided what they've asked him about?'

'Francis didn't say a lot yesterday evening. Wasn't here much, actually. There were some local friends he'd fixed to meet in the pub.' Debbie Carlton looked troubled. 'Funny, he seems to think he can just behave exactly the same in Fedborough, like nothing had happened, like we were still together.'

'Must be hard for you.'

'Mm. I supposed it's always the case, in any divorce, that there's a winner and a loser. He's got his new life, two homes on opposite sides of the world, and . . .' She gestured feebly round her Italianate sitting room. '. . . and I've got this. But he doesn't seem to be aware of the difference.'

'Are you sure that's not just a ploy, part of some one-upmanship game he's playing with you?'

'I don't know. I really don't know how Francis's mind works. If the divorce has taught me nothing else, it's made me realize how little I knew the man I spent five years of my life with.'

'So he hasn't passed anything on to you that the police told him?' Carole eased the question in. 'Anything you didn't already know? Whether they've got any further in their thinking about the case?'

Debbie Carlton shook her blonde head. 'If they have given Francis any information, he hasn't confided it in me. But then I'd been quite surprised if he did.'

'Why?'

For a moment she seemed to contemplate another

answer, but then just said, 'We're divorced. The time for confiding in each other – if it ever existed – is long past.'

'All right, so you don't know anything about the *police's* thinking on the case. What about *your* thinking on the case? Your ideas advanced at all?'

Debbie Carlton looked up sharply. 'Why should they have done?'

'Having lived in Pelling House, you can't pretend not to be interested in what happened there.'

'I'm not pretending that.'

'And the fact that your ex-husband has come all the way across the Atlantic must mean—'

'Is that what they're saying?'

'I'm sorry?'

'Are the Fedborough gossips saying that Francis must've had something to do with the torso, otherwise he wouldn't have come back?'

'I've no idea what they're saying, Debbie. I don't live in Fedborough.'

'No, of course you don't.' But Debbie nodded to herself, as if some conjecture had been proved correct. 'I bet that's what they are saying.' She smiled wryly. 'I don't think Francis'd like that, knowing that the whole town thinks of him as a murder suspect. He has a rather high opinion of himself, he wouldn't like the idea of not appearing respectable.'

'And if people were thinking as you suggest . . .' asked Carole gently, 'do you think there'd be any reason for them to do so?'

There was a nanosecond of consideration before Debbie said, 'No. No, of course there wouldn't be.'

Carole wondered about the level of innocence in this reaction. She couldn't forget Jude's suggestion that Debbie might be deliberately directing suspicion towards Francis, and continued her probing. 'But you've just admitted you don't know your ex-husband very well.'

'No, but Francis . . . It's unthinkable. He has his faults . . . He's vain and a bit tight-fisted . . . but there's no way I could see him as a murderer.' And yet her words slowed down, as if the idea were taking root, as if for the first time she was seriously contemplating the possibility of her former husband having some connection with the dead body. 'Anyway, we've no idea who the torso belonged to. If, when we get that information, it turns out to have been someone who Francis knew or . . . I suppose in those circumstances, we might all have to think differently about what went on.'

Though her words expressed token resistance, fascination with the new thought was still growing in Debbie Carlton's mind. Or, alternatively, that was the impression she was trying to give.

There was the sound of a key in the front door, and she tensed. They were both silent as quick, heavy footsteps mounted the stairs.

Chapter Seventeen

'Bloody police! Are they trained in techniques to make everyone feel guilty? I came back from the States to do my duty as a British citizen and . . .'

His words petered out when he saw that Debbie was not alone.

'Francis, this is Carole Seddon. Carole, my hus– my *ex*-husband, Francis.'

He dutifully shook her hand, but did not look pleased to see her. Francis Carlton was bulky, probably round six foot four, but there was a fastidiousness about him, which was at odds with his size. It showed in the high shine on his brown loafers, the crispness of his button-down collar, the crease of his light grey trousers, the 'English-style' cut of his American sports jacket (so different from anything purchasable in England). Most of all the fastidiousness showed in the flat oblongs of his spectacles, rimmed in matt black metal.

Debbie Carlton was visibly nervous in her ex-husband's presence. She gestured to the coffee tray, but he dismissed the suggestion with a shake of his head. Then he looked at her quizzically, demanding an explanation for the presence of a visitor.

'I've been showing Carole some fabrics.'

'Ah yes, of course. The *interior designer*.' He spoke the

words with a contempt that was utterly diminishing. Debbie was not going to get any support in her new career from that direction.

Francis Carlton looked at his watch. 'I must go and wash my hands,' he said. 'Absolutely filthy, the desk they had me sitting at.' Realizing this might have given Carole some clue as to where he'd been, he moved brusquely towards the bathroom.

'Are you going to want something for lunch?' asked Debbie.

'No. Meeting some people,' he called over his shoulder as he left the room.

'Am I meant to know where he's been?' Carole murmured.

Debbie shook her head. 'No. Francis wouldn't like that. As I say, he's very concerned about his image of respectability.'

'In that case, I'd better pretend I didn't hear what he said when he came in. Have you any idea how long he's going to be staying with you?'

'He hasn't said. I wouldn't think long. He'll want to get back to Jonelle.' Still unable to say the name without an edge of distaste, she chuckled bleakly. 'That is, of course, assuming the police allow him to go.' In response to Carole's startled expression, she said, 'Just a joke. Sorry. Me being vindictive.'

But was it just a joke – or part of a strategy of deception? 'Do you have any other reason for saying that – apart from being vindictive?'

'No,' Debbie almost snapped.

'But for Francis to have come all this way—'

Again there was the sound of the front door being unlocked. This time Debbie Carlton did not become more tense. More relaxed, if anything. She knew it was her mother.

Billie Franks arrived in the sitting room, looking exactly the same as she had on the previous occasion. She may have been wearing different clothes, but she was the kind of woman who always wore the same kind of clothes, so they made little difference. The tight grey perm looked as if it had been assumed like a helmet, and the basket was still clutched to her broad stomach.

'Morning, love. Oh, hello, Mrs Seddon.' The recall was instant. She took in the books of fabric samples. 'You going to go ahead with the decorating, after all, then, are you?'

'Well . . .'

'Be good if you do, because Debbie gets such a pittance from that husband of hers that—'

'Mum . . .'

'And she's a very hard worker. Real perfectionist. Gets that from her dad. He never left the shop till the last thing had been put away and the last surface polished. Closed to customers at five-thirty sharp, but he was never home till—'

'Mum, Carole doesn't want to hear this.'

Billie Franks took the point, and was silent. Carole smoothed down her skirt. 'I'd better be off, actually . . .'

'Not on my account. I just dropped in on the way to see Debbie's dad, like I do every morning. Don't let me disturb you.'

'Well, I . . .' Politeness dictated that Carole probably should leave. But then again, when would she get a better chance of pursuing her investigation with some of the principals in the case? She relaxed into her chair.

'Is he back?' Billie asked her daughter.

'In the bathroom.'

'Has he told you what the police interrogated him about yet?' The old woman had no reticence about discussing in front of a stranger where Francis had been. Indeed, she seemed to relish the opportunity.

'No.'

'So you don't know if they've asked him about his other women?'

Debbie Carlton shook her head, her expression now indicating that this might not be appropriate conversation. Her mother, undeterred, addressed herself directly to Carole. 'I never trusted that young man from the first moment Debbie introduced him. Only ever going to think about Number One, I could tell that.'

'Mum . . .'

But Billie Franks wasn't going to be diverted. 'And when Debs told me they was going to get married, I couldn't have been more upset. I wanted her to marry someone nice from round here, someone from Fedborough, who'd care about her and look after her properly and give her lots of babies and—'

'Carole doesn't want to hear all this, Mum.'

Nothing could have been further from the truth, but more revelations were stopped by Francis Carlton's reappearance from the bathroom.

He stood facing his ex-mother-in-law. The temperature in the room dropped by ten degrees. Then, clutching her basket righteously to her, Billie Franks announced, 'I'll give your love to Dad, Debbie', and left the flat.

Francis Carlton made no reference to what had just happened. Instead, he walked across to a coat rack and said, 'Must've left the mobile in my raincoat pocket.' He retrieved it, and looked again at his watch. 'Still a bit early to ring Florida. Want to check how Jonelle is. She's been feeling pretty ropey in the mornings . . . you know, with the morning sickness . . . because of the baby.'

He moved to the door. 'I'll be back later.'

No gesture this time at a polite farewell to Carole. He didn't want to lessen the impact of his parting shot. Carole felt sure it was the first time the baby had been mentioned, and a look at Debbie's face confirmed that. She was almost as pale as her hair, her red lips a wound-like gash in the whiteness. Tears sparkled in the dark blue eyes.

Carole had no idea of Debbie Carlton's gynaecological history, whether she had ever tried to have a child, whether she had been unable to, whether even that had been the reason for the failure of their marriage. All she knew was that Francis Carlton's announcement had hurt his ex-wife deeply. And also that breaking the news that way, casually, with a stranger present, had been a deliberate act of vindictiveness.

'I'd better be on my way,' she said. She couldn't think of any help to offer that wouldn't be emotionally intrusive. Jude would have been fine in such a situation, she'd have found the right words, she'd have provided comfort. But Carole Seddon didn't have those skills.

Fortunately, Debbie Carlton's shock and self-pity didn't last. Quickly, she converted them into anger. 'God, he's a bastard!'

'Well, I'm not really in a position to—'

'If I'd still had a sneaking residual shred of affection for him, what he just said would have removed it. That was the first time he'd told me Jonelle was pregnant.'

'I rather thought it might have been.'

'He did it simply to hurt me, to see me react with

pain.' Debbie rose from her chair, seething. 'Well, I'm not going to give him the satisfaction. Francis thinks he's destroyed me. He hasn't! I'm a lot tougher – and a lot more determined – than he's ever imagined. While we were married, I did play the doormat for him – I thought that's what wives did – but I'll be damned if I'm going to let anything he does get to me now!'

'Good for you, Debbie.'

'I put up with all his arrogance and infidelities . . .'

Casually, Carole picked up the word. 'Yes, your mother mentioned infidelities . . .'

'For a long time I didn't realize what was going on. Traditional wifely role of "being the last to know". And when I did find out, I even kind of accepted it. He met them in London, didn't foul our own footpath down here. He wouldn't have liked that, tarnishing his image in Fedborough. You know, Francis has always had a rather chilling ability to divide his life into compartments. Me down here, lovers in London, and never the twain shall meet.'

'And what if the twain had met?'

'Sorry?'

'What if someone from his London life had come down here, a woman had appeared, threatening his respectable Fedborough image?'

'He wouldn't have let that happen. If any woman came down here after him, Francis would have just got rid of her.'

Debbie Carlton's hand leapt up to her mouth, as she realized the appalling implication of what she had just said.

Chapter Eighteen

Jude had suggested that they meet on Fedborough Bridge at twelve. Carole was there first. The water was high, flowing perversely upstream, as the tide from the sea was at its strongest. Occasional spars of wood and plastic bottles swirled on the green-grey surface. What lay beneath was as unknown and secret as Fedborough itself.

She looked upstream to the cluster of boatsheds and the silting-up excavation which Roddy Hargreaves had apparently once envisioned as a marina. The dilapidated buildings looked bleak and hopeless. Surely the local authority wouldn't allow the site to stay that way much longer, an ugly canker on Fedborough's 'West Sussex Calendar' charm.

The abandoned business brought a sudden chill of melancholy into Carole's heart.

Then she saw Jude coming down the High Street, her clothes – today a thin Indian print skirt and long chiffon scarf over a blue T-shirt – drifting as ever around her. She looked untroubled, benign, as though living in the world she should be living in. Not for the first time, Carole envied that certitude. For her, life had always been a process of adjustment, trying to match her angular contours to the ill-fitting frame in which she found herself.

Like the child holding the bag of sweets, she decided

to ration out her own revelations and hear Jude's first. 'How was Harry?'

'Getting better. Now I've given him the freedom actually to talk about what he saw in the cellar, he's turned into the complete Hercule Poirot.'

'And have his "little grey cells" come up with anything useful?'

'Not really. I'm afraid his theories feature too many aliens for my taste. One interesting thing he did tell me, though . . .'

'Hm?'

'Well, Harry had been worried about the police. You know, Grant went on at him about how irresponsible he'd been cutting the seals on the cellar door, so Harry was expecting a big rocket when the police came back to Pelling House to continue their investigations.'

'And?'

'And they haven't come back. Which might suggest that, so far as the police are concerned, they've got all the information they want. Even that they might be close to solving the case.'

Which coincides, Carole thought, with them talking to Francis Carlton. But she didn't voice the connection yet. She was still rationing out her sweeties.

'I find talking to Harry useful,' Jude went on. 'He helps as a sounding-board, helping me to sort out my own thinking about the case.'

'I thought that was my role,' said Carole in a moment of potential spikiness.

Easy as ever, Jude defused the situation. 'You are. You both are. The more input of ideas we get, the better. Being a sounding-board isn't a competitive activity. If one person's doing it, doesn't mean that nobody else can.'

'No.' Carole wondered for a moment whether her life had always sought for exclusivity. Even from school days she'd wanted a one-to-one 'best friend', not a wide social group. And the difficulty of achieving that goal had maybe turned her inward, made her appear standoffish. In her marriage it had been the same, wanting David exclusively for herself. His desire to mix with more people was one of the elements which had started the frost between them. Even with Ted Crisp there had been—

Fortunately, Jude's voice cut through the cycle of self-recrimination. 'You get anything interesting from Debbie?'

'Well, yes.' And it struck Carole that she had really had a rather constructive morning. 'For a start, I met Francis.'

'The ex-husband?'

She nodded. 'And I found out that, throughout their marriage, he was a serial philanderer.'

'Ooh.' Jude rubbed her hands together with glee. 'This sounds terrific. Lovely stuff. You know what we need?'

'What?'

'A couple of large white wines and some South Downs Something-or-other from the menu at the Coach and Horses. Once we're equipped with those, you can give me all the dirt.'

Giving the dirt about Francis Carlton had to be deferred. When they entered the pub, they found it full of lunch-time eaters and drinkers, but alone at the bar sat Roddy Hargreaves.

Oblivious to the weather, he was still wearing his Guernsey sweater, and he looked isolated. Presumably that day his cronies all had wives or jobs to go to. Without their support, he slumped on his stool. There was whisky in front of him rather than beer, and the intense way he concentrated on the glass suggested he'd been drinking for some time.

'Hello,' said Jude, as they waited for a barman to be free. 'How're you, Roddy?'

Very slowly, he removed his gaze from the whisky, but found it more difficult to focus on her.

'Jude,' she supplied. 'Remember, we met here last week. And this is my friend Carole.' (This time, Carole was too intrigued to find the introduction embarrassing.)

'Ah.' He seemed puzzled to be given the information, but was instinctively courteous. 'Good afternoon, ladies.'

A barman, the same one as on their previous visit, had arrived. 'Two large Chilean Chardonnay, please,' said Jude. 'And can I get you one, Roddy?'

'Wouldn't say no to the same again.'

'Large Johnnie Walker,' the barman noted impassively.

'Do you mind if we join you?' said Jude, drawing up a barstool before Roddy had time to answer. 'Are we going to get something to eat?'

'I wouldn't mind a sandwich,' Carole replied primly.

'You eating?'

Roddy shook his head. 'Some days eating seems rather to slip down my list of priorities. Today is one such day.'

They got in an order for 'Generous Sussex-style Tuna Sandwiches', without pursuing the interesting question of where one might catch a 'Sussex-style Tuna'. Both of them wondered whether Roddy Hargreaves would need a prompt to continue talking. He didn't.

'Seem to remember you said you didn't come from Fedborough.'

'Fethering.'

'Ah, right. Thought you must be from out of town.'

'Why?'

'Because you came right up and talked to me.'

Jude looked puzzled. 'Why shouldn't we?'

He took a long swallow of whisky. 'Have you ever lived in a small country town?'

'Fethering's not very big.'

'No, it's virtually a village. But it's on the sea, which somehow makes it different. Lets in some air. Different in a land-locked little country town like Fedborough.'

'I'm sorry,' said Carole, once again demonstrating her lack of people-skills, 'but what on earth are you talking about?'

'I'm talking about gossip. Have you any idea how corrosive gossip can be in a place like this? I'm used to it – or I should be. Soon as Virginia and I moved here, we very quickly got used to the idea that we couldn't clear our throats without everyone knowing. It was a bit of a shock, because we'd come down from London. You can be anonymous in a city. Forget that down here. Whatever we did in Fedborough, we just fed the local piranhas a bit more of ourselves. I heard about my plans for converting the old boatsheds down by the bridge almost before I'd made the decision to do it.

'And, of course, when all that started to go wrong, the gossips were in seventh heaven. What a lot of new scandal Fiona Lister and her coven had to get their teeth into. And then my marriage crumbled – partly because of all the gossip, let me tell you – and they were even more ecstatic. When Virginia walked out on me, they all thought Christmas and their birthdays had come at the same time.'

Gloomily he emptied his whisky glass. 'But all that'll be as nothing to what's about to happen now.'

'What do you mean?' asked Jude.

'I'll be shunned. At the moment they think I'm just an old piss-artist . . . not very admirable, perhaps, but nice and safe. A cautionary tale to bolster the harpies' rectitude. "There but for the grace of God we will never go." A mess, but a harmless mess. They won't think that any more. Nobody'll want to talk to me.'

'Nonsense,' Carole snapped. 'Your friend James Lister has invited us to dinner tomorrow night. And he said it was your birthday, and you'd definitely be there too.'

'Did he? Oh yes, I remember. He managed to persuade the lovely Fiona that I would behave myself.' The bleary eyes looked sceptical. 'I wonder if my invitation will still stand tomorrow.'

'What's happening tomorrow?' asked Jude softly.

'You'll find out soon enough.' He tapped his glass sharply on the counter. 'Could you give me another of those, please. Lee? Are you two ladies ready for another?'

'No.'

'No, thank you.'

'It's a mess,' Roddy Hargreaves went on, 'a total bloody mess. Drink gets you into it, and drink's the only way out of it.' He shuddered. 'Imagine what life would be like if you were sober all the time, if you had to face the reality without alcohol blurring the edges a bit. Intolerable.' He took a long pull from his whisky glass. 'Oblivion's the only hope.'

'When you talk about drink getting you into a mess . . .' Jude began cautiously, 'are you talking about the time when your wife left you? You said last week that all that period was a blur.'

He focused on her for a moment of stillness. 'You're a very intelligent woman. You're exactly right. That is the time I'm talking about. That's the time I can't remember anything about. But that's the time they keep asking me about.'

' "They" being the police?' asked Carole.

He nodded, rubbing a large hand over his purple nose. 'Yes. I'm a coward, really. I was brought up to believe in honour and bravery and facing up to things. Whatever questions arose in life, the Jesuits had an answer to them. Just a matter of having faith. Faith and character. That's the kind of school my parents sent me to. But every time my character was put to the test, it proved unequal to the challenge. Same goes for my faith too, I'm afraid. I just always escaped into this.' He looked down at the glass.

'When did Virginia walk out?' Jude asked softly.

Whatever his vagueness about other details, he knew that instantly. 'Three and a half years ago. February it was.'

'Where did she go?'

'I don't know.' He seemed near to tears. 'She needn't have gone. I still loved her. We could have made it work . . . if only I had been there.'

'Where were you?'

He chuckled bitterly. 'Drunk. Oh, geographically I was there, but so far as being actually on hand, I . . .' The sentence petered out. 'Everything had gone wrong with the business. I'd had to sell what was left, just the strip of land on the riverbank and the buildings there. Got less than I'd paid for them, and I never saw back anything for the money I'd spent on dredging and . . . Anyway, that was collapsing, and there were all kinds of practical things I should have been arranging, but I couldn't face it. The new owner wanted all my stuff out of the boatsheds, so I paid Bob Bracken – the old bloke I'd bought the business from in the first place – to clear them for me, and I . . . I just escaped . . .'

'Where to?'

'France. I just couldn't face this place. Fedborough.' He spoke the name with undisguised distaste. 'I couldn't stand the thought of all those smug bastards sniggering behind their hands at me, so I just got a lift to Newhaven, caught the first available ferry, and got stuck into the duty-free.'

'How long were you away?'

Roddy Hargreaves let out a sigh of uncertainty. 'I don't know, three days, four days. A real bender. A real escapist's bender.' His head sagged on to his chest. 'And when I came back, Virginia had gone.'

'Leaving a note?' asked Jude.

'Leaving nothing, except a big hole in my life.'

'And she hasn't contacted you since?'

He shook his head wearily. 'Why should she? She'd given me enough chances, I'd rejected all of them. I knew what she was telling me. The message got across all right. Actions, as they say, speak louder than words.'

'Are you telling us,' said Carole in her sensible, practical voice, 'that the people in Fedborough are suggesting you had something to do with Virginia's disappearance?'

Roddy laughed, without humour. 'Of course they're suggesting that. And they're right. I let her down, I let down my faith too. I was an inadequate husband to Virginia, so she disappeared. I caused it all right.'

'But are people in Fedborough saying more than that – that you actually did away with your wife?'

A silence followed Carole's question. He looked at her for a long moment, apparently having difficulty understanding. Then, choosing the words carefully, as if speaking a foreign language, he said, 'It's very hard to answer questions about something you genuinely can't remember. We're talking about a lost weekend here . . . rather longer than a weekend, in fact. And all I know is that I went to France, and I was blind drunk for some days, and when I came back, Virginia had gone. Not a cast-iron alibi, is it? Happens to be true, but I've got no one who can . . .' He negotiated the word with great care. ' . . . corroborate that for me. So I've neatly set everything up for the Fedborough gossips to have a bloody field day.'

He slammed his empty glass down on the counter in frustration. 'Lee! Could you fill this up for me, please?'

The young barman looked awkward and mumbled, 'Erm, Janet said we shouldn't serve you any more . . .'

'Well, thank you very much.' Some alcoholics would have made this the start of a furious tirade, but Roddy Hargreaves wasn't that kind of drunk. His anger vanquished by upbringing, he spoke the words of thanks with great courtesy, then stumbled off his stool and swayed like a sailor finding his land-legs. 'Fortunately I do have alternative supplies at home, so am not entirely dependent on the Coach and Horses' service policy to maintain my necessary intake.'

He smiled at the squirming barman, turned and gravely touched his forehead to Carole and Jude. 'Excuse me, ladies. I hope you understand I have to leave. A great pleasure talking to you.'

Then, with eccentric dignity, he tottered out into the

sun of Pelling Street. Curious tourist eyes followed him. There was a ripple of nervous laughter. So far as they were concerned, he was just another small-town drunk, but Carole and Jude knew that Roddy Hargreaves was – or could have been – so much more.

Chapter Nineteen

As James Lister had said, he and his wife lived in Dauncey Street, far away – well, at least fifty yards – from the Bohemian excesses of Pelling Street. The house was a three-storey Victorian edifice, unadorned almost to the point of being forbidding. Indeed, when Carole and Jude arrived in the rain of the Friday evening, the house looked positively unwelcoming. But it was solid, respectable and undoubtedly worth a lot. There had been money in being a butcher in Fedborough.

Not that his wife chose to draw attention to James Lister's commercial origins. When the Tournedos Rossini were being served at dinner and he mentioned the fine quality of the beef, he was cut short from the other end of the table by his wife's voice saying, 'I don't think we need to talk about *meat*, James.'

Blushing like a schoolboy who had told a dirty joke at a maiden aunt's tea party, James Lister was duly silent, enabling his wife to steer the conversation to more rarefied planes. 'Do tell us about your plans for the Art Crawl, Terry.'

Fiona Lister's voice was, like her person, so encrusted with gentility that it had to be hiding something less genteel underneath. Though probably in her late sixties, she was one of those thin straight women whose looks don't change much throughout their adult life. She was dressed in a white blouse with a plain collar and a grey silk dress. Though the clothes were undoubtedly expensive, they made her look like a failed nun. And also somehow gave the impression that she'd worn the same style for many years.

Her dinner menu hadn't changed for a while either. Though beautifully presented, the food came from the *ancien régime* when Constance Spry and *cordon bleu* had ruled the kitchens of Britain; before that mildest of revolutionaries, Delia Smith, had achieved her *coup d'état*; and long before the excesses of fusion added by ever-wilder television chefs.

Each course looked exactly as it must have done in the recipe book photographs. Not a lemon slice was misaligned on the smoked salmon pâté. For the Tournedos Rossini, the toast, the *foie gras* and the disc of entrecote were piled in perfect symmetry, identical on every plate. Glacé cherries and angelica sticks made an exquisitely regular clock-face on the yellow surface of the sherry trifle; the sponge fingers were exactly parallel around the Charlotte Russe.

The choice of wines was also from another generation, the existence of the New World unacknowledged. James Lister poured copious amounts of Châteauneuf-du-Pape and an icy sweet Niersteiner. When it came to coffee (and After Eight mints), the guests would be offered Cointreau, Benedictine and Kümmel.

The overall effect was rich and rather cloying.

The guest list for the dinner once again included the Durringtons and the Rev Trigwell. Jude wondered if this helped to explain the unexpected invitations to herself and Carole. Without desperate infusions of new blood, perhaps all Fedborough dinner parties ended up with exactly the same personnel.

There was another couple she hadn't met. The fact that they were gay clearly gave Fiona Lister quite a *frisson*. She kept making unambiguous remarks, destined to show what a broadminded hostess she was to have friends 'like that'. She was so determinedly relaxed with the gay couple that the effect was very unrelaxing.

Terry Harper, the one to whom she'd addressed the question about the Art Crawl, was the older. A neat man with short grey hair styled like one of the lesser Roman emperors, he wore owl-like tortoiseshell glasses and an immaculately cut charcoal sports jacket. His partner was thin and dark, Mediterranean looks at odds with his very English name, Andrew Wragg. He wore tight black leather trousers and a shimmering black V-necked sweater, deliberately contrasting with the collars and ties of the other male guests. Had someone else turned up to one of her dinner parties dressed in that way, Fiona Lister would have been vocal in her disapproval, but the fact that Andrew had seemed to give her some kind of charge. She was being so daring, inviting someone 'like that'. She beamed indulgently whenever he spoke, impressed by the astonishing breadth of her own mind.

Andrew could have been as much as twenty years younger than Terry, and he was clearly the volatile element in the partnership. He flirted outrageously with the other guests, regardless of gender, and was prone to calculatedly shocking remarks. Terry looked on benignly, a parody of the steady older man, with a lot of raised eyebrows and comfortable 'What on earth can I do with him?' grimaces.

Terry Harper, it was established when Jude and

Carole were introduced, ran the Yesteryear Antiques, which James Lister had pointed out during his Town Walk as being Fedborough's former grocery. Andrew Wragg was some unspecified kind of artist, and worked in the studio that had been converted from the smokehouse behind his partner's shop.

The Art Crawl turned out to be the one Debbie Carlton had described to Carole, and, as its organizers, Terry and Andrew were more than happy to talk on the subject.

'I'm quietly confident it's going to be rather good this year,' said the older man. He spoke with the same restrained neatness as he dressed.

'Remind me, Terry – when does the thing actually start?' asked Dr Durrington.

Fiona Lister saw it as her duty to provide the answer. 'Really! Don't you pay any attention to what's going on in this town, Donald?'

Joan Durrington also looked daggers at her husband, but said nothing and took a sip of her mineral water.

The doctor's protestations that he was kept rather busy in his practice were swept away by his hostess. 'There's Fedborough Festival literature and posters all over the town. There's even a big banner out on the A27. The Festival starts with the Carnival Parade on Thursday night, and the Art Crawl is open to the public at two o'clock on Friday. Open two to six every afternoon of the Festival. You really ought to know that, Donald – particularly since one of the artists is exhibiting in your house.'

She sounded genuinely offended that any prominent citizen of Fedborough should remain ignorant of what was going on in the town. Donald Durrington looked suitably chastened. 'I'm sorry,' he mumbled. 'Joan deals with all that sort of thing.'

His wife's expression suggested this was not an arrangement with which she was happy. It also suggested their marriage was not necessarily an arrangement with which she was happy.

'Yes, just a week to go,' said Terry Harper. 'All in place, though. I think it'll work well.' He smiled coyly. 'Though I'm afraid we may have put one or two backs up around the town.'

'One or two?' screeched Andrew. 'Always had a way with the old understatement, didn't you? I think he's offended so many people, soon he's going to need police protection.'

'Why is that?' asked Fiona Lister with steely gentility. 'Who have you been offending, Terry?'

He made a shrugging gesture of studied innocence. 'All I've done is to suggest that we should broaden the range of artists we include. Get some of the bright new talent from London, from Paris, from Hamburg, Amsterdam. As a result, of course, there is inevitably less room for some of the local artists . . . no, sorry, I'd better qualify that . . . some of the local people who *think* of themselves as artists.'

There was a sparkle in Fiona Lister's eyes as she leaned forward to listen. Her highly sensitive gossip-antennae informed her that bitchiness was imminent.

Terry Harper listed some of the locals who'd featured in previous years' Art Crawls, but whose work didn't meet the more exacting artistic standards his regime was introducing. Andrew Wragg chipped in to the aspersions with his own scurrilous addenda. They were clearly going into a practised routine; some of Terry's lines showed signs of long honing.

None of the names meant anything to Carole or Jude, so they just sat back and let the malice flow around them.

Terry: 'His idea of mixed-media is about as original as cheese and pineapple chunks on a cocktail stick.'

Andrew: 'And the cheese in his case'd only be bog-standard Cheddar.'

Terry: 'I mean, her little whimsical pictures of kittens'd be all right on the front of a chocolate box.'

Andrew: 'Oh yes, lots of people like a nice bit of pussy.'

Terry: 'Goblins and elves carved from driftwood must be useful for something . . .'

Andrew: 'Kindling, perhaps?'

' . . . but you can't call them art,' Terry Harper concluded. 'No, so I'm afraid a lot of the local amateurs and weekend painters have had their noses rather put out of joint. But I just think that in the arts you have to have the highest standards possible.' He spoke with regret at the hard task he had set himself, but was obviously enjoying every minute of it. He loved being in charge of the Fedborough Art Crawl Hanging Committee. And his attitude to hanging was reminiscent of Judge Jeffries.

'So who of the locals has survived?' asked Fiona Lister eagerly, storing information for future slights and put-downs.

'Well . . . Alan Burnethorpe's still in there, of course, but then his drawings are quite superb.'

James Lister chuckled. 'I always like his stuff. Doesn't leave a lot to the imagination. After last year there was no one in Fedborough who didn't know what the lovely Joke looked like in the altogether.'

He was all set to bracket the speech with another chuckle, but catching Fiona's eye, let it wither instantly on the bough.

Terry Harper sighed coyly. 'And I'm afraid there's someone else in this room who's survived the cull.' He sent an indulgent look across to Andrew Wragg. 'Because I just haven't got the strength for any more tantrums. I knew if I excluded him, I'd never hear the end of it.'

'That's not the reason. Don't listen to him!' shrieked the younger man in mock-affront. 'I'm going to be represented because I'm bloody good! In years to come, art-lovers will make pilgrimages to the Fedborough Smokehouse to see where I worked. And all of you lot'll be boasting that you once were once at the same dinner party as Andrew Wragg!'

He was so over the top as to be humorous, and he duly got his laugh. But Carole had the feeling he more than half believed what he was saying.

'What about Debbie Carlton?' asked Fiona Lister in acid tones. 'Have her little watercolours survived the cull?'

'Oh yes,' Terry replied. 'Debbie's one of the few genuinely talented artists in Fedborough. Present company, of course, excepted,' he added quickly before Andrew could say anything.

This was clearly the wrong answer so far as Fiona Lister was concerned. 'Her parents always said she was very gifted.' She sniffed. 'Couldn't see it myself. Billie and Stanley were very tickled when she got into art college. Can't imagine why. It's not a proper training for anything. At least our children all got professional qualifications, didn't they, James?'

Her husband hastily agreed that indeed they did.

With trepidation, the Rev Trigwell tiptoed into the conversation. 'Of course, Fiona, you must have seen a lot of the Frankses in the old days . . . what with their grocery being right next door to your butcher's . . .'

From the frown it prompted, this hadn't been the right thing to say either. Carole got the feeling that the only right thing to say after Fiona Lister's every pronouncement was 'Yes'. From the subdued way her husband was behaving that evening, it seemed to be a lesson he had learnt early in their marriage.

'Did you hear,' Fiona went on, after a withering look at the vicar, 'that Francis Carlton had been back in Fedborough this week?'

'Oh, yes!' squealed Andrew Wragg. 'Owning up to the police about all the women he'd chopped up in the cellar of Pelling House.'

Fiona Lister spoke, darkly portentous. 'He certainly did have other women friends, after he'd been married to Debbie.'

'Having women friends,' said Jude, who was getting a bit sick of all the prejudice flying about, 'doesn't automatically mean chopping them up.'

'It could do,' her hostess riposted. 'The kind of man who betrays his wife is capable of all kinds of other moral lapses.'

'I don't agree with that. You can't apply the same standards to sexual behaviour and criminal behaviour.'

Fiona Lister turned the beady majesty of her stare on Jude. She was not used to having her opinions challenged, least of all in her own house. Jude, who had never been afraid to express her views on anything, seemed blithely unaware of the beam of disapproval focused on her.

The Rev Trigwell tried to ease the conversation, and

regain some of the ground he'd lost by his previous remark. 'Very sad that things didn't work out with Debbie and Francis.'

Fiona Lister was implacable. 'Her parents gave that girl too much freedom. Too full of her own opinions, if you ask me. That kind can never make a marriage work. You need discipline. Marriage may not be fun all the time, but you have to stick with it. All our children's marriages are still intact. Aren't they, James?'

Her husband, who hadn't heard the subject that was being discussed, took the safe option of saying that indeed they were.

'It hit her parents very hard when Debbie and Francis divorced,' Fiona went on. 'The shock was what started Stanley's illness, wasn't it, Donald?'

'Oh, I don't think one can say that,' the doctor equivocated. 'He was deteriorating long before Debbie's marriage went wrong. Anyway, no one really knows what brings on Alzheimer's.'

'In Stanley's case it was Debbie getting divorced.' Fiona Lister would never change an opinion simply because there was an expert on the subject present. 'Have you seen him recently, Donald?'

'Couple of weeks back. The Elms is part of my patch, so I do go down and check over the old lot on a fairly regular basis.'

'Any change with Stanley? I met Billie in Sainsbury's the other week and she said he was improving.'

'I'm afraid there's little chance of that. Alzheimer's is a degenerative condition.'

Carole wondered whether the doctor should be talking about one of his patients in this way. Surely even someone in Stanley Franks's condition had the right to medical confidentiality. She thought how much she would dislike meeting her own doctor socially, sitting down to meals with someone to whom she had entrusted embarrassing physical secrets. But perhaps that was inevitable in a small community like Fedborough.

She was also beginning to wonder why she and Jude had been invited to the dinner party. Once they'd said they came from Fethering, nobody had asked them any further personal details. Fiona Lister wasn't, as her husband had said, interested in new people; she just wanted to appropriate new people before anyone else in Fedborough got their hands on them.

The assumption seemed to be that the immigrants from Fethering should be deeply honoured to be included in conversations about Fedborough people they didn't know and were never likely to meet. Jude, having experienced the same at the Roxbys', had issued a warning in the car on the way over, but Carole had thought she was exaggerating.

And, what's more, they didn't seem to be getting any very useful information about the case. The torso had been mentioned, yes, but only surrounded by unsupported rumour.

Even as Carole had this thought, though, Joan Durrington, who had not spoken before, filled the silence with an announcement. 'Did you hear that the police have identified who the torso was?'

Chapter Twenty

Her husband's voice rumbled disapproval. 'I think I was told that in confidence, Joan.'

'Well, you told me.'

'Yes, but a doctor's wife . . . there are certain kinds of accepted obligations that go with the job.'

The way the couple looked at each other suggested that they were digging over an old argument. But the defiance in Joan Durrington's eyes also suggested to Carole that the doctor's wife was less mousy and anonymous than her manner might suggest.

'You can't leave it there, Joan,' said Terry Harper.

'No, you can't!' Andrew Wragg squealed in agreement. 'Come on, give us the name! We want to know which of the fine upstanding pillars of Fedborough society cut his mistress down to size in such an imaginative way.'

This sally didn't go down well with the assembled company. Carole reckoned the offence was caused, not by the tastelessness of the image, but by the implication that respectable men in Fedborough might have mistresses.

Joan Durrington's moment of self-assertion had passed. 'You'd better ask Donald. He was the one the police talked to.'

Fiona Lister turned her beady eye on the doctor. 'Well, don't keep us in suspense.'

He immediately became formal and professional. 'The police consulted me about some medical records . . .'

'Whose?' demanded Andrew Wragg. 'Come on, give us the dirt!'

'Obviously I can't tell you that.' It was the answer Andrew had been expecting; indeed, to get that answer had been the only reason he'd asked the question. Terry Harper's eyes rolled heavenwards in fond despair at the incorrigible nature of his partner.

'And in the course of conversation they told me there would soon be a press conference when the identity of the deceased would be announced.'

'Has the press conference happened yet?' asked Carole.

'I don't think so. The implication was that it'll be tomorrow.'

'Hm . . .' James Lister stroked his moustache thoughtfully. 'I wonder if that's why Roddy isn't here tonight . . . ?'

'What do you mean by that?' his wife snapped.

'I was just thinking, if the body does turn out to be Virginia . . .'

Fiona was not persuaded by this idea. 'Nonsense, that has nothing to do with it. The reason Roddy isn't here is the usual one. He's drunk. It's his birthday, for heaven's sake, probably been celebrating all day. He's lost the few manners he ever had.' Carole thought that was unfair. Roddy Hargreaves was certainly a drunkard, but he had seemed to her almost excessively courteous.

Fiona was returning to a theme she'd started on earlier in the evening, when it became clear that Roddy wasn't going to turn up. He was very inconsiderate, and had ruined her seating plan. Everything had been arranged for ten people; nine was a much less convenient number. She'd been persuaded – against her better judgment – to invite Roddy because it was his birthday and – as ever – he'd disgraced himself. There was no doubt where the fault lay: where it always lay in their marriage. James shouldn't have issued the invitation.

Joan Durrington's wavering assertiveness returned. 'Roddy was certainly in a very bad state round the time Virginia disappeared.'

'What do you mean by "a bad state"?' asked Carole.

But the direct question frightened the doctor's wife. 'Oh, I don't know . . . just . . . well . . .'

Fiona Lister saw an opportunity to go back on to the attack. 'Roddy was falling apart. He'd got all these marina plans that Alan Burnethorpe had done for him, and he'd started work on them, but he was running out of money fast.'

'Didn't his wife have any money to bail him out?' asked Jude.

'I'm sure she did,' Fiona replied. 'She came from an aristocratic background, after all. But she must've realized that giving money to Roddy would be tantamount to pouring it down a drain. He just didn't face up to things at all. I'm sure he could have got his affairs back in order, but he hid away from reality . . . in a whisky bottle, or in the Coach and Horses.' The look she darted at her husband showed that not only did she dislike her husband's friend, she also disapproved of their meeting place.

James tried to salvage some justification for Roddy's behaviour. 'Oh, he didn't just drink round that time. He was trying to sort himself out. He talked to you about it, didn't he, Philip?'

The Rev Trigwell looked embarrassed, which wasn't

difficult, since he always looked embarrassed. 'Well, there were one or two conversations that . . .'

'What did he talk about?' asked Carole, once again favouring the direct approach.

The vicar reacted as if a godparent had asked him to drown the baby in the font. 'Oh, I couldn't possibly, I mean, there are things I'm not allowed to—'

'Professional confidentiality,' Donald Durrington offered supportively.

'Exactly, yes.'

'Why, did Roddy talk to you in the confessional?'

'No, no, it was just a friendly conversation.'

'He is Catholic, after all, though, isn't he?' Carole had decided that she didn't like any of the people sitting round the dinner table – except for Jude, of course – and she didn't really care whether or not she was being rude to them. 'You're not a Catholic priest, are you?'

'Good heavens, no.' Thinking his response might have been too vehement, the Rev Trigwell's face grew blotchier as he immediately started fence-mending. 'That is to say, I've nothing against the Catholic Church. They do some wonderful work, and in these days of increased ecumenicalism our communities are getting closer all the time. Though obviously my own training and conviction persuades me more towards the Church of England, I still don't think one should dismiss too easily the—'

Carole cut through all this. 'So you can't tell me what Roddy Hargreaves talked about to you. Fine.' She turned to her hostess. 'You were saying he was in a bad way, and there were problems with his marriage – is that right?'

'All I was saying was that with a man in the state Roddy was in . . .' Fiona replied darkly, 'anything could have happened.'

Once again Carole asked for clarification.

'I'm just saying he might have got into an argument with Virginia . . .'

'And ended up killing her and dismembering the body?' suggested Jude with characteristic frankness.

Fiona Lister coloured. 'No, I didn't say that. I was just suggesting that . . . Roddy and Virginia weren't getting on very well round that time.'

Carole shuddered inwardly at the power of these insinuations. In spite of her denial, Fiona Lister had been virtually implying that Roddy Hargreaves had murdered his wife. His paranoia in the Coach and Horses about the gossips of Fedborough seemed to have been justified. Carole needed to know more. 'What was Virginia Hargreaves like?'

This was clearly a subject that their hostess felt much happier with. 'Oh, an extremely nice person. Her father was actually titled, you know. Virginia mixed a lot in aristocratic circles as a child, knew the Royals very well. She could have used her own title, if she'd chosen to. But she didn't . . . much . . . very nice and unassuming in that way, Lady Virginia was. Charming. And lovely to look at. Early forties, I suppose when she left Fedborough. Lovely blonde hair . . . well, blonded probably . . . and of course beautifully spoken. It's such a pleasure to hear good vowels, isn't it?' Fiona Lister somehow contrived to make this another criticism of her husband. 'Just so sad that a person of Lady Virginia's breeding should end up with someone like Roddy.'

Carole thought this was a bit rich, coming from a butcher's wife. 'Roddy seems to have breeding too.'

'Oh yes, I'm sure he went to the right schools and all that kind of thing, but I was talking about *character.*

Virginia never drank to excess.' Fiona flashed another venomous look at her husband.

'And where's Virginia Hargreaves now?' asked Jude.

'*According to Roddy*,' Fiona's words were weighed down with scepticism, 'Virginia went up to London when she left him.'

'And when exactly are we talking about here? About three years ago?'

'Yes. End of February.' James Lister gave what he hoped was a winning smile. 'Friday the twentieth, I remember. Because you gave one of your most successful dinner parties that evening, Fiona.'

But the attempt at ingratiation cut no ice with his wife. With another shrivelling glance at him, she went on, 'Virginia had a flat up in London, I believe. But when I last asked him, Roddy said he thought she was living in South Africa, where apparently she had a lot of friends. But, as I say, that's only Roddy's version.'

'Did they have children?' asked Carole.

'No.'

'But they still had a bloody *au pair*!' The last look from his wife had stung James Lister into raucousness. 'Which always seemed a bit excessive to me.'

'You wouldn't understand, James. Anyway, *au pair*'s the wrong word. But someone like Virginia Hargreaves had her charity work to do. She couldn't afford to be bothered with domestic details all the time. Some people are just used to growing up with servants.' Fiona Lister beamed magnanimously at the Rev Trigwell. 'As you can imagine, I had to make a few adjustments myself when I got married.'

The vicar smiled weakly. Carole wondered what it must be like inside the Listers' marriage, how James survived his wife's constant reminders that she'd married beneath herself. She also wondered how much higher up Fiona had really been in the social pecking order. The implication of having grown up with servants didn't ring true. The Listers' was just another battle of one-upmanship within the wafer-thin layers of the middle classes.

'Still, the *au pair* did all right out of it,' Terry Harper observed languidly.

That got a tart response from Fiona Lister. 'If you call marrying Alan Burnethorpe "doing all right". I would have thought it was not an unmixed blessing.'

Jude, who'd met Mrs Burnethorpe, asked, 'Oh, was Joke the Hargreaveses' *au pair*?'

Fiona, happy to be back in her role of Fedborough information officer, was quick to reply. 'As I said, *au pair*'s, really the wrong word, because that does imply an element of childcare. Joke had been working as an *au pair* for another family in Fedborough, but I suppose for Virginia Hargreaves she was more of a . . . housekeeper and social secretary. Anyway, that's how Alan met her. He's been practising as an architect here for years. Has his office on that lovely old houseboat down by the bridge . . . do you know the one I mean?'

Carole made the connection with the fine refurbished Edwardian vessel James had pointed out on the Town Walk, but Jude, for reasons of her own, said, 'No, I'll make a point of looking out for it next time I'm down that way.'

'Anyway,' Fiona went on. 'Alan couldn't have avoided meeting Joke. He was round Pelling House so much working on the marina plans with Roddy.'

'And they fell in love?' asked Jude ingenuously.

James Lister, caution loosened by wine, let out a

guffaw. 'Fell in *lust*, let's say. Quite a dishy little number, that Joke, isn't she? I must say I wouldn't . . .' He caught his wife's eye and backed off. 'There are a few men round Fedborough who wouldn't kick her out of bed.'

The blaze in Fiona Lister's eyes indicated that he hadn't backed off far enough.

Jude continued to nudge the conversation forward. 'But it wasn't just an affair. They did get married.'

'Oh yes,' her hostess agreed. 'A very correct little aspirational Dutch miss, our Joke is. Alan was still married to Karen and just looking for a good time, but Joke wasn't having any of that.'

'Or he wasn't getting any of that until he agreed to marry her!'

The look with which Fiona Lister greeted her husband's joke would have frozen the jet of a hosepipe at fifty metres.

'Always on the lookout for a new woman, though, Alan is,' said Terry Harper, maliciously casual.

'Ooh, you're so right!' Andrew Wragg agreed gleefully. 'We were talking just now about men in Fedborough having mistresses. A lot of tempting singles and divorcees around this place, you know. Positive hotbed of rampant crumpet, Fedborough is. Or so I've been told.' He flicked a dark eyebrow in an exaggerated gesture of relief. 'Thank God at least I'll never have *that* problem.' He smiled coyly at Terry. 'Plenty of others, but not that one.'

Jude remembered the excessive pressure of a hand on hers that evening at the Roxbys. 'Are you saying that Alan Burnethorpe has mistresses?'

'He may have done while he was married to his first wife. He's very happy now with Joke, I believe.'

The frostiness of Fiona Lister's response showed that

she was not enjoying the directness of her Fethering guests. They were not suitable for one of her famous dinner parties. Who invited them? Once again, poison shot across the table towards James.

Carole Seddon, who in her Fethering environment would have behaved very differently, was enjoying the insouciant freedom of being discourteous. 'Oh, did he? How many mistresses?'

'I don't think we should discuss that,' pronounced Fiona Lister, all girls' school headmistress.

'Ooh, but I think we *should*!' Andrew Wragg had caught on to the game that Carole and Jude were playing, and wanted to join in. He was also worried that they might be threatening his pre-eminence as the most outrageous person present. 'For someone whose architectural practice is based here in Fedborough, Alan Burnethorpe does have to do a remarkable number of trips up to London.'

'Are you suggesting he's got a little mistress tucked away up there?' suggested Jude, also beginning to have fun for the first time in the evening.

'Why stop at one? He may have dozens,' Carole contributed. This was most unlike her. She hadn't even met the man in question and she would never normally have participated in this kind of vulgar gossip. But she was really enjoying it.

Terry Harper joined in. 'That's before you include all the ones he's got down here. Easy for an architect. You go round to these houses. The husband's away at work . . . the wife tells him what she wants done . . .'

There was a chuckle from down the table. Terry's point had been made, but James Lister couldn't resist the cue to complete the innuendo. 'And he does it for her! Or should I say *to* her!' In case anyone hadn't got the joke, he added, 'He gives her one!'

His wife's thin face had turned dusty purple. 'Please! I must ask you to stop this conversation. At my dinner table I cannot allow my guests to pass around malicious gossip!'

No, thought Carole, supplying the unspoken final words to Fiona's speech: Because that's *my* job.

Chapter Twenty-One

The next day, the Saturday, the rain continued, and the promise of a good summer now seemed to have been a false one. Carole and Jude monitored the media all through the day but there was nothing on until the early evening television news.

The young female presenter, whose smile worked independently of the sense of what she was saying, announced, 'Police reveal identity of Fedborough corpse,' and cut to a senior police officer who had long ago had the smile trained out of him. He was at a press conference, where he announced gravely, 'The limbless body discovered two weeks ago in a house in Fedborough, West Sussex, has been identified after extensive forensic examination. It belonged to Mrs Virginia Hargreaves, a former resident of the town.'

As the presenter, smiling inappropriately, moved on to the fortunes of the local football teams, Jude crossed the room to turn down the television sound. Carole kept on saying she ought to get a remote control, but that kind of thing was low on Jude's priorities.

The two women looked at each other. 'So the gossips of Fedborough were right,' said Carole.

'Some of them. I'm sure at least as many had other

theories about the torso's identity and have been proved wrong.'

'Still, at this moment Fiona Lister is no doubt rubbing her hands with glee and waiting to hear the news of Roddy Hargreaves's arrest.'

'Or is Alan Burnethorpe shaking in his shoes because Virginia Hargreaves was his mistress and he killed her *in a fit of jealous passion*!' Jude's impersonation of Andrew Wragg on the last few words was uncannily accurate.

'They were a strange lot last night, weren't they?'

'Do you think, to an outsider, they'd seem any stranger than a group of Fethering locals?'

'Maybe not.' Carole narrowed her pale blue eyes with concentration. 'So clearly, to solve this case, we have to concentrate on the period round Virginia Hargreaves's disappearance.'

'If the case still needs solving.'

'What do you mean, Jude?'

'I'd have thought, now the police know who it was that died, they'd be pretty close to knowing how she died.'

'And who – if anyone – caused her death.'

'Even if she wasn't murdered,' Jude reminded her friend gently, 'someone cut off Virginia Hargreaves's arms and legs.'

'Yes . . .' Carole shook her head slowly from side to side. 'Things don't look very good for Roddy.'

Later that evening she found out that things looked even worse for Roddy. Debbie Carlton rang with the news that his dead body had been found floating in the Fether.

Chapter Twenty-Two

And, so far as Fedborough was concerned, that was it. The mystery was solved. Three and a half years previously, Roddy Hargreaves had killed his wife, dismembered her, and hidden her torso in the cellar of their home, Pelling House. When he knew the police were close to identifying the body, he had taken his own life. Case closed, so far as Fedborough was concerned.

On the Saturday evening Jude received a phone call that could have suggested this was the official view as well. Harry Roxby was on the line, elaborately conspiratorial, living up to the hilt his role as private investigator. 'The police came again today,' he whispered.

'Oh?'

'They took the seals off the cellar door.'

'The ones you'd sawn through?'

'Yes.'

'Did you get into trouble over that?'

'No. I was dead lucky. One of the cops was all set to bawl me out, but Mum sort of smoothed it over. She said I'd been very traumatized by what had happened and I was in a fragile emotional state . . .'

'Are you?'

'Well . . .' He giggled nervously.

'Sleeping better?'

'Yes. What you said was good. Now I'm thinking of the case as something that needs investigating, I sort of feel more, I don't know, further away from it . . .'

Excellent, thought Jude. That was the aim of the exercise. 'So the cop backed off, did he? Didn't bawl you out any more?'

'No. After what Mum said, he didn't seem that bothered. Just removed the remains of the seals, and said we could use the cellar again like normal.'

'Which might suggest the police have concluded their investigation.'

'Yes.' He sounded wistful at the thought of his detective game ending. 'So they reckon that this Mr Hargreaves killed his wife?'

'I can't be certain what the police think, but I'll bet that's what a lot of people in Fedborough are saying.'

'Mm,' he mumbled gloomily. 'I haven't even met Mr Hargreaves, which makes me feel, I don't know, sort of cheated over the case. Like I haven't got the whole story.'

'Happens a lot in police work.' Jude was joking, but there was sympathy in her voice too.

'I don't know,' said Harry disconsolately. 'Even if the police have got the right solution, it still leaves a lot of loose ends untied.'

'Like what?'

'Well, where the body's arms and legs went, for a start.'

'You're right. Trouble is, Harry, we don't have access to police files. Who knows, the limbs may have been found a long time ago, and the cops only needed the torso to match them up.'

'Perhaps.' He sounded even more despondent. 'Why would someone cut off a body's arms and legs?'

'Well, if we put aside sadism or a psychopath getting a cheap thrill . . .'

'Yeah.' A bit of interest crept back into his voice. 'I saw a video about a guy who did that. Somebody I knew in London had this great collection of that kind of stuff.'

Jude didn't want to go up that alley. 'As I say, putting sadism on one side, the most usual reason for dismembering a body would be ease of disposal.'

'Oh, I get you. So someone – perhaps the woman's husband – killed her, cut her up, and got rid of the arms and legs . . . Where do you reckon he'd have done that?'

'Lots of places around here. Bury them up on the Downs. Chuck them in the sea. Or the Fether, maybe. When the tide's going out, they'd get swept out into the Channel in no time.'

'Yes.' Harry was more enthusiastic. Now he felt he was back being an investigator. 'But if that's what happened, why didn't he get rid of the torso too?'

'Maybe he was interrupted? Someone got suspicious of him?'

'Frustrating not knowing more, isn't it? I think it's unfair that the police keep all the information to themselves.'

'The full details would usually come out later in court . . . but of course that'd only happen if someone was charged with the murder. If the gossip's right and the police do reckon Roddy Hargreaves killed his wife, then the whole story'll never be known.'

'No . . .' The boy was cast down again.

'But the police may not be right,' said Jude encouragingly. 'There may still be something to investigate. So, Harry, I'm relying on you to keep thinking about the case and listening to what people say. You might come up with that vital detail that turns the whole thing on its head. You might be able to prove that the police were wrong, and that Roddy Hargreaves wasn't a murderer.'

'You're right.' Now she'd given him his role back, Harry Roxby sounded positively perky. 'Don't worry, Jude. My investigation of the case continues.'

'That's what I like to hear, Sherlock.'

On the Sunday morning Carole and Jude went for a walk on Fethering Beach. As if apologetic for the recent rain, the day was exceptionally fine, the sky a gentle blue, and the beige sand stretched for miles. Gulliver circled ecstatically around them. He appreciated having the attention of two people, and he loved the intriguing smells of the low tide flotsam and jetsam. A late June day scampering across the pungent sand, with infinite sniffing detours, was his idea of dog heaven.

The two human beings with him were less cheerful. The sadness of Roddy Hargreaves's death, and the unsatisfactory way in which it might tie up the mystery of his wife's death cast a pall over both the women.

'I don't want to leave it like that,' said Jude.

'But how else can we leave it?' asked Carole. 'We have no information. We don't even know for sure that the police do think Roddy killed her.'

'No, and we probably never will know.' Jude picked up a stone and threw it into the retreating sea. Her mood was uncharacteristically despondent. 'I don't think he did kill her, though.'

Carole was silent for a moment, before saying, 'Nor do I.'

'But why do we think that? Given how little hard fact

we've got about the case, why are we both convinced Roddy didn't do it?'

'I suppose . . .'

'It's because we liked him, didn't we? We met him, and though we could recognize he was an alcoholic and a man with problems, we both had a gut instinct that he wasn't the kind of man who'd commit a murder.'

Carole, reluctant to admit to such an irrational impulse as 'gut instinct', had nonetheless to admit that Jude had a point.

'So, just for a moment, let's pretend that our gut instinct is right.'

'Why?'

'Because in my experience gut instincts usually are.'

Carole awarded that a rather frosty harrumph.

'Come on, if Roddy didn't do it, who did?'

'We're back to the same thing, Jude. We have no idea. We don't have enough information.'

'Then we'd better get some more information, hadn't we?'

'About what? About whom?'

'Roddy'd be a good person to start with. If we find out more about him, maybe we can actually prove he didn't do it.'

'All right. So who do we know who can tell us about Roddy?'

'James Lister, I suppose. If we can talk to him without the dreadful Fiona present.'

'Yes. Or . . .' A smile irradiated Carole's thin features. 'There's someone else.'

'Hm?'

'At the dinner party on Friday, Jude, don't you remember? Someone admitted he'd had "one or two conversations" with Roddy Hargreaves round the time Virginia disappeared.'

'Yes.' Jude smiled too as she nodded agreement.

'You know,' said Carole Seddon, 'I think I might go to church in Fedborough this evening.'

Chapter Twenty-Three

It was a long time since Carole had been to any kind of church service, and even longer since she had been to Evensong. The liturgy sounded unfamiliar and awkward. She must have gone to church a few times since the Prayer Book had been modernized, but it was the rhythms of the older version that had stayed with her from schooldays, when non-attendance had not been an option.

The biblical readings were even worse. Again, she had grown up with the King James Bible, and its rolling cadences were deeply etched on her subconscious. The version that was now being used had clearly been assembled by people with no sense of rhythm at all, and every clumsy phrase just made her aware of the perfect symmetries it had replaced.

The language might have been more effective if presented with conviction, but the Rev Trigwell's tremulous delivery suggested that he himself was uncertain of the text's validity. Idly, as she listened, Carole wondered whether it was possible for a Church of England vicar to show conviction. As a religion, Anglicanism was so wishy-washy. A passionate Anglican was an oxymoron, and the idea of an Anglican fundamentalist simply laughable.

She tried to think back to a time when she had had

faith, and couldn't find it. Till her mid-twenties she had been a regular church-goer, but that wasn't the same thing at all. Attendance had been a social convention, a polite ritual which had nothing to do with belief.

And, looking round the congregation in All Souls Fedborough that June evening, Carole Seddon didn't see much evidence of passionately held faith there either. The turn-out was better than most churches had come to expect in the first decade of the twenty-first century. At least two-thirds of the pews were full, but all with the same kind of people, respectable matrons with dutiful, suited husbands in tow. No ethnic diversity, and no children. Perhaps there was a Family Service on Sunday mornings, Carole reflected; there might be more of an age range on show in the church then.

The congregation were mostly regulars. At least they were very prompt on belting out the liturgical responses, all of which were different from the ones preserved in the amber of Carole's memory.

And they certainly knew the hymns, which again weren't ones she recognized. She wouldn't have minded giving 'Rock of Ages' or 'O God our help in ages past' a good seeing-to, but since the words were unfamiliar, she had to fall back on the silent and inaccurate lip-synch she'd relied on in her early days at school. Mouthing something and sounding only the occasional final 's' or 't' has been a church stand-by of the unaccustomed and the tone-deaf for centuries.

Still, the respectable people of Fedborough treated the verses on their photocopied sheets as if they were proper hymns and delivered them with great gusto. Behind her, Carole could hear one female voice soaring and swooping over the others. Its owner might once have been a good singer, but somewhere along the line had got the idea she could create her own descants to dance around the words, independent of the tune everyone else was singing. She didn't understand the choral principle of sublimating the individual in the group creativity.

A surreptitious look around brought Carole no surprise. The owner of the voice was Fiona Lister. Beside her, in a stiff suit, stood James, with the expression of a man who'd much rather be slumped in front of the television watching golf.

But in his face there was also a resignation. He had long ago recognized that he couldn't escape. Church-going was one of the rituals in the freemasonry of Fedborough respectability. If Fiona said it had to be done, it had to be done. James Lister couldn't perhaps help having been a butcher – though that still remained very regrettable – but in every other way he would have to conform to the middle-class stereotype.

At the end of the service, Carole deliberately dawdled. She had caught the eye of – and been graciously acknowledged by – Fiona Lister, to whom she mouthed a 'Thank you so much for Friday night.' She also spotted the Durringtons leaving the church some way ahead, but they didn't see her. Wondering whether the Roxbys might have considered church as a quick route into Fedborough society, she looked around, but saw no sign of them.

As the congregation filed out, they passed the Rev Trigwell in the porch. He did a lot of hand-shaking and feeble laughing, but *bonhomie* did not come naturally to him. He seemed, as ever, unrelaxed and gauche. A spike of his thinning hair was pointing upwards, and the red blotches on his face looked almost painful.

When Carole reached him, he took her hand in a

double handshake of unconvincing heartiness. 'Well, goodness me. All the way from Fethering. I'm honoured. Has news of the quality of my sermons travelled so far?'

His words contained the ingredients of insouciant small talk, but seemed to cost him a great effort to produce.

Carole had decided at the Listers' dinner party that directness was going to be her most effective approach with the Rev Trigwell. 'No,' she said. 'I just wanted to talk to you.'

'Oh?'

'About Roddy Hargreaves.'

His second 'Oh' was much gloomier. And it was followed by an 'Oh dear'.

The All Souls vicarage was a large building, but the Rev Trigwell only really lived in two rooms. They gave the appearance of having been furnished from second-hand shops by someone who had no interest in furniture. There were no pictures or personal photographs on the walls or mantelpiece. Philip Trigwell seemed as reluctant to impose his personality on his surroundings as on other people.

'I'm not married,' he announced, as if he had to get that out of the way before they moved on to anything else. 'I mean, I don't mean that I'm . . . I never have been married. I'm not married.'

'No.'

'Could I get you a cup of tea?'

He seemed relieved when Carole declined the offer. Her refusal was instinctive. The vicarage was not exactly dirty; it just had the feeling of being unused and unvisited. If she had agreed to tea, the Rev Trigwell might have taken some time to find a second cup.

'So . . .' They were sitting opposite each other in anonymous armchairs. He rubbed his hands together in a manner that anyone else would have made breezy. 'Poor old Roddy Hargreaves, eh? Sad business.'

'But presumably the Lord giveth . . .'

'Sorry?' He looked genuinely puzzled by the words.

'The Lord giveth and the Lord taketh away. Isn't that how we should think about death?'

The Rev Trigwell nodded his head slowly up and down as though considering a novel idea. 'Well, it's an approach, certainly. I didn't know you knew Roddy Hargreaves well.'

'I didn't.'

'Oh.'

'Only met him for the first time last week.'

'Ah. Well, he was a . . . He had his faults . . .' Suddenly this sounded too definitive a statement. 'That is, not very serious faults. I mean, he was unreliable, and he certainly drank too much . . . but I like to think his heart was in the right place.'

The vicar sat back, relieved to have achieved a perfect balance, venturing no opinion that hadn't been cancelled out by its opposite.

Carole was silent, which she somehow knew would make him uncomfortable.

It did. 'So if you didn't know him well . . .' Philip Trigwell went on awkwardly, 'presumably you're not really here for grief counselling.'

'No.'

'People do come to me for that.' He spoke doubtfully.

'I like to think I give some kind of help, some comfort . . . but I'm not really sure.'

'Presumably you can recommend the consolations of religion?'

'Oh yes.' He sounded unconvinced by the efficacy of the cure. 'I can do that.'

Carole decided it was time to move on. 'At the Listers' on Friday James said that Roddy Hargreaves had talked to you during the time when everything was going wrong for him, when his plans for the marina weren't working out . . .'

'Yes, yes. James did say that, yes.'

'Did Roddy come to you . . . sort of voluntarily . . . in search of help? I mean, was he a church-goer?'

'No. No, he wasn't. I've never seen him in All Souls. He was a Catholic, as we said. No, he just, erm . . .'

'So you went to see him?'

'Um . . . well . . . I suppose, in a way, yes. That's sort of how it happened.'

'You just recognized that he was in trouble . . . ? Here was someone who needed help . . . so you did your Good Samaritan act and went to see him?'

'Well, it wasn't quite like that, really, because the Good Samaritan actually found the man who fell among thieves injured by the roadside, and Roddy wasn't really injured in that way . . . he was just, erm . . . things weren't going very well for him . . .'

Carole began to wonder whether Philip Trigwell was deeply stupid, or whether sounding stupid was just a by-product of his embarrassment.

'But you did decide, off your own bat, that you should go and see him?'

'Well, erm . . . It was suggested to me that, erm, I

should perhaps have a word . . . I wasn't sure it would do any good, but . . .'

'Who suggested that to you?'

'Fiona Lister.'

That figured. The Queen Bee of Fedborough, trying to ensure that nothing happened outside her control. It would have been totally in character for her to order the Rev Trigwell to go and see Roddy Hargreaves, regardless of the man's religion and of how little either would have welcomed the encounter.

'She's a strong character,' Carole observed.

'Yes, yes, she is. Very strong.' Thinking 'strong' might be too strong a word, he immediately counterbalanced the statement. 'That is, she's a very good person, very thoughtful, very concerned for everyone's welfare, but perhaps she does sometimes . . . rather impose her views on . . . I mean, I'm not using "impose" in the sense of putting any pressure on people . . . Fiona's a very public-spirited person, and does a lot for charity, but she's . . . she's . . . well . . . As you say, she is a strong character,' he finished lamely.

'So when you went to see Roddy Hargreaves, was he receptive?'

'Receptive?'

'Did he take notice of the religious consolations that you offered him?'

'Oh, I didn't mention religion.' The Rev Trigwell was slightly appalled by the idea. 'I didn't want to cram that down his throat. Wouldn't do that to a Catholic, anyway. They can get funny about things like that. They seem to have such certainty about their religion.' He sighed wistfully. 'No, I just told Roddy I gathered he was in a spot of bother . . . was there anything I could do to help?'

'And was there?'

'Well, yes. I mean, it wasn't a . . . sort of therapeutic or counselling service. It was a purely practical thing he asked me to do for him.'

'What?'

'Give him a lift.'

'Sorry?'

'He wanted to get away. Things had been bad for a while. I think Roddy'd just had enough and he kept saying he wanted to go to France for a few days. And he knew he'd been drinking too much for too long to be safe driving, so would I give him a lift to Newhaven?'

'And did you?'

'Yes.' Even after such a length of time, the Rev Trigwell still sounded relieved. Giving someone a lift was so much easier than giving someone the consolations of religion.

'You took him to the ferry terminal?'

'Yes. He was very pleased, I remember, because he just got there in time to catch one. He hadn't got any luggage with him, so he bought his ticket and rushed on just before they pulled up the gangplanks.'

'Have the police asked you about this?'

'No.' He was genuinely puzzled by the question. 'Why should they?'

'Well, it's just . . . Roddy's dead. The torso that was found in Pelling House has been identified as belonging to his wife. There are a lot of people in Fedborough who're saying he must've killed her.'

'Are they?' His surprise still seemed authentic. 'Oh, but I can't imagine that.'

'Why not?'

'Roddy didn't seem that kind of person. I mean, as I said, he wasn't perfect. He certainly drank too much, and he was rather irresponsible, but I don't think there was any evil in him.'

'No.' The vicar's gut instinct was exactly the same as hers and Jude's. But she needed more than gut instinct. 'Did you tell anyone that you'd taken Roddy to Newhaven?'

'No, I didn't. He'd asked me not to . . . which I did find potentially a bit awkward. I try to avoid lying as a general rule. But nobody asked me anything about his movements, so it turned out all right. Mind you . . .' He coloured. 'I did have an awkward moment that very afternoon . . .'

'The afternoon you'd taken him to Newhaven?'

'Yes.'

'This would have been a Friday?' He nodded. 'And we're talking about . . . what? Late February three years ago?'

'It would have been around then, yes. I suppose I could check, see if I can be more specific about the precise date . . .' He sounded dubious about the prospects for success in any such search.

'Don't bother about that. You said you had an awkward moment that Friday afternoon . . .?'

'Yes. I'd just got back from Newhaven and parked the car when I remembered I was out of eggs, so I hurried down to the grocer's, because it was just before closing time, and in the shop I met Virginia.'

'Virginia Hargreaves?'

'Yes.'

'And I thought – wouldn't it be awkward if Virginia asked me if I'd seen Roddy, because then I'd either have to tell a direct lie or go against what he had asked me to do . . . so it was potentially very awkward. But . . .' He wiped his brow at the recollection. 'She didn't ask me anything about Roddy . . . so it was fine.'

'But did you tell anyone else about giving Roddy the lift?'

'No. Thank goodness nobody else asked, so I managed to avoid that particular moral dilemma.' He spoke as if avoiding moral dilemmas was a rarity for him.

Carole's mind was racing. She had to talk to Jude. She had to tell Jude about the connections that were forming in her mind.

She contrived to leave the vicarage quickly, but without overt rudeness.

Philip Trigwell stood wringing his hands in the doorway as he saw her out. 'I'm sorry. I probably haven't been much use to you. I often wonder if I'm much use to anyone . . . you know, my parishioners or . . .' He sighed. 'Life's not easy, is it?'

'No, it's not,' said Carole Seddon, as she started towards the parked Renault. 'But having a strong faith must help, mustn't it?'

'Yes,' the Rev Trigwell agreed wistfully. 'It would, wouldn't it?'

Chapter Twenty-Four

'. . . which must mean that Roddy Hargreaves couldn't have killed his wife,' Carole concluded triumphantly. 'He was in France at the time. The Rev Trigwell saw him on to the ferry and then met Virginia afterwards.'

Jude was uncharacteristically cautious. 'Ye-es. We'd have to check the actual timing of her disappearance.'

'Oh, come on. We know we're talking about late February three years ago. Friday the twentieth, to be precise, as James told us. Roddy talked about three or four days of his "lost weekend" in France and said that when he got back, presumably round Tuesday the twenty-fourth, Virginia had gone.'

'But if he'd killed her, he would have said that, wouldn't he?'

'What, so you're suggesting the trip to France was just to provide an alibi?' Carole demanded scornfully. 'That's why he involved the Rev Trigwell? Roddy caught the next ferry back to England, murdered his wife and pretended he'd been in France all the time? And I suppose he was only pretending to be drunk out of his skull, was he?'

'That's what a premeditating murderer would do, isn't it?'

'Yes. But I can't see Roddy Hargreaves in the role of

premeditating murderer. He wasn't sufficiently organized to do anything like that. He was a complete mess.'

'That's how he presented himself, yes. But that could have been an elaborate double bluff.'

'For heaven's sake! Why're you being so pussy-footed?'

This outburst brought a slow smile across Jude's rather beautiful face. 'Just playing devil's advocate.'

'Why?'

'Somebody's got to. Normally I can rely on you to take the job.'

'Oh, Jude . . . !'

Jude continued to smile in the silence. After some moments of resistance, Carole couldn't help smiling too. Jude had that effect on people. As they sat there that Monday morning over coffee in the cluttered sitting room of Woodside Cottage, Carole felt great gratitude for the fact that they'd met. Not that she'd ever put the feeling into words. Carole Seddon had a deep distaste for hearts worn on sleeves.

'Don't worry. If it's any comfort to you, I think you're right.'

'Thank God for that.'

'But we do need to find out more about the weekend when Roddy claimed to be away.'

'*Was* away.'

'Probably. We still need to know more about it.'

Carole conceded grumpily that this was true. She'd wanted a bigger reaction to what she'd found out from the Rev Trigwell. And though she knew that Jude was only teasing her, Carole Seddon had never enjoyed being teased.

'All right then. Who do we talk to? Who might know about what Roddy was up to?'

'James Lister. We keep coming back to him. Regular drinking companion of Roddy's.'

'Yes . . .' A new thought struck Carole. 'I wonder when James retired . . .'

'Mm?'

'Well, we know he was a butcher – much as Fiona would like to keep that fact a secret. And he's now . . . what? When we did the Town Walk, he said he was over seventy. So I wonder when he retired.'

'Why's it relevant, Carole?'

'Simply because Philip Trigwell said he'd met Virginia Hargreaves in the grocer's. Presumably he meant the one that Debbie Carlton's parents used to run . . . which is now an antique shop.'

Jude caught on. 'And which was next door to the butcher's, formerly John Lister & Sons, now an estate agent's.'

'Exactly. And I was wondering whether James Lister was still plying his trade on the weekend Virginia Hargreaves disappeared.'

'Carole, you aren't making a connection between butchery and dismemberment, are you?'

A shrug. 'Well, it's a thought. I'd imagine removing arms and legs is an easier job for a professional than an amateur.'

Jude's brow wrinkled as she assessed the idea. She pushed a flop of blonde hair off her forehead. 'I have the same problem with James in the role of murderer as I do with Roddy. Or at least with Virginia in the role of victim. Now, if Fiona had been dismembered . . . well, yes, that would make sense.'

Carole grinned grimly. 'Anyway, it's all worthy of investigation. I'm sure we'll find out that Roddy Hargreaves couldn't possibly have killed his wife.'

'Yes . . .' Jude tapped her chin as she remembered something. 'And there's another person we should talk to as well.'

'Who's that?'

'The old bloke Roddy bought the boatyard from.'

'Do we know who that is?'

'Ted Crisp knows.'

Carole froze at the name. Her carapace of reserve was immediately rebuilt around her. The thawing of the last couple of weeks was undone in an instant.

'I thought I might go down and have lunch at the Crown and Anchor. I don't suppose—'

'No, Jude!'

Her primary purpose could not be fulfilled, because Ted Crisp wasn't on duty at the Crown and Anchor. It hadn't occurred to Jude before, because he seemed to be a fixture in the pub, but of course the landlord must have days off. There was a pattern even to lives as apparently disorganized as Ted Crisp's.

But her trip wasn't wasted. As she approached, Jude had seen a familiar figure getting out of a BMW he had just parked and going into the pub. Alan Burnethorpe, dressed in his uniform collarless black shirt and black jeans. She remembered Ted telling her that the architect who'd worked with Roddy Hargreaves was an occasional visitor to the Crown and Anchor.

Jude had checked her pace and wandered down to the sea front for a moment to give Alan Burnethorpe time to buy a drink. She felt it would be easier to approach him once he was comfortably ensconced in the bar. He could certainly be a useful source of background information about his former client.

When she finally entered the Crown and Anchor, Jude couldn't see any sign of the architect. Only when she had ordered a white wine and a Tuna Bake from the unfamiliar girl who seemed to be in sole charge did she spot him, tucked away in a booth, deep in conversation with a heavily built man in a smart sports jacket and oblong glasses. She picked up her drink and sidled casually into the booth next to them.

'. . . overnight flight to Miami,' the one she didn't know was saying, 'which will be as uncomfortable as ever.'

'Surely you go First Class or Club?' said Alan Burnethorpe.

'No. It doesn't take that long.'

'Oh, come on. You can afford it.'

'That's not the point.'

'You always were a bloody cheapskate, Francis.'

This ready identification was extremely convenient from Jude's point of view. She felt confident that the large man was Debbie Carlton's ex-husband, and she settled down with interest to hear what he had to say. Making her presence known to Alan Burnethorpe was an option she would decide whether or not to exercise later.

'I'm not a cheapskate. I'm just not going to give Debbie the satisfaction.'

'Don't know what you're talking about. What satisfaction?'

'The satisfaction of making me shell out for a First Class ticket.'

'Sorry, you've lost me, Francis. What is this?'

'Look, I don't want to be over here. I want to be in Florida with Jonelle. I only came back because the police were getting suspicious of me.'

'About Virginia's body?'

'Yes.' There was a silence between the two men. Then Francis Carlton asked, 'Haven't been in touch with you, have they?'

'The police? No. I don't think anyone knows there's any connection between her and either of us.'

'I don't know whether the police knew anything about me and Virginia. If they did, they kept quiet about it when they questioned me. Mind you, of course, at that stage the body hadn't been positively identified as hers.'

'No,' Alan Burnethorpe agreed. There was another awkward silence. 'I should think we're all right now, anyway.'

'Roddy Hargreaves's suicide puts a lid on the investigation?'

'I'd have thought so. That must be what the police are thinking. Certainly what all the snoopers and harpies of Fedborough are thinking.'

'So Roddy's really done us a favour,' said Francis Carlton slowly.

'Ensured that there'll be no more investigation of Virginia's past . . . Yes, I hope so. We're both off the hook.'

'And I really don't think anyone in Fedborough has a clue that either of us had affairs with Virginia. So far as they're concerned, she was a nice aristocratic lady who only went up to London to sit on charity committees.'

'As opposed to sitting on . . .' The architect, maybe aware of its tastelessness, thought better of continuing the line. 'Anyway, it was all a long time ago. I broke up with Virginia when I met Joke.'

'And with her and me it was just sex, really. Very good sex, it has to be said. I don't need to tell you about that four-poster bed she had in London, with the design of vines climbing up the pillars and—'

'No, you don't,' said Alan Burnethorpe curtly.

'OK. I don't actually think many people in Fedborough even knew Virginia had a flat in London. And nobody knew what she used it for.' Francis chuckled harshly. 'There was a marked lack of curiosity about anything she did away from Fedborough. Which is good news for both of us. We can congratulate ourselves on having got away with it, having evaded the beady eyes of the town.' Francis Carlton let out an audible shudder. 'God, I'd forgotten how claustrophobic that environment can be.'

'It's not so bad.' Instinctively, Alan came to the defence of his home town.

'You may not find it so, but I do. Maybe it's all right for you "Chubs". You're just like Debbie, she seems to enjoy all that shopkeepers' gossip. Well, it's not for me. I tell you, Alan, I wouldn't dare be having this conversation with you anywhere in Fedborough.'

'Maybe not, but we're fine here. This place is very quiet. I use it quite a bit.'

'Like you used to use your office on the houseboat? Bring a few little friends here, do you?' Francis nudged.

'Francis, I've got Joke. I'm a happily married man.'

'But the way he said it prompted a laugh of male complicity.

'Yes, of course. How is married life?'

'It's fine.'

Francis Carlton picked up on the automatic nature of the reply. 'Really?'

'Well . . . It's all a bit familiar. I've got two small

children. I had two small children before, when I was married to Karen. I don't find the new set much more interesting than I found the first lot.'

'And how's married sex?'

'Fine. Fine . . . so long as I get the occasional outside diversion.'

Another masculine chuckle from Francis. 'You don't change, do you, Alan?'

'What about you? You working your way through the busty cheerleaders of Florida?'

'As a matter of fact, I'm not. I don't expect you to believe this – because the idea's so alien to your nature – but, since I married Jonelle, I've been entirely faithful to her.'

'Oh. Well, congratulations.' It was Alan's turn for a male-bonding chuckle. 'Still, if she's pregnant, that's going to have an effect on your sex-life. You'll have to develop some outside interests to get you through that.'

'No.' Francis Carlton spoke with a new seriousness. 'The pregnancy is what makes me certain that I'll stay faithful to Jonelle. That really means a lot to me. Maybe if Debbie had been able to have children I might have stayed with her . . .' He quickly dismissed the idea. 'Anyway, Jonelle and me is for keeps.'

'Are you saying you don't think you'll ever make love to another woman?'

'I hope not.'

'God, Francis, you're no fun any more.'

'Two Steak and Kidneys.' The girl from behind the bar brought over the men's food. Jude made a silent prayer that the service to her might be slow. She was getting more information than she had dared imagine, and didn't want the arrival of her Tuna Bake to draw attention to her presence.

There were sounds of the men salting and peppering and starting in on their food, and Jude wondered for a moment if she had heard all she was going to get, but fortunately Alan Burnethorpe picked up the conversation again. 'Do you know, Joke never had a clue that Virginia got up to naughties in London. And she was living and working in Pelling House all that time.'

'Yes, but that was in Fedborough, Alan. Like I said, all the fine people of Fedborough cared about was Virginia's title. And they spent so much time feeling sorry for her because of Roddy's drunken behaviour, it never occurred to them she might have failings of her own.'

'Mm.'

'I mean, apart from being good in bed – and I won't take that away from her, she was extremely good in bed – Virginia wasn't really a very nice person. She wasn't on speaking terms with any of the rest of her family, I know that for a fact.'

'Might not have been her fault. Perhaps they were even more unpleasant than she was.'

'All right, that's possible. But presumably, if any of her family had taken any interest in her, she couldn't have vanished off the face of the earth so effectively for the last three and a half years.'

'No.' Alan Burnethorpe was thoughtful.

Francis Carlton chuckled. 'Good thing for you Joke didn't know about Virginia's little London habits. Otherwise she might have found out that you shared them for a while. That wouldn't have been conducive to domestic harmony, would it?'

'You're right. She'd have taken a pretty dim view of me having screwed her employer. Or anyone, come to that. Joke has a distinctly old-fashioned attitude to adultery,' Alan concluded gloomily, as though his wife's scrupulousness was a cross with which he had been unfairly burdened.

'So when did you last see Virginia?' asked Francis.

'About a week before she disappeared – or perhaps now we should be saying "before Roddy topped her". We had an assignation in London for that Friday, and I remember I was getting a bit uptight about it, because things had started up with Joke, and I knew soon I was going to have to tell Virginia it was all off. Anyway, she saved me the trouble.'

'What do you mean?'

'She phoned me at the office and said she was ill. Couldn't make our meeting in her flat on the Friday.'

'Did she say what was wrong with her?'

'No. Quite honestly, I didn't care. Just breathed a big sigh of relief. Then the next week all Fedborough was talking about the fact that Virginia'd upped sticks and walked out on Roddy. So I was off the hook.'

'Very convenient,' said Francis Carlton.

'Yes,' Alan Burnethorpe agreed, without intonation.

There was a bit of steak-and-kidney-chomping before he went on, 'You still haven't explained what you meant by "not giving Debbie the satisfaction" of you buying a First Class ticket.'

'Ah, no. Well, I told you I only came over because the police were making some nasty insinuations on the phone . . .'

'What kind of insinuations . . . assuming at that stage they didn't know the body was Virginia's?'

'Just asking how often I went down to the cellar in Pelling House, that kind of thing. It wasn't actually what they were asking that got me worried; it was the tone in which they were asking it. I decided the only way to kind of clear my name was to come and talk to them face to face. And when I got here, I discovered why they were so suspicious of me.'

'Had they had an anonymous tip-off or something?'

'Exactly that. A letter, saying if they wanted to know how the torso got into the cellar at Pelling House, they should ask Francis Carlton.'

There was a silence. Jude held her breath. She noticed with annoyance that the barmaid had disappeared into the pub kitchen. Oh dear, she didn't want this moment ruined by the arrival of a Tuna Bake.

'Did you see the actual letter?'

'No. But obviously it came from Debbie.'

'What makes you say that? Debbie's not vicious. I think she's got a rather forgiving nature.'

'Oh, come on, Alan. You've been divorced. You know divorce isn't a great recipe for sympathy between a man and a woman. Debbie may appear to you to be "forgiving", but she hates me. She hates the fact that I've got Jonelle. She hates the fact that I'm happy. She'd do anything to shaft me. And making me have to shell out the cost of an airline ticket from Miami—'

'Even just an economy one.'

Francis ignored the interruption. 'That'd give her a great charge. Pathetic, but it's the only way she could think of to get at me, and take me away from Jonelle, even just for a few days. I bet Debbie had the idea the minute she heard about the discovery of the torso.'

'Did she sound gleeful when she heard you were going to come over?'

'She's too subtle to do that. Besides, if she had started crowing, I might have smelt a rat. No, it was very simple.

Debbie just wanted to cause me maximum inconvenience – and do something that'd upset Jonelle too. Petty revenge, that's all.' He coloured at the recollection. 'God, I bawled her out when the police told me about the anonymous letter.'

'Did she admit she'd sent it?'

'No, of course she didn't! She denied it. But then she would, wouldn't she?' Francis Carlton realized his anger was taking him over and paused to regain control. When he spoke next, his voice was quieter, but very tense. 'I can't wait to get on that plane tonight. I tell you one thing, Alan, whatever else I do in the rest of my life, I'm never coming back to bloody Fedborough.'

Having voiced the thought, he seemed anxious to depart as soon as possible. Alan Burnethorpe made a half-hearted offer to pick up the tab, which Francis accepted with alacrity. In spite of his denials, he really was very mean. Even with Jonelle's money, he would remain mean. Jude wondered whether his new wife had yet found out about this little characteristic of her husband. To Jude's mind, it was the worst flaw a man could have.

With hurried insistence that he must go and get his bags from Debbie's and perfunctory thanks for the lunch, Francis Carlton was suddenly gone. The barmaid at that moment appeared with the Tuna Bake, so Alan Burnethorpe had to wait at the bar before he could settle up.

He looked across to where the girl was, and Jude shrank into her booth. But she wasn't quick enough. Alan Burnethorpe didn't make any acknowledgment, but there was no doubt that he'd seen her.

And no doubt he'd deduced that Jude had overheard his conversation with Francis Carlton.

Chapter Twenty-Five

'You know Debbie. Do you think it's in her nature to send anonymous letters?'

'I don't know her that well, Jude. And, anyway, divorce tends to change people's natures,' said Carole with feeling. 'When a relationship comes to an end, perfectly rational adults start behaving like playground bullies. I'm always amazed at the levels of petty vindictiveness that divorce can bring on.'

Jude nodded. She had witnessed the same. May even have witnessed the same in her own life, Carole thought suddenly. Again, she felt frustrated by how little she knew of her friend's past. Now the subject had come up, maybe it would be a good moment to fill in some of the gaps.

But, as ever, the opportunity passed, as Jude said, 'And, from what you say Debbie and Francis respectively got out of the settlement, I'd imagine she was pretty bitter.'

'She tried to sound grown-up and philosophical, but clearly she was very hurt. Her with her little flat in Fedborough, and him with his rich wife and two homes. And that was before she found out about the baby.'

'Yes.'

'That really hit her hard. I told you.'

'Mm . . .'

The pensive silence that ensued offered another opportunity to elicit a bit of information. Carole snatched it. 'Do you regret not having children, Jude?'

Her friend looked up, smiling mischievously. 'Who says I haven't had any?' And, once again, before the supplementary question could be put, Jude had moved on. 'I can see the satisfaction in it, from Debbie's point of view. She hasn't got much she can do in the way of revenge. Dragging Francis all the way back from Florida, putting him through a few nasty grillings with the police . . . not bad, is it?'

'I suppose not,' said Carole grumpily, still resentful of the way Jude had evaded the personal question. Unambiguously that time, as well; Jude had definitely been playing with her curiosity.

'Mind you,' her neighbour went on quickly, 'if Debbie was responsible for the anonymous letter, then that probably rules out Francis Carlton as a suspect.'

'It was only her desire for revenge that made him look like a suspect in the first place?'

'Exactly. So that might rule him out, in spite of the fact that we now know that he had an affair with the dead woman.'

'Strange, isn't it,' said Carole, 'that, whenever murder's discussed, anyone who's had an affair with the victim becomes an immediate suspect . . .'

'Why's that strange? Seems pretty logical to me.'

'I suppose I meant strange in the way it comments on human relationships. If you love someone, that means you want to kill them.'

' "Yet each man kills the thing he loves . . ." '

Carole hadn't expected Jude to quote Oscar Wilde.

She kept encountering inconsistent details in her friend's character. Carole Seddon liked to categorize people; then she knew what she was up against. But Jude made that process very difficult.

'Anyway,' Jude went on, 'Francis Carlton wasn't the only one to have had an affair with the lovely Virginia Hargreaves.'

'Alan Burnethorpe too.'

'Yes. The saintly image she projected seems in retrospect a little tarnished. How did she get away with it, in a wasp's nest of gossip like Fedborough? Do you really think they were all seduced by the glamour of her title?'

'Yes,' Carole replied firmly. Then, in response to Jude's sceptical look, she went on, 'You haven't lived down here as long as I have. There's a level of snobbery associated with the aristocracy you just wouldn't believe. Everyone wants to invite them to everything, and they're given a much freer rein than ordinary people. There'd have to be a really monumental scandal for people in a place like Fedborough to start thinking badly of someone with a title.'

'I thought that kind of nonsense had gone out in these so-called egalitarian times.'

'Don't you believe it.'

'Hm. Right.' Jude rubbed her hands together in a business-like manner. 'So . . . where do we go next? Presumably Francis Carlton is back in the States. Be good to talk to Debbie again – and I'd like to meet her this time. Have you run out of credibility on interior design consultations?'

'I think I have a bit. Unless I actually say I'm going to go ahead with the job.' Her face clouded at the recollection this brought to her – of the euphoria prompted by her relationship with Ted Crisp, which had made her full of plans for brightening up her life. 'And I'm certainly not going to do that,' she concluded tartly.

'Ooh, but just a minute, though . . .' A new thought came to Carole. 'If we wait till Friday, we've got the perfect opportunity to go and see Debbie.'

'What?'

'The Art Crawl we heard so much about from Terry Harper.'

'Right. Debbie Carlton's exhibiting. Yes, I remember him saying that.'

'So we can wander at will through a selection of the private homes of Fedborough . . . on the pretext that we're art-lovers. Debbie described the Fedborough Festival Art Crawl as a Snoopers' Charter.'

'Good. Any other houses we ought to investigate?'

'Wouldn't mind having a look in Terry Harper's. I don't know whether he's actually part of the Crawl, but there's nothing to stop anyone from walking into an antique shop.'

'I get you. You're thinking that used to be the grocer's?'

Carole nodded. 'The last place, from the information we have, where Virginia Hargreaves was seen alive. On February the twentieth, three years ago.'

'Yes.' Jude ruefully jutted out a lower lip. 'Though it has to be said that the information we have is verging on the sketchy. We really need to find out more detail about Virginia Hargreaves's last weekend.'

'Which brings us back to James Lister.'

'Right. How're we going to justify getting in touch with him again? The Listers' house isn't part of the Art Crawl, is it?'

'No.'

'Actually, I can't see the lovely Fiona being that interested in art . . . though I suppose she might have her husband's balls mounted and framed.'

Carole blushed instinctively. Lines like that always made her blush . . . though she couldn't help finding the image rather funny.

She made no comment on it, however. 'Not a problem. We have the perfect excuse to get back in touch with the Listers.'

'What?'

'Have you called them to say thank you for the delightful evening on Friday?'

'No, I haven't yet.'

'Nor have I.' Carole reached for the phone.

Fortunately, James Lister answered. His wife was off poisoning the atmosphere somewhere else. He was fruitily grateful for her fulsome thanks. 'It was my pleasure. Can't have enough pretty women around me, you know. Though don't let the wife hear me say that.' He chuckled rather feebly. Even when she wasn't there, Fiona still cast a shadow of anxiety over his life.

'Well, it was a great pleasure, James. So kind of you to invite us.'

'We enjoyed seeing you.'

'And do thank Fiona for the magnificent dinner, won't you?'

'Yes, of course.'

'And I hope we'll see you again soon, James.'

'Yes.' He hesitated. 'When you say "we", you mean you and your friend Jude?'

'That's right.' Carole winked at Jude across her sitting room. 'Have you heard from her since Friday?'

'No, but don't worry. I'll pass on the thanks from both of you to Fiona—'

'That seems rather—'

'Did you hear, incidentally,' James Lister went on, 'the reason why poor old Roddy Hargreaves wasn't with us on Friday?'

'Yes, I did. A terrible tragedy.'

'Mm.'

'It must be dreadful for you, James.'

'Why?' He sounded instantly suspicious.

'Well, to lose one of your regular drinking mates.'

'Oh, yes. Well, that happens, I'm afraid. Increasingly, these days.'

'But it won't stop you using the Coach and Horses?'

'Good Lord, no.' He let out a heartily masculine laugh. 'Death's a tragedy, but stopping going to the pub would be an even worse tragedy.'

'So you'll still be there on a regular basis?'

'You bet, young lady. Six o'clock on the dot every weekday evening. Erm, except Fridays, that is, because, erm . . . well, as you know, Fiona gives her dinner parties then.'

'Of course. Well, James, thank you again for last week . . .'

'From you and Jude, yes.'

' . . . and I'll hope to see you in the Coach and Horses one of these evenings.'

'That'd be splendid,' said James Lister, not realizing he had just made a definite appointment.

But he didn't look surprised when Carole and Jude appeared in the Coach and Horses shortly after six that evening. In fact, he was delighted to see them. James Lister was alone at the bar. His cronies hadn't turned up. One of them would never turn up again. Maybe the others wouldn't appear at all that evening. The women saw him before he saw them; he looked old and forlorn.

But he perked up the minute he caught sight of them. 'Well, this is a double pleasure. Fiona will be so interested to hear that I've met up with you again. So what brings you here?'

Carole gaped. She hadn't thought to prepare a cover story.

'Oh, we're just stupid, Jimmy,' said Jude smoothly. 'I'd got it into my head that this Art Crawl thing, you know, that Terry Harper was talking about at your dinner party . . . well, I thought it started today.'

'No, that's Friday. Third of July. Well, most of the Private Views are on Thursday evening. Fiona and I will have to put in an appearance at a few of those.' His tone of voice didn't suggest he'd had an overnight conversion to the joys of visual art. 'But the Crawl proper opens to the public on Friday afternoon.'

'I know now. I've seen the posters all over the town. Anyway, since we'd come here on a wasted journey, we thought we'd have just a quick drink before we went back to Fethering.'

'Your mistake is my gain,' said James Lister with elaborate courtesy.

'Stupid of me.' Jude shook her head pitifully.

He responded to the dumb blonde routine. 'Women, eh? Can't be trusted out of the kitchen. Or the bedroom.' He cackled. Carole and Jude resisted their instinctive responses to his words and smiled winsomely. They weren't going to put this information opportunity at risk. 'Now come on, let me get you pretty little things a drink.'

Skittishly, Jude requested a white wine. Carole did the same, although she was less good at being skittish.

When they were supplied with glasses, Jude looked around the bar and sighed. 'Sad to think last time we were in here we were talking to Roddy Hargreaves.'

James Lister looked suitably reverent. 'Yes. Poor bugger – pardon my French. I knew he was in a bad way, but I didn't ever imagine he'd go and do that.'

'Do what?' asked Jude innocently.

'Well, jump in the river.'

Carole joined in the questioning. 'Is everyone in Fedborough assuming it was suicide?'

'Obviously. What's the alternative?'

'He might just have fallen in. He drank a lot. Very unsteady, I would imagine, when he was walking around.'

'Oh yes, but he knew the riverbank well. He wouldn't have fallen in by accident.'

'Someone might have pushed him in,' Jude suggested innocently.

'Why would they do that?'

'I've no idea.'

'Well, I'm sorry, my lovely young thing . . .' James Lister took the opportunity to give Jude's shoulder a more than avuncular pat. ' . . . but I'm afraid the truth is poor old Roddy topped himself.'

Jude continued to play the innocent. 'Why would he do that?'

'Once the police had identified Virginia's body, he knew it was only a matter of time before they arrested him. He couldn't face that, so . . .'

'Are you saying he murdered his wife?'

'That's what everyone in Fedborough's saying.'

'Is everyone in Fedborough usually right?' asked Carole.

'About most things, I'd say, yes. Once you hear a rumour in this town, nine times out of ten it'll turn out to be true.'

Neither woman believed this, but they both nodded, unwilling to stop his flow.

'Poor old Roddy.' James Lister shook his head lugubriously. 'Must've been nursing that ghastly secret all these years. Probably what drove him to drink.'

'But I thought he drank a lot while his wife was still around,' Carole objected.

'Yes, but he was worse after she'd gone. Now we know why.'

'How long ago was it all this happened?' asked Jude, still playing the *ingénue*.

'Three . . . three and a half years. I know that, because it was my last year in the business. I sold out . . . I suppose about six months after Virginia disappeared.'

'Must've been a wrench for you after all that time, giving up the family business.'

'Well, in some ways it was. In a lot of other ways I was pleased to be shot of the whole thing. Butchery's changed, you know, not the profession it was. When I started, Fedborough could support two butchers. There was my dad's, and old Len Trollope on the corner of Dauncey Street. And both of them thought their business would be passed on from father to son for all eternity.

'But now every supermarket has its own meat counter, it's hard to make a living as the old traditional local shop. And butchers nowadays have all this Brussels and BSE nonsense to deal with . . . I think I got out at the right time. Didn't do too badly out of it, either. Property prices in Fedborough have gone up very satisfactorily, you know.'

'Good,' said Carole, reckoning that was the required response.

'Oh yes.' He nodded, pleased with his business acumen.

'So were you one of the last people to see Virginia Hargreaves alive?' asked Jude breathlessly.

The idea of being part of the drama appealed to him. 'Yes, I suppose I was.'

'Ooh, how horrid,' said Jude, continuing to play daffy. 'Do you remember when it was exactly?'

He smoothed his white moustache with the effort of recollection. 'Let me see. I think it was late on the Friday afternoon before she vanished . . .'

Neither Carole nor Jude made any reaction, but the same thought was in both their minds: when Roddy was already on the ferry to France.

'Mm, because I remember, just before closing time, I'd dropped into Stanley Franks's shop next door . . .'

'The grocer's?'

'That's right. He sold up round the same time I did. But we were still both in business then . . .'

'I gather he's now very ill,' said Carole.

'Yes, poor bugger – pardon my French again. Physically in very good nick, I gather, which means he'll probably last for years. But the mind's totally gone. Very sad. He used to be so good at what he did. All right, I know running a shop's not the most glamorous of professions . . .' (a fact of which his wife had left him in no doubt over the years of their marriage) ' . . . but there's a lot of skill involved in doing it well, and the best people in the retail trade really take a pride in their work. I like to think I was one of those, but I couldn't hold a candle to Stanley Franks. He was a real perfectionist, ran that shop like a finely oiled machine. Spotlessly clean, all the best produce, a lot of it prepared on the premises. Really sad to see him now.

'Used to be a great drinking mate of mine, Stanley. You know, we'd both built up our businesses in the town next door to each other, but . . .' He shook his head gloomily. 'Used to go and see him when he first moved into The Elms, but pretty soon stopped. No point. He didn't know who I was.'

'I met his wife, Billie. She said she thought he was getting better.'

'Deluding herself, I'm afraid, Carole my love. There's no way back from the road old Stanley's gone down. Billie's had a rotten deal of it. Had to sell the family home and move into a houseboat to pay for his care and, as I say, he looks like he could last for ever. Don't know what she'll do when the money runs out.' His head shook mournfully.

'Sorry,' Jude prompted, 'but you were telling us about the last time you saw Virginia Hargreaves.'

'Oh, right, so I was.' With relish James Lister resumed his position centre stage of the tragedy. 'When I popped into Stanley's shop that afternoon, Virginia was there and I remember thinking at the time . . . she looks in a bad way.' He paused for effect.

'What – ill?'

'Could have been ill. Certainly pale and drawn. But I thought she looked more . . . emotionally upset.' He nodded sagely. 'I remember, I said so that evening at our Friday-night dinner party. I said, "Virginia Hargreaves is looking in a bad way. I don't think things are too healthy in that marriage".' He let the meaning sink in, while Carole and Jude thought how typical it was that private grief should be dissected round the Listers' dinner table. 'Little did I know how prophetic my words would be,' James concluded.

After a suitably impressed pause, Carole asked, 'But didn't anyone in Fedborough think to enquire where she had gone?'

'Not really. Everyone knew things had been sticky between her and Roddy. The surprise really was that she hadn't walked out earlier. I think the general assumption was that she had gone back to stay with some of her aristocratic relations.'

Ah yes, thought Carole, the title once again working its magic. Fedborough had been honoured by the presence in its midst of a member of the peerage; not good form to pry after she'd graciously moved back to be among her own kind. Though, if Fedborough had pried, it would quickly have found out that she wasn't on speaking terms with any of her own kind.

James Lister's face took on an expression of pious thoughtfulness. 'If only I'd asked Virginia what the trouble was when I saw her that Friday afternoon, perhaps I could have saved her.'

'I don't think you should blame yourself,' said Carole, managing not to smile.

'No. But one does,' he said gravely. 'When something like this happens, inevitably one does.'

Jude took up the baton of investigation. 'Jimmy, you don't know of anyone who saw Virginia Hargreaves after you did?'

He shook his head. 'Somebody may have done,

but . . . Didn't realize at the time it would be important, so I never thought to ask.'

'And I don't suppose,' said Carole, 'that you remember when you next saw Roddy after that weekend?'

'Matter of fact, I do.' He barked a laugh. 'Typical of the disorganized bugger.' Too caught up in his narrative, he forgot to ask for his French to be pardoned. 'I get a call from him on the Tuesday evening. He's just come off a ferry at Newhaven, he's smashed out of his skull . . . would I "be a mate" and pick him up?'

'And did you?'

'Yes.' Remembered guilt flashed across his face. 'Fiona has her Church Choir rehearsals on a Tuesday.'

'And what kind of state was Roddy Hargreaves in?'

'Totally paralytic. He must've been drinking solidly for two or three days. I assumed he'd been doing it because the boatyard business had gone belly-up, but of course now I realize he had something on his mind he wanted to forget even more – the murder of his wife.'

'Did he actually tell you how long he'd been away?' asked Carole casually.

'No, he wasn't coherent enough for that.' James Lister flicked his moustache as a new thought struck him. 'Or perhaps he was just pretending to be incoherent . . . ? Yes, perhaps he was completely sober, and he'd only gone to France to establish an alibi.'

'How do you mean?'

'Well . . .' The butcher warmed to his new role of criminal investigator. 'Let's say he'd killed Virginia over the weekend, on the Saturday . . . Then he'd nipped over to France on the Sunday and pretended he'd been there longer than he had.'

'Yes, that makes sense,' Carole lied. She exchanged a

flick of the eyelids with Jude, as Roddy Hargreaves's real alibi seemed to be confirmed.

'Have the police talked to you about any of this?' asked Carole.

James Lister was affronted. 'Good heavens, no.'

'If they have decided Roddy Hargreaves murdered his wife, you'd have thought they'd have asked around the town.'

'Well, they haven't talked to me.' His tone implied the end of that topic of conversation.

'Speaking as a professional . . .' Jude contrived to get a Marilyn Monroe breathiness into her voice. ' . . . would it be easy for someone untrained to dismember a corpse?'

James Lister guffawed. He was much happier with this subject. On his home ground. 'Depends on the quality of the job you were after. Any idiot with a chainsaw could cut a body up. If you wanted it neatly jointed . . . well, for that you'd need someone qualified.'

'Mm . . .' said Jude coquettishly. 'Interesting.'

Chapter Twenty-Six

The original concept of the Art Crawl had been a brilliant one, but Terry Harper's attempt to improve the quality of the art on show was not popular with Fedborough opinion. Almost as enjoyable as snooping round the houses of people one knew vaguely was the opportunity of being disparaging about the creative efforts of people one knew vaguely. When the artist in question was not on the premises, but in London, Paris, Hamburg or Amsterdam, the pleasure of murmuring 'I wouldn't give house-room to *that*' was considerably diminished.

The fact that the art on display was of a higher standard than in previous years did not make a blind bit of difference. Nobody in Fedborough knew anything about art, anyway. They took much more pleasure in sniggering at a local amateur's random spars of driftwood impaled by rusty nails or leather bookmarks embossed with Celtic runes than they did in appreciating a delicate watercolour, a subtly lit photograph or a thought-provoking collage of disaster images by a professional artist.

The people of Fedborough did not know much about art, but they knew what they liked – and that was stigmatizing the excesses of other people in Fedborough. So before Carole and Jude started their tour at three o'clock on the Friday afternoon, that year's Art Crawl had already received the communal thumbs-down.

The system was blissfully simple. Throughout the Fedborough Festival, some twenty-five houses around the town opened themselves up as impromptu galleries between two and six every afternoon. In each one, visitors could pick up a map which marked the venues, with the names of the artists exhibiting and brief descriptions of the work on show. There was no obligation to complete the full circuit. One could take in a couple of artists, stop for tea in one of the many teashops or buy the odd antique, and then take in a couple more. All the art on display was available for sale, and quite a lot of it got purchased.

The Art Crawl, for whatever reasons, brought a large number of people into the town, and was deemed a good thing by the local Chamber of Commerce.

Interest in the Art Crawl, and in the many other events of the Festival, would build up over the ten days of its duration, but on the Friday afternoon the town was relatively empty. Which suited Carole and Jude perfectly.

They had had no doubt as to what should be their first artistic port of call. Jude had yet to meet Debbie Carlton, and they were delighted when they emerged at the top of the stairs, to find the artist alone in her flat.

She had moved most of the furniture out of the sitting room to make more space for the anticipated art-lovers. There were many more paintings on the walls than there had been before. All were in the same style, evoking drowsy afternoons in Italy, but they demonstrated infinite subtle variations. Debbie Carlton fully justified Terry Harper's description: 'one of the few genuinely talented artists in Fedborough'.

'This is Jude, my neighbour. I've been going on so much about your paintings, she was desperate to come and have a look.'

Jude slipped easily into the slight exaggeration. 'You bet. And from a quick look I can tell Carole was absolutely right. Wonderful stuff.'

Debbie Carlton glowed. Though she claimed to be suffering from a hangover following her Private View the night before, she looked very pretty that afternoon, casual in clown-like dungarees, almost beautiful, and totally relaxed. Carole was even more aware of the tension that her ex-husband's presence had engendered.

'You're my first visitors. I've been sitting here for the last hour wondering if anyone was going to come, and wondering if I dared go off to the loo, in case someone did.'

'Feel at liberty to do so now,' said Carole. 'We'll guard your premises against international art thieves.'

Debbie grinned. 'The urge has gone away. Just nerves, I expect. This is a different kind of tension for me. I got terribly nervous yesterday before the Private View, but then at least I knew everyone was going to arrive at about the same time. Waiting around like this is a sort of extended torture.'

'Well, I hope our arrival has taken the curse off it,' said Jude, whose eyes were darting round the paintings on the wall.

'Yes, I think it has.'

'Ooh, I love that one!' Jude swooped towards a small close-up of a terracotta urn from which sharp green plant tendrils trailed. 'It is for sale, isn't it?'

'They're all for sale. Except for the ones with red

stickers on. Those were bought at the Private View last night.'

'Great! I'll have this one! How much?'

Carole Seddon looked on, open-mouthed. What Jude had said was the wrong way round. You didn't decide to buy something and then ask the price. The correct procedure was to find out the price, assess whether you could afford the object in question and whether it might not be better to consider the decision overnight. If the sums made sense, and you were feeling particularly impulsive, then you might proceed to make the purchase on the spot.

Jude didn't work that way. On being told the catalogue listed seventy-five pounds, with a cry of 'Cheap at the price', she immediately whipped a cheque-book from her bag and started writing. Flamboyantly, she ripped the cheque out and handed it to a delighted Debbie Carlton.

This little transaction raised two intriguing questions for Carole. One was an old, recurrent one: where did Jude get her money from, what did she live on? Carole was no nearer to answering that than she had been when her new neighbour first moved in to Woodside Cottage.

The answer to the second question had proved equally elusive. Ridiculous, given the length of time they'd known each other, but Carole still didn't know Jude's surname. It hadn't been volunteered on their first meeting, and the longer time went on, the more difficult for Carole became phrasing the direct question on the subject.

But Jude had just produced a cheque-book; and surely printed on her cheques must be her full name. Carole tried, without being too conspicuous, to lean across and read what was on the cheque. But the transaction was too quick. Debbie immediately placed the cheque in a cash-box she hoped would fill up over the next ten days, and by the time Carole looked back, Jude had replaced the cheque-book in her bag. Carole's frustration was unrelieved.

Hard on the heels of that annoyance came another troubling thought. If Jude had just bought a painting, shouldn't Carole do the same? She was the one, after all, who had had more contact with Debbie Carlton. She, if anyone, was Debbie's friend. Didn't etiquette demand that she should go against her nature and make a comparable impulse buy? She liked Debbie's paintings, there was no problem with that, but she couldn't make a snap decision like Jude just had. And should she go for one at the same price as Jude's? Though how could she know it was the same price as Jude's? The prices weren't marked on the paintings; they were on the set of printed sheets piled up beside Debbie's cash-box. And if she looked at one of those sheets before deciding on which painting to buy, might her behaviour not – by comparison with Jude's spontaneity – appear calculating or mean?

This characteristic spiral of thought in Carole's mind was fortunately interrupted by an equally characteristic direct question from Jude. 'You used to live in the house where the torso was found, didn't you, Debbie?'

'That's right.'

'I don't know if you heard, but I was present at dinner with the Roxbys the night it was discovered.'

'How horrible. Did you actually see the thing?'

Jude nodded, and Debbie Carlton smiled sympathy. Carole was once again amazed at her friend's ease in reaching a state of intimacy with complete strangers.

'Did you know her?' asked Jude.

'Virginia Hargreaves? I knew her to say hello to. Because my parents have always lived in Fedborough, even when I wasn't living here I'd often come back. So I'd see Virginia in the High Street or in my parents' shop. They used to run the grocery in the town.'

Jude reacted as if this was new information to her. Then, casually, she asked, 'Everyone seems to be assuming the husband killed her. Do you go along with that?'

Debbie Carlton splayed out her hands in a gesture of ignorance. 'What else is there to think? I must say I'm surprised, because, from what I'd seen of Roddy, he appeared to be just a fairly harmless piss-artist. Hard to imagine him as a murderer, but . . . who knows what goes on inside a marriage? People tell me my marriage to Francis looked fine from the outside, so . . .'

'But was Virginia Hargreaves universally liked?' asked Carole. 'We've found it difficult to get anyone in Fedborough to say a word against her.'

Debbie Carlton let out a derisive snort of laughter. 'Oh, they were just impressed by her title. And now it's even worse, because "not speaking ill of the dead" comes into the equation. But no, there were a few people who'd had their set-tos with the lovely Virginia.'

'What kind of people?'

'People who weren't impressed by her title and made no secret of the fact. Or people who tried to be competitive with her socially.'

'Like . . . ?'

'Well, I guess the main one would be a woman called Fiona Lister . . . don't know if you've come across her . . . ?'

They explained that she had been their hostess for dinner the previous Friday.

'My, you are honoured. I was never granted the dubious pleasure of an invitation to one of La Lister's *soirées* – and for a very obvious reason.'

'What?'

'Trade, Carole, trade. My parents' grocery was right next door to James Lister's butcher's. All Fiona's money may have come from trade, but she didn't want her social life to do so as well. She aimed for something much more *genteel.*' There was an uncanny evocation of Fiona Lister in the way Debbie shaped the word.

'And is that why she fell out with Virginia Hargreaves?'

'Spot on. Fiona has always seen herself as the Queen Bee of Fedborough society, and Virginia was a rival for that title.'

'She wasn't a great entertainer too, was she?'

'No. Rather the reverse. I can't ever remember Virginia doing any entertaining at Pelling House. But, you see, she didn't have to. She got invited everywhere simply by virtue of who she was. People in Fedborough fell over themselves to include her in everything. So, without making any effort at all, Virginia Hargreaves was always going to win over Fiona Lister. Virginia was born into the aristocracy and, however much social-climbing effort Fiona Lister made, she would remain, at bottom, the wife of the local butcher.'

'Was there a moment when things came to a head?' Jude asked eagerly. 'When the two of them actually came to blows?'

'No, no. Coming to blows was very much not Virginia Hargreaves's style.' Debbie smiled mischievously. 'I did hear a rumour from Mum about something that'd happened, though, but I'm not sure if it's true.' She read the avid anticipation in the two women's faces and went on, 'Still, one of those things that *should* be true, even if it isn't. Apparently, according to Mum, Virginia and Roddy were once invited to one of La Lister's *soirées*. And Virginia sent a note back, saying that it was an extraordinarily kind thought, but she was afraid they wouldn't be able to attend, *because it wasn't really their kind of thing*.'

Carole winced. 'The Snub Direct.'

'Exactly. And entirely unanswerable, from Fiona's point of view. Virginia had very firmly put her in her place. People of Virginia's background didn't mix with butcher's wives, and that was all there was to it.'

'Sounds like something out of Jane Austen,' said Jude.

'Believe me, it could easily have happened here in Fedborough. And, what's more, it still could today.'

Carole nodded. She had lived long enough in Fethering to find the anecdote utterly believable. 'Interesting that last Friday Fiona Lister was almost fulsome in her appreciation of Lady Virginia.'

'Easy to do that now she's not around,' said Debbie. 'Easy – and rather useful – for Fiona to imply, without fear of contradiction, that they were part of the same social circle.'

'Did your husband know Virginia Hargreaves . . . ?' asked Jude casually.

Debbie shrugged. 'I'm sure he'd met her. He was friends with Alan Burnethorpe who married Virginia's housekeeper, so they probably knew each other.'

Jude and Carole exchanged a covert look. Debbie Carlton's innocence sounded genuine. She appeared completely unaware of her ex-husband's closeness to Virginia Hargreaves. Or of Alan Burnethorpe's, come to that.

'Has Francis gone back to the States?' asked Carole, also affecting ignorance.

'Yes. Back to his born-again marriage and prospective family.' She could not keep the bitterness out of her voice.

'Hm. In retrospect . . .' Carole mused, 'it seems strange that the police dragged him all the way over here to talk to them.'

'Why?'

'Well, given the fact that the murder victim – or perhaps we should just say the body – turned out to be Virginia Hargreaves, who lived in Pelling House long before you took possession of the place, why on earth would the police have any suspicions of Francis?'

'I've no idea.'

'I heard a rumour round Fedborough . . .' Carole kept her voice deliberately light. ' . . . that they'd had a tip-off.'

'The police? A tip-off about Francis?' She seemed suddenly to remember. 'The anonymous letter?'

'Yes. The anonymous letter which pointed the finger of suspicion firmly at him. You do know about that?'

'Francis mentioned an anonymous letter, but I thought he was just being paranoid. But if there really was one . . . Bloody hell!' Debbie said, on a sudden spurt of anger. 'I'd like to get my hands on whoever sent it.'

'Why? Because you're sorry about the emotional trauma caused to Francis?'

'No. Because I'm sorry about the emotional trauma caused to me by having the selfish bastard staying here!'

Carole and Jude exchanged another momentary look. Either Debbie Carlton was a much better actress than either of them had ever considered likely, or she had had nothing to do with the anonymous letter that fingered her ex-husband.

'Well, we're on the case,' said Jude, in a parody of a cop show. 'Leave it with me. I'll find out who sent that anonymous letter and, when I do, you will be the first to know.'

'Thanks.' Debbie grinned.

'Meanwhile,' said Carole, 'if you could ask around in Fedborough . . . ? You're much more likely to find out something than we are.'

'I'll put my mum on to it. If there are any secrets to be found out in this town, she'll root them out. I will unleash the not-inconsiderable power of Billie Franks.'

'Right,' said Jude. She turned ruefully towards Carole. 'Oh well. I suppose we'd better move on . . . assimilate a bit more culture. Though I must say, Debbie, I'm absolutely delighted with my purchase.'

'I'm glad you like it. If you don't mind, I want to keep the exhibition intact until the end of the Festival . . . so if you could pick up the painting then . . . ?'

'Suits me fine.'

'Let me just take your address.' She wrote it down at Jude's dictation. Then, proudly, Debbie Carlton detached a red circular sticker from a sheet and placed it on the frame of Jude's painting. 'Looks good. The more of these, the merrier. Maybe it'll convince people they're missing something by not buying my paintings.'

'Yes . . .' said Carole awkwardly. 'I, er . . . I think they're lovely. I'm sure I'll . . . er, in a few . . . Do you mind if I take one of these catalogues?' She was blushing at her clumsiness, but totally incapable of overcoming the habits of a lifetime to make an on-the-spot purchase.

'No, of course. And do take your Art Crawl maps.'

'Oh yes.' Carole picked up two of the folded bright blue sheets. 'Thank you. So I'll hope to be back . . . you know, to have another look . . . when I've made up my mind about the, er . . .'

They were interrupted by the arrival, unannounced as ever, of Billie Franks. She recognized Carole and was introduced to Jude. After the briefest of conversations, the two women left, Jude calling out to Debbie as they went, 'Let me know if you find out anything about that anonymous letter.'

On the street outside, Carole still felt gauche and stupid. So much of her life seemed to have been wasted in introverted anger at her own gracelessness.

As a result, she was surprised to hear Jude murmur, 'Well done.'

'Why? What've I done?'

'Very clever.'

'What?'

'Pretending you hadn't decided which painting you wanted.'

'Oh?'

'Leaving the door open to go back and conduct further investigation. Nice thinking.'

Carole Seddon smiled, as if to say, Yes, it had been quite a clever idea, really.

Chapter Twenty-Seven

The Smokehouse Studio, as Andrew Wragg had left them in no doubt the previous Friday, was on the Art Crawl map, but Yesteryear Antiques, formerly Stanley and Billie Franks's grocery store, wasn't. Not that that stopped Carole and Jude from going inside.

The shop appeared to be unoccupied, so they had an opportunity to browse through the goods on offer. The word 'Yesteryear' should have been a clue that Terry Harper specialized in domestic antiques. There was a lot of Victorian kitchen furniture and equipment, instruments like patent apple corers, knife sharpeners and marmalade cutters. One table was devoted to old butcher's tools, another to a rich variety of tea-caddies. There were besoms, washboards and mangles. Bottles of dark blue and pale green glass stood in ordered rows. On the walls, between multi-drawered apothecary's chests and elaborate hatstands, hung old metal advertising signs, puffing the custards, beef extracts and health drinks of an earlier age.

Another side of the main room concentrated on relics of the outdoor life. Deckchairs with fading stripes stood alongside white-painted cast-iron tables and chairs. Fine salt-glazed chimney-pots held sprays of garden tools and farming implements, hoes, rakes, billhooks and fruit-pickers. There were elegantly shaped watering cans, wooden trugs and manual hedge-clippers.

Despite the profusion of objects, the impression was not of disarray. A designer's eye had put everything in its place and, though in another setting the goods might have looked like junk, everything in Yesteryear Antiques had been punctiliously restored and polished. The quality standards maintained by Terry Harper in his choice of stock were extremely high. So, Carole and Jude observed when they looked at the tags, were his prices.

At the back stood a tall dresser with many drawers and shelves, which must have been retained from the shop's former life as the local grocer's. Some of the tools, utensils and containers on sale probably replicated ones that had once been part of the shop's equipment in those days. There was a kind of irony in that. Carole wondered whether Billie Franks got a sense of *déjà vu* if she ever went into Yesteryear Antiques.

Brass rings clattered on a brass rail as a velvet curtain was swept aside, and Terry Harper appeared from the back of the shop. 'Sorry, just on the phone. I . . .' Then he saw who his visitors were. 'Well, good afternoon. How lovely to see the pair of you.'

'We were just passing,' said Jude. 'Doing the Art Crawl and—'

'*Don't* talk to me about the Art Crawl!' On his own Terry Harper seemed more camp than he had at the Listers' dinner party. The round tortoiseshell glasses looked impossibly affected. Maybe it was only by comparison with Andrew Wragg's flamboyance that he'd seemed restrained; or maybe when his partner was present he deliberately cultivated the image of straight man in the double act.

'Honestly, it's the *artists* who're supposed to suffer from artistic temperament, not the people who're just allowing their houses to be used. You wouldn't believe the fuss I've had from the good burghers of Fedborough about security details and insurance. I tell you, this is the last time I work with *amateurs*! If I ever do anything else like this – which I must say, given my current aggravations, is extremely unlikely – then it'll be with professional galleries. Members of the public are *such* a nightmare!'

'We've just made a start on the Crawl,' said Jude chattily. 'Seen Debbie Carlton's stuff – lovely. I bought one of hers.'

'Ooh, hooray, an actual *purchaser*! Someone who's more interested in the art than in what books people have got on their shelves. You must go and see Andrew's work – particularly if you're quick on the draw with a chequebook.'

'I only buy stuff I really fall for.'

'Hm. Not sure whether the *wunderkind's* work is something one would actually *fall* for. But it is very good. Very challenging. He's building up quite a reputation,' Terry concluded proudly.

Carole indicated her Art Crawl map. 'Andrew was going to be our next port of call. The Smokehouse Studio.'

'He's just down the alley behind here.'

'Why's it called the Smokehouse Studio?' asked Jude.

'Because that's what it used to be. Don't know whether you know, but this used to be the Fedborough grocer's . . .'

'Yes, we had heard.'

'And next door – the one that's now an estate agent's – used to be the town butcher – and behind that was the smokehouse they used for home-curing all their bacon and stuff like that. It was on the market at the same time as this place. The people who bought the butcher's didn't want it, but I did.'

'That's where Andrew works?'

'Right. When I thought about buying this place—'

'When was that actually, Terry?'

'Three, three and a bit years ago.'

'Did you buy it directly from Stanley and Billie Franks?'

'Yes. They'd let it run down because they knew they were retiring soon, so I got it at quite a good price. Needed a hell of a lot doing, though. Everything was in a terrible mess, really filthy.'

'Were they giving up the business because Stanley was starting to get ill?'

'I've always assumed so. Certainly Billie was the one who did the negotiation of the sale. Mind you, Stanley must've been late sixties by then, so maybe that's when they'd planned to retire, anyway.'

'Sorry, I interrupted you. You were talking about when you were thinking of buying this place . . .'

'Yes, well, I knew, if Andrew was going to come with me, I'd have to find him a studio space, and the smoke-house was ideal.' For a moment, Terry Harper betrayed deep insecurity, the fear that Andrew Wragg would walk out if his every whim was not catered for. 'That's really what sold the place to me.'

He moved quickly on, perhaps embarrassed about the lapse into self-revelation. 'Anyway, the conversion job is just wonderful. You'll see it in a minute. You cannot begin to imagine the state the smokehouse was in when I bought the place – much worse than in here. Hadn't been used for a while – except as a kind of storeroom. Full of all kinds of junk, packing cases, rusty tools – a real glory-hole. But local architect – Alan Burnethorpe, don't know if you've met him . . .'

Jude nodded. 'He's the one who's got an office on a houseboat down at Fedborough Bridge?'

'That's right. Done a lovely refurbishment on that. Alan's very clever, and he's known every building in this town all his life. Very sympathetic to their history. He did a wonderful job on the smokehouse too, kept a lot of the original features – the kiln, that kind of thing – and really created this magical space. Andrew's very happy with his studio.' He spoke the last words with relief, again revealing an edge of paranoia.

'We look forward to seeing it,' said Carole formally.

'Not to mention seeing Andrew's *challenging* art,' said Jude.

Carole looked around Yesteryear Antiques. 'You've done wonders with this place too.'

'Yes, well, I wanted to keep that old-fashioned-shop *feel*. Fits in with the kind of stock I carry.'

'You must be something of an expert in social history.'

'Just a bit.' He picked up the top copy from a pile of hardback books, and coyly straightened the tortoiseshell glasses on his nose. 'This is one of mine.' *The Edwardian Kitchen* by Terence Harper. 'I'm working on a new book, about Edwardian garden furniture. At least I am when I get any time . . . which in the last few months, with this endless Art Crawl palaver, hasn't been very often.' He gestured round his Aladdin's cave of domestic treasures. 'Anything I can interest either of you in?'

Oh dear, thought Carole, how embarrassing. He thinks we're here as customers.

As ever, Jude smoothly defused the situation. 'Sorry,

there's too much to take in in one visit. I'd like to come back and have a really good riffle around. But this afternoon we're concentrating on art, not antiques.'

'Right you are.' Terry Harper seemed unoffended. Jude had again found the right words. 'Well, give my love to Andrew. Tell him I'm expecting him to join me for a G and T at six-thirty sharp.' Again he allowed them a glimpse of his possessive anxiety. 'But it's lovely to see you two. People like us must stick together in a place like Fedborough.'

'Like us?' said Carole. 'What do you mean?'

'We *sexual minorities*.' He breathed the words and winked. 'I'd have known, incidentally, even if Fiona hadn't pointed it out. But, as I say, we must stick together. Not the most broad-minded place on earth, Fedborough.'

As they emerged from Yesteryear Antiques, Jude could no longer control her pent-up laughter. 'Isn't it wonderful?' she crowed. 'Thanks to the wagging tongue of Fiona Lister, all of Fedborough thinks we're a lesbian couple. Isn't that the funniest thing you've ever heard?'

Carole's frosty expression suggested she had heard funnier ones.

Chapter Twenty-Eight

The Smokehouse Studio lived up to Terry Harper's glowing preview. Alan Burnethorpe's conversion had been imaginative, but respected the existing features of the building. The original structure was little more than a large shed with a slate roof. The interior walls had been stripped back to their russet brickwork; the supporting beams buffed down till the fine light grain showed through. On one side of the roof the slates had been retained, on the other, the spaces between the bare rafters had been glassed in. These windows could be opened by a ratchet mechanism, so that a healthy breeze diluted the warmth of the July sun.

At the back of the large room, a wall had been built to slice off some of the space. Two doors in this presumably led to a bathroom and utility area. But the most striking feature of the studio was the old smoking kiln, a brick cylinder which tapered upwards like an inverted funnel till the chimney found its way out through the roof.

The large doorway in this structure had been bricked into a recess, which contained the matt-black pillar of a Scandinavian wood-burning stove. The studio that Terry Harper had had built for his partner reflected the strength and the insecurity of his love. Andrew Wragg could have no complaints about the working space that had been provided for him.

Everything was meticulously tidy. The untouched canvas on an easel in the centre of the room contrived to look neat, even the array of brushes and acrylic paints were somehow regimented.

Only the paintings themselves showed wildness and indiscipline. Terry Harper had described the work as 'challenging'; the word Carole would have chosen was 'dreadful' – in both senses. There was a fury in the screaming splashes of colour across Andrew Wragg's canvases. None of the shapes that struggled and strangled each other in the compositions was representational, and yet they were very evocative. They spoke of deep anger, and even deeper pain.

The artist himself also looked angered and pained. When Carole and Jude entered, he was sitting in a throne-like wooden chair, flicking restlessly through a design magazine. His eyes rose from the page to greet them.

'Thank God,' he drawled. 'I was beginning to think the world had ended out there and nobody had told me.'

'I'm Carole and this is Jude, my . . . er . . .' Terry Harper's recent misunderstanding about their relationship was still unsettling her. ' . . . my neighbour,' she concluded firmly. 'You remember, we met at . . .'

'At the infinitely dreary James and Fiona's. Yes, I remember.'

Andrew Wragg seemed out of sorts, tired and listless. When they were on their own, it seemed, the partners reversed roles. Terry was the extravagant queen, Andrew the restrained introvert.

'Do I gather from what you said,' asked Jude, 'that we're your first visitors?'

'Yes. The avid art-lovers of Fedborough are somehow managing to curb their wild enthusiasm for my work.' He hadn't risen when they'd entered, and now he slumped further into his chair. 'God, it's a dreary place. You two are not from here, are you?'

Carole shook her head.

'No, I remember it came up in conversation on Friday. Buggered if I can remember where you did come from, though.'

'Fethering.'

Andrew Wragg groaned. 'That's just as bad. Costa Geriatrica. The entire south coast is God's waiting room, a repository for washed-up widows and washed-out maiden aunts. Why do you live down here?'

'It's . . . convenient,' was the only answer Carole could come up with.

'Convenient for what?'

'Well . . . shops . . . the sea . . . the Downs. Anything you might need.'

'Assuming you don't need intellectual or creative stimulus.' He turned his gaze on Jude. 'And why do you live down here?'

She shrugged easily. 'Everyone's got to live somewhere.'

'Do you think you'll stay here for the rest of your life?'

'I very much doubt it.'

Carole was amazed how much the words hurt her. She had come to rely on Jude too much. She was stupid. She shouldn't have let her guard down. Life worked better for Carole Seddon when it was strictly circumscribed and self-contained.

'Where would you move to then, away from this rural mausoleum?' asked Andrew Wragg.

'Quite fancy Ireland,' Jude replied lightly. 'Where would you go to?'

'London. If I stayed in this country. Otherwise, I don't know. South America perhaps. Somewhere that's got a bit of life. Somewhere where you don't have to explain what an artist is.'

'You're not seriously thinking of moving, are you?' asked Carole.

'If I could, I'd be off tomorrow.'

'Why can't you?' asked Jude.

'Well, I . . .' He sighed and ran a hand through his short black hair. 'There's Terry and . . . That's not going to last for ever, but . . .' He sprang suddenly from his chair. 'God, I hate this place!'

Carole was beginning to understand the reasons for Terry Harper's anxiety. It wasn't just paranoia. His lover's recurrent threats of leaving were real enough. The older man was living on borrowed time in the relationship.

'Did you know Fedborough before you moved into this place?' asked Jude.

Andrew shook his head. 'No. Terry and I met in London. He kept saying he wanted to move back down here, but I didn't think he really meant it.' Another gloomy shake of his head. 'Now I know he did.'

Carole picked up on a detail. 'You said "move *back* down here". Terry had lived here before, had he?'

'Oh yes. Fedborough born and bred. Terry is a . . . what? "Pilchard" is it they say locally?'

'Chub.'

'Right. A *Chub*.' He handled the word as though it were unwholesome. 'So Terry thinks this is seventh heaven. He's back where he grew up, sniggering gleefully at all the local gossip and intrigues. He loves it.'

'Whereas you,' Jude murmured, 'from what you've been saying, don't.'

'That is a very accurate assessment of the situation. Terry's got it so wrong. He thinks everyone round here is tolerant of the fact that we're gay. It's rubbish. They're all sniggering behind their hands at us. Harpies like Fiona Lister like to show how broad-minded they are by inviting us round, but she's absolutely riddled with prejudice. She only wants us there as performing animals.'

'A role which, it must be said, you lived up to fully last Friday.'

'Oh, sure. They wanted a screaming queen, I gave them a screaming queen. Besides, I was very pissed. Only way I can get through an evening like that.' He let out an exasperated sigh. 'Fedborough is about as tolerant of anyone different as a fundamentalist town in the Deep South of America.' He smiled crookedly at the two women. 'Still, I'm sure I don't have to tell *you* that.'

Carole's eyes blazed. She was about to put him right on his misconception, but Jude mimed an infinitesimal shake of the head. Not the moment to rock the boat. They were still pursuing an investigation; mistaken assumptions about their sexuality could be corrected at another time.

'If he was living in London before you moved down here,' said Jude slowly, 'then presumably Terry never met Virginia Hargreaves?'

'Oh God, yes. He knew everyone in Fedborough.'

'Did he get on with her?'

'I don't know. I don't think he had a lot to do with her. But she was part of his precious Fedborough. You see, even when he was supposed to be living in London, he came down here every weekend. His mother was still living up near the Castle. That's one of the reasons why he said we had to move down here, so that he could be nearer to her. Then, when she popped her clogs, my understanding was that we'd hightail it straight back to London.'

He looked at them grimly. 'Terry's mother died six months after we moved and look . . .' He gestured round the studio, whose earlier charm had been diminished by his obvious discontent. 'Here I still am.'

'So what do you think will get you out of Fedborough?' asked Jude gently.

'My talent,' he replied. 'I'm bloody good. Nobody else is doing stuff like this. I don't want you to think I'm included in the Art Crawl simply because I sleep with the guy who's organizing it.'

'We never thought that,' said Carole. Mind you, now he'd planted the idea in her mind, it began to take root there.

'No, my stuff's truly original. That's why the bloody arts establishment has been so slow to recognize me for what I am. But it'll happen, I never doubt that. And when my talent as a painter's properly recognized, then I'll be able to afford to go wherever in the world I want.'

Before they left, Carole and Jude took a detailed look at the work on show. Though they didn't put the thought into words, both of them reckoned it would be a long time before Andrew Wragg was likely to get out of Fedborough.

Chapter Twenty-Nine

'I shouldn't.'

'Oh, come *on*!'

What they were discussing was a Cream Tea. Cream Teas belong by rights to the West Country, where there is a tradition of meals featuring the local clotted variety. But the tourist industry has never been too picky about geographical exactitude, so all of Fedborough's teashops offered the speciality, and the Olde Cottage, in which they sat, was no exception. When Jude made the suggestion, Carole had objected that she'd had a perfectly good lunch and tea wasn't a meal she normally ate. Jude instantly overruled her and gave the order to the eleven-year-old waitress in black dress and frilly pinny.

Carole looked round the teashop with some embarrassment, fearing to see anyone she might recognize. Though certain that she wasn't lesbian, she worried how deep the misinformation might now be engrained in the communal consciousness of Fedborough.

Jude grinned. She knew exactly what was going through Carole's mind, but made no comment. Instead, she asked, 'So where are we?'

'Well, we've ruled out the possibility that Roddy Hargreaves did it, haven't we?'

'Yes, because that makes for such a boring solution.'

Carole deemed this answer to lack sufficient *gravitas*. 'We have a better reason than that. A witness, the Rev Trigwell, who saw Roddy on to the ferry on the Friday, the twentieth of February, and who later saw Virginia alive in the Franks's grocery. And another witness, James Lister, who picked Roddy up from Newhaven on the Tuesday, the twenty-fourth of February. Which, assuming our suspect wasn't bouncing back and forth across the Channel like a yo-yo, would seem to provide him with an alibi for the time of his wife's death.'

'Yes.' Jude beamed to greet the arrival of the underage waitress with their cholesterol-fest. Tea-pouring and the smearing of scones with cream and jam followed. Once they were settled into their food, Jude went on, 'We may have got Roddy's movements sorted, but we still need more information about what Virginia got up to that weekend. Who actually was the last person to see her . . . and indeed what was wrong with her? Remember, she was too ill to make her assignation with Alan Burnethorpe.'

'Yes. I must say,' Carole observed, 'that the charms of Virginia Hargreaves – or Lady Virginia or whatever she was – seem to diminish with every new detail we find out about her.'

Jude nodded. 'Sounds like Roddy got as rough a deal in the marriage stakes as poor old Jimmy Lister. Maybe that's why they enjoyed drinking together so much, to commiserate about their mutual misfortune. You know, Fedborough's track record on marriage doesn't seem very good, does it? We haven't met any happy couples here, have we?'

'Your friends the Roxbys seem OK.'

'Yes, so long as Kim agrees exactly with everything

Grant says, they're fine. Mind you, they're new to the place. The creeping Fedborough infection hasn't got to them yet.'

Carole wiped a crumb of scone from the corner of her mouth. 'The one married person I've met here who seems absolutely devoted is Billie Franks . . . Which is rather sad, really . . . given that her husband doesn't even know who she is.'

Suddenly Jude tapped her Art Crawl map on the table. 'I've had a thought!'

'What?'

'We haven't exhausted the Snoopers' Charter yet.' She looked at the large face of the watch attached by a ribbon to her wrist. 'Can you cope with a bit more art?'

'In the hope that it isn't like Andrew Wragg's, yes.'

'At the Listers' last week Terry said that Alan Burnethorpe would be showing his drawings during the Festival, didn't he?'

'Yes.' Carole nodded with satisfaction as she got the drift. 'And Joke Burnethorpe used to be Virginia Hargreaves's housekeeper.'

'So she might well know about her employer's movements on the weekend she disappeared.'

'*And*,' said Carole triumphantly, 'Fiona Lister also said last week that the Durringtons' house was part of the Art Crawl. If Virginia Hargreaves had been ill, the local doctor might have known something about it. Whether he'd tell us, of course, is another matter. Hippocratic oath and all that.'

'From what I've seen of Donald Durrington, medical confidentiality doesn't seem to be at the top of his priorities. And his wife might be prepared to be indiscreet, anyway. They appear to be another mutually loathing Fedborough couple.'

Carole looked down at her map. 'Trouble is, this only lists the artists who're exhibiting. Doesn't say who owns the houses.'

'We can nip back into Yesteryear Antiques. Terry'll know.'

'Yes. Good.' Carole looked at her watch. 'Art Crawl finishes at six, doesn't it?'

'Hm. We'd better split up to save time. I'll do the Burnethorpes, because I did meet them at Grant and Kim's, so I'd have some justification for starting a conversation. You do the Durringtons.'

'OK.'

'Besides, better if we're not seen together too much, eh?' Jude winked and giggled.

Carole didn't giggle. She still wasn't finding Fedborough's error very amusing.

The stuffier, more traditional architects of Fedborough lived up in Dauncey Street. The more Bohemian feel of Pelling Street was entirely appropriate to the image Alan Burnethorpe tried to project, that of the imaginative mould-breaker, the architect as artist. And his home, Number 47, was an excellent testament to his skills.

As with the smokehouse, he had captured the historical essence of the building and enhanced it with the ultra-modern. But the effect was totally different. Andrew Wragg's studio had started life as a simple shed structure and it was to that bareness of brick and rafters Alan Burnethorpe had returned. 47 Pelling Street, on the other hand, had been built as a tribute to the success of an early nineteenth-century merchant, and that was the style which its restoration endorsed.

The long through-sitting-room which had been requisitioned as a gallery for the duration of the Fedborough Festival, was decorated in dark wood colours and purple, contriving to present overtones of a heavily upholstered Victorian parlour. But at the same time there was a sense of space, accentuated now all of the furniture had been removed to make room for art-lovers.

The two chairs and table which did remain were strikingly modern, minimalist confections of exposed wood and leather. But their colours toned with the others in the room, soothing away any danger of strident anachronism. In the same way, the brass light fittings on the walls, starkly contemporary in design, diffused a light that was golden, mellow and contemplative. Alan Burnethorpe certainly knew his job.

When Jude entered, clutching her Art Crawl map, Joke Burnethorpe was sitting on one of the minimalist chairs, dealing with a couple who had just made a purchase. On the table in front of her was a pile of catalogues. Unlike the photocopied sheets in Debbie Carlton's flat, these were glossily produced, with the logo of Alan's architectural practice on the front.

Joke was dressed in a v-necked white T-shirt, black jeans and clumpy black slip-on shoes. Such artless simplicity, Jude recognized, didn't come cheap. A woman more interested in fashion than she was would have wanted to know the identity of the labels.

There was no question, though, that with her square-cut blonde hair and exquisitely judged make-up, Joke Burnethorpe looked stunning. She really did have a fabulous figure.

Joke was the kind of woman, Jude knew, whom all men would undress with their eyes. How generous, therefore, of her husband to save them the trouble. As James Lister had suggested, the walls of the Pelling Street house were decorated with an abundant selection of images of the naked Joke.

The drawings showed her in a variety of abandoned poses, though to Jude's mind they were too punctiliously accurate in execution to be erotic. Still, she wasn't a man. Quite possibly a masculine reaction would be different.

The art-buying couple's paperwork was completed, and they left with expressions of satisfaction at their deal. Joke looked across at Jude.

'Oh, hello, we met that evening at the Roxbys.' The 'that' was a 'dat', still the only give-away to Joke's foreign origins.

'Yes. Jude.' She avoided the problem of her name having been forgotten.

'Of course. And I am Joke.'

'I remember.' Jude gazed round appreciatively at the walls. 'These look wonderful. Are they all of you?'

Joke Burnethorpe preened herself as she replied, 'Most of them. A few down the end date from before Alan met me. Other women.' The way she said the last two words managed to combine both confidence and disparagement.

'I look forward to having a good look at all of them. I was told, whatever else I missed in the Art Crawl, I must make sure I saw Alan Burnethorpe's work.'

'Who said that?'

Jude was momentarily flummoxed. The recommendation had been pure invention. 'James Lister,' she said quickly.

'Ah yes.' Joke gave a cunning smile. 'The way he reacts to these, you'd think he'd never seen a naked woman before.'

'Which, given who he's married to, may well be true.'

It was an uncharacteristically bitchy line for Jude. And also risky. If Fiona Lister turned out to be Joke Burnethorpe's closest friend, the remark wouldn't be conducive to increased intimacy.

But, as was so often the case, Jude had judged her effect exactly right. The Dutchwoman's face broke into a wide grin, revealing perfectly schooled teeth. 'Yes, I'm afraid the Listers aren't our favourite people. He spends all his time ogling me and she's just malicious.'

'So you're not on their Friday-night dinner-party list?'

'No.' She shook her head firmly. 'I think Alan maybe was before he and I got together, but not now.'

'Any particular reason?'

'Fiona Lister invited him once when we were just going round together, before we got married. And Alan said, fine, could he bring me? Fiona said no, she didn't think it would be suitable to invite *servants* to her dinner parties.'

'Ah.'

'The sheer arrogance. I was very angry. If my parents in Naaldwijk had ever heard about it, they would have been furious. Fiona Lister is only a butcher's wife, after all, not a member of the Royal Family.'

Jude giggled. 'I did recently hear another story, the kind of mirror-image of that one.'

'Really?'

'About Virginia Hargreaves . . .'

At the mention of the name, a shadow of caution came into Joke's blue eyes. 'Oh?'

'You used to work for her. Perhaps you can tell me if it's true or not. That Fiona Lister invited Virginia Hargreaves to one of her *soirées*, and Virginia turned her down flat like a bedspread, on the ground that *it wasn't her sort of thing*.'

Now Joke saw the funny side. 'I don't actually know if that's true, but it would have been in character. Just the sort of thing Virginia would do. She never did anything she didn't want to – and she didn't . . . what's the expression you have? "Suffer idiots gladly" . . .?'

' "Suffer fools gladly".'

'Right. Well, that's it. She didn't.'

Jude made as if to laugh again, but stopped herself. 'Terrible, what happened to her, wasn't it?'

'Virginia? Yes, awful.'

'Must be ghastly for you, having actually lived in the same house as them.'

'Well, it is ghastly now, now I know what happened. At the time I wasn't aware of what was going on, so it didn't really worry me.'

'But you must have noticed that there were tensions in the marriage?'

Joke shrugged. 'Yes, but I put that down to what was happening with Mr Hargreaves's business and, you know, how much he drank, which was a result of the same thing. But they led fairly separate lives. I don't think Virginia was too worried, so long as she could do her own thing.'

'And what was her own thing?'

'Going up to London a lot, you know, to do her charity work.' The words were spoken without irony. Virginia Hargreaves's housekeeper had been as incurious as the rest of Fedborough about what her employer got up to in

London. Jude had the feeling that Alan Burnethorpe's secret past was safe.

'Tell me,' she began, but she was interrupted by a clattering thump from another part of the house, followed almost immediately by anguished childish screams. 'Should you go and do something about that? I'll keep an eye on things here if you—'

'No,' said Joke sleekly. 'I have an *au pair* to do that kind of thing for me. That's what she's paid for.'

The words were spoken with enormous satisfaction and Jude thought what an unattractive role being an *au pair* for Joke Burnethorpe would be. There is no worse employer than the one who previously suffered the indignities of your job.

Yes, thought Jude, as she looked around the splendour of the sitting room. However high up Joke's parents might be in the society of 'Gnarled-vague' (wherever that might be), their daughter had still come a long way to be queening it in Pelling Street, Fedborough. She had a very nice standard of living for a girl not yet thirty. And she had it because she was married to Alan. Jude wondered about what she'd overheard in the Crown and Anchor, how he'd bemoaned his new wife's 'old-fashioned' attitude to adultery. Now she'd seen the house, she reckoned Joke might be unlikely to put all that at risk, even if it did mean turning a blind eye to her husband's occasional sexual peccadilloes.

Still, time enough for such thoughts. Jude knew she mustn't waste this opportunity to tap into the memory of the garrulous Joke.

'Did the police talk to you?' she asked.

'About what?'

'Virginia Hargreaves's disappearance.'

'No. At the time no one knew she had disappeared. Everyone here in Fedborough thought she had just walked out on Mr Hargreaves – and very few people blamed her for that. He didn't report her missing, or make any attempt to find her . . .'

'Which, if he had killed her, is hardly surprising.'

'No.'

'What kind of state was he in after she'd disappeared?'

'I didn't see much of him. It was just round that time, you see, that Alan and I were getting together. I was going to move in with him to his house. Karen, his wife, had gone off to her mother's with the children. I'd given in my notice to Virginia.'

'So when were you actually going to leave Pelling House?'

'That Friday of the weekend she disappeared. That's what I did.'

'So you didn't see her over that weekend?'

'No. Alan suddenly surprised me with a trip to Paris. He arranged that I should be at Waterloo on the Saturday morning. I had no idea what was happening, and then suddenly he showed me the Eurostar tickets. It was fabulous. We had a wonderful romantic time.'

A second alibi in France, thought Jude. Not that Joke really seemed to need an alibi. On the other hand, she'd raised the possibility that Alan might not have an alibi for the Friday night. Jude would check that in a moment, but needed to ask other questions first.

'So you didn't see whether or not Virginia Hargreaves had packed up all her belongings when she moved out?'

The blonde head shook. 'I didn't go back to the house after that.'

'So the last time you saw her was the Friday?'

'I have just told you that.'

'Yes, I'm sorry. And you spent the Friday night with Alan?'

'In his house. Alan himself had to be in London that night but, as I say, we met at Waterloo on the Saturday morning.'

Jude quietly filed away this information. 'And you and Virginia parted on good terms?'

Joke's lips twisted negatively. 'She had rather got up my nose just before I went. I was trying to move my stuff out, get it to Alan's place, and she kept insisting I should stay and look after her.'

'Oh yes, of course, she was ill.'

'Not very ill,' said Joke dismissively. 'Only a tummy bug. Something she had eaten – and of course she blamed me, because I did the cooking. But Virginia was always a terrible invalid, make a fuss about everything, had to be waited on hand and foot all the time. She was a very selfish woman.'

Another infant wail erupted from the interior of the house. This time it sounded as though the child in question was being impaled.

'I'd better go and do something about that,' said Joke peevishly, and went to the door. 'The girl has no idea how to deal with Linus when he gets hysterical. If you wouldn't mind staying just till I come back . . . in case anyone comes in to see the drawings?'

'No problem.'

Since she could no longer pursue her investigation, Jude did what she was meant to be in the house for, and took a look at Alan Burnethorpe's drawings. From somewhere in the house, she could hear Joke berating the inadequacies of her luckless *au pair*.

Terry Harper had been right. Alan was extraordinarily good. But Jude still got the impression he had the skills of a draughtsman rather than an artist. The nudes were immaculately executed, but by a detached observer, not by someone who engaged with them at an emotional level.

She moved on through the exhibition, adding to her detailed knowledge of Joke's anatomy, and imagined how much James Lister would relish doing the same – particularly if he could convince Fiona it was in the name of art.

But in the drawings on the far wall the subject had changed. They were all still nudes, but these were of a variety of women. These were the ones which pre-dated Alan's meeting with Joke.

One of the pictures showed a woman post-coitally splayed on rumpled sheets. She was blonde, trim-figured, late thirties perhaps. One of her hands suggestively caressed a wooden bedpost carved with the design of a climbing vine. The image of this woman glowed with all the sensuality the other drawings lacked. She oozed sex from every pore.

Jude could not claim to recognize the body from the mummified torso she had seen in the cellar of Pelling House, but, with the bedpost as a clue, she knew instinctively that the subject of the drawing had been Virginia Hargreaves.

'Enjoying the view?' asked a cold male voice behind her.

Jude turned to face Alan Burnethorpe, who was looking at her with undiluted suspicion.

He opened his mouth to speak, but a door behind him clattered open. 'God,' Joke drawled as she came in, 'it's impossible to get a decent *au pair* these days!'

Chapter Thirty

The Durringtons' house was a large Edwardian pile in Dauncey Street, which figured. Respected local doctor, pillar of the community, Donald Durrington's natural habitat was Dauncey Street. As she followed her Art Crawl map towards the front door, Carole Seddon wished she knew more about him. Had he been a Fethering general practitioner, she would have got some feeling of his reputation, but all she had to go on in Fedborough was the impression he'd made on her at the Listers' dinner party.

That impression had been of someone world-weary, disengaged and not as discreet about professional secrets as he should have been. If that last extrapolation were correct, then it could be good news for the cause of her investigation.

But she couldn't get the 'feeling on the street' about the doctor, those little nuances of resentment and approbation. In every practice there'd be some patient who claimed a male doctor lingered unnecessarily long over a gynaecological examination, some mother complaining that he wouldn't make a house call when her child was seriously ill, some bereaved relative bitterly resenting his diagnosis of what had been wrong with the deceased. Equally, there would be ecstatic wives praising the doctor's early recognition of their husband's prostate cancer, mothers whose babies had been nurtured back from the edge of dehydration, patients with undying gratitude for the seriousness with which he had approached their Irritable Bowel Syndrome. But to know whether the balance of Donald Durrington's local image was favourable or unfavourable Carole Seddon would have had to live in Fedborough for a while. So she was left to rely on her instincts.

When she entered the large hallway of the Dauncey Street house, she didn't think those instincts were going to be much help to her. The girl who was acting as curator for the art exhibition Carole had never seen before. Late teens, she wore the scowl of bored resentment that went with her age. Along with the photocopied catalogue sheets on the table in front of her lay a magazine with the latest boyband on the front. Its disarray suggested the girl had read every last statistic of the members' taste in fast food and quality of first snogs.

Carole felt disappointment for which she knew there was really no justification. What had she expected to find when she came into the house? Donald Durrington sitting waiting, ready with a filing cabinet full of medical records for her to riffle through at will? Was the smooth run of investigation that she and Jude had experienced in Fedborough about to come to an end?

This thought revived an earlier doubt. She remembered discussing with Jude how easy the first bit of their investigation had been, how ready people had been to talk to them. At that stage, endorsed by his transatlantic dash to clear his name, their suspicions had been moving towards Francis Carlton. And the police's interest in him had been prompted by an anonymous letter. Carole reminded herself that they still hadn't identified the sender of that letter. Debbie Carlton had seemed genuinely sceptical about its existence, but then if she actually was the sender, that's how she would behave. The anonymous letter needed following through . . .

As she processed these thoughts, Carole decided she'd better maintain her cover story and look at the art on display in the Durringtons' hall. She was, after all, meant to be a mere punter on the Art Crawl. But, so far as the teenage guardian of the art was concerned, Carole's masquerade was wasted. The girl had shown no acknowledgment of, or interest in, her arrival.

The artist's name was foreign, Polish perhaps, a jumble of letters which looked like an anagram. What he – or she – did wasn't Carole's kind of stuff. Whereas Andrew Wragg's paintings had been troubling in their violence, these were equally troubling in their blandness. They were abstracts too, abstract to the point of being comatose. Pale washes of blue, grey and white lay lethargically across the canvases. Titles like *Serenity VI, Tranquillity IX* and *Acquiescence XIII* raised the unwelcome prospect that somewhere existed at least five more *Serenities*, eight more *Tranquillities* and twelve more *Acquiescences*. The paintings were the visual equivalent of musak.

Still, Carole did her stuff. She moved through to the dining room, where the exhibition continued. The Durringtons' furniture, sideboard, large table and set of matching chairs was dull, but still more interesting than the paintings. These were so like the exhibits in the hall Carole wondered how even the artist himself – or perhaps herself – could tell them apart. The titles – *Consent VIII, Satisfaction X* and *Wish-Fulfilment XIX* – seemed to have been selected totally at random.

She was looking at the photographs on the mantelpiece, presumably of Durrington children, though of an age by now to have moved away from home, when she heard an interior door open into the hall.

'Can I go?' asked the teenager's voice immediately. 'You said three hours. It's over that.'

'Have you had many people?' Joan Durrington's voice was deeper and more assertive than it had been at the Listers' dinner party.

'Hardly any. There's some woman through there now, but she's only about the third.'

'If you stay till six, I'll give you another couple of pounds.'

'Hardly worth it,' the girl's voice said. 'Fixed to meet my boyfriend down the Stag half-five.'

'Oh. All right. Well, there's the money we agreed.'

No thanks were expressed as the cash was presumably pocketed.

'Can you do tomorrow afternoon?'

'Don't know that it's really worth my while,' said the girl. 'Ten quid for three hours. Do better than that picking down the mushroom farm. Anyway, it's the weekend.'

'But I thought we agreed. Are you saying you won't be back tomorrow?'

'That's right. See you. Cheers!'

'You little bastard!' Joan Durrington's voice called after the retreating girl. The front door slammed shut.

The doctor's wife was still standing looking at the door, when Carole appeared a little sheepishly from the dining room.

She cleared her throat. 'I was just, er, looking at the paintings.'

Joan Durrington turned. She was wearing jeans and a

T-shirt, which emphasized her thinness. The blonded hair was scraped back by a couple of grips, exposing the white at her temples. Without make-up, her face looked a lot older, its grey puffiness explained by the cigarette that drooped from her lips.

'So what did you think of them?' she asked, her voice a little uncertain, as though she had only recently learned the language.

'Not really my sort of stuff,' said Carole discreetly.

'Nor mine. Looks like décor for changing rooms in a swimming pool.' The crow's-feet round Joan Durrington's faded blue eyes tightened. 'We've met, haven't we?'

'Carole Seddon. At the Listers' last week.'

'Oh, right. Yes, of course.' The doctor's wife swayed a little and put a hand on the catalogue table to steady herself. Surely she can't be drunk, thought Carole, not at half-past five in the afternoon.

Joan looked at *Tranquillity IX* and shook her head. 'Why do we get landed with garbage like this? We've done this Art Crawl since it started, six years ago, and we've had some pretty hideous stuff in here. Nothing as dreary as this, though.'

'Why do you keep doing it then, opening up your house?'

An unamused smile. 'Because my husband Donald is such an important figure in Fedborough society. He's senior partner in the local medical practice, so he can't be seen to be standoffish, can he? Doctors have to have the common touch. So when some local committee member says, "Oh, Dr Durrington, can we use your house again for the Art Crawl?" the big-hearted medico says, "Yes, of course. I'd love to have members of the public traipsing through my house, nothing I'd like more." But, remarkably, when it comes to the Fedborough Festival, and the exhibits have to be put up and somebody has to keep an eye on all the members of the public traipsing through the house, Donald is not here. Busy life, being a doctor, so many calls on your time. Need a loyal wife to see that everything's kept going at home.'

Carole was now in no doubt. Joan Durrington was drunk. As if to confirm it, the doctor's wife swayed again, tottered and would have fallen if Carole had not moved forward to take her arm. The smell of gin was very strong.

'Sorry.' The fuddled blue eyes found hers.

'Do you want to go and lie down?'

'No, I bloody don't!' Joan Durrington broke free. 'That's all Donald ever says to me. "Don't you want to go and lie down?" Why? So that I can see an example of his famous bedtime manner? I tell you, it's a long time since he practised his bedtime manner on me.'

She moved savagely to the front door, and snapped the latch shut. 'Bad luck anyone else who wants to come and see these lousy paintings. It's nearly six, anyway, isn't it?'

'Yes.' Carole's social instincts told her she should leave, that she shouldn't be witnessing the woman's distress. But her burgeoning detective instincts told her to stay as long as possible.

'You don't live in Fedborough, do you?'

'No. Fethering.'

The reply seemed to reassure Joan Durrington. With someone who didn't live in Fedborough, someone who wouldn't instantly report her actions round the town, she dared to take a risk. 'Come and have a drink with me,' she pleaded.

'Well . . .'

'Come on. I haven't seen anyone all day, except for that blasted girl.' She led the way through a door at the back of the hall. Without further protest, Carole followed.

The Durringtons' kitchen, like their dining room, was furnished efficiently, but impersonally. Everything was stowed away and tidy. Only the half-full bottle of Gordon's gin, the glass and the ashtray on the scrubbed table looked out of place.

Joan opened the fridge. 'You drink gin, don't you?'

Carole didn't as a rule, but she wasn't going to do anything to threaten the intimacy that had suddenly been offered.

'I've even got some tonic and lemon,' said the doctor's wife, as if this somehow made getting drunk in the afternoon socially acceptable. 'Do you know,' she continued with a sudden gleeful chuckle as she fixed Carole's drink, 'Donald's been highly praised for his work with alcoholics. Referring them, putting them on drying-out programmes, rehabilitating them . . .' She managed the long word with an effort. 'He's asked to write papers on the subject, speak at seminars . . . He's a saint, not a man.' She thrust the full glass on to the table in front of Carole. 'Funny no one ever seems to ask him where he does his research.'

'Has he tried to help you?'

Joan Durrington, who was lighting up another cigarette, squinted in bewilderment at her guest, trying to come to terms with the oddness of the question. 'He doesn't notice me. We share a house, but he has about as much interest in me as in the wallpaper. All Donald thinks about is keeping up his image in Fedborough as a caring professional and model citizen.'

'Surely that's not easy for him . . .' Carole suggested gently, 'if you often get like this?'

'I don't often get like this. I am very well behaved. In public I've never been seen to drink anything stronger than mineral water. What a perfect doctor's wife I am.' Joan Durrington topped up her own glass, dispensing with tonic, ice and lemon, and took a long swallow. 'It was just something Donald said this morning which made me realize . . . that he didn't even think of me as a human being . . .' Tears threatened. She took another fierce swig from her glass to stop them.

'But you're letting me see you like this. Aren't you afraid I'll gossip about you, spread the story of your secret?'

Joan shook her head. 'You're not from Fedborough. You're not part of Fiona Lister's Thought Police.'

Carole was divided between glee at her good fortune in finding her potential witness in such a communicative mood, and pity for the woman's state. She quickly decided that the pity didn't really help, though the communicativeness could be very useful to her.

'What will Donald say when he comes back and finds you've been drinking? Will he be angry?'

'God, no! He won't give me that satisfaction. He will be infinitely understanding, just as if I was one of his patients. He finds it easier to deal with me as a malfunctioning organism than he does as a human being. And I dare say he'll decide I need a break, and I'll be sent away somewhere.'

'Won't people in Fedborough be suspicious of the real reasons why you've gone away?'

'No. Because Donald will be the one who tells them. And he's a doctor, so he must be right. And I'm known to "have trouble with my nerves" and be "highly strung". Donald is thought locally to be rather magnificent for the way he copes with me. "A man like him needs stronger support at home. Pity that such a dedicated professional has to keep being diverted from his work by his wife's illness." That's what they say . . . little knowing that he's the one who caused his wife's "illness" in the first place.'

'Couldn't you just leave him . . . if staying is making you so unhappy?'

Joan Durrington let out a harsh bark of laughter. 'And go where? I stayed while the children were around, thought I owed it to them, and kept looking forward to the time when they'd moved on and I would up sticks and away. But that moment never seemed to arrive. And now . . . I'm older than Donald, you know. I'll be sixty next birthday. Hardly a great time for opening a new chapter in my life.'

'It can be done,' said Carole stoutly. 'I got divorced. I've made a new life for myself.'

'And how old were you when you and your husband split up?'

'Late forties.'

Joan Durrington let out a short derisive sigh, as if her point had been made. 'No, I'm stuck . . .' She looked fuddled for a moment. 'What was your name again?'

'Carole. Carole Seddon.'

'That's right. As I say, I've come too far. If I'd really wanted to do something, I should have done it years ago, while I still had something to offer, before Donald drained all the confidence out of me. Sod the children, I should have just upped and gone. Now . . .' An infinity of hopelessness lay in that monosyllable.

She took refuge once again in her glass. Carole matched the action with a considerably smaller sip. On the rare occasions she drank it, she was always surprised how nice gin and tonic was. But mustn't get into the habit. For Carole Seddon, spirits symbolized excess.

'You remember at the Listers' last week, Joan . . .' she began tentatively, 'you were the first person to mention that the police had identified Virginia Hargreaves as the mysterious body?'

'Yes.' The response was toneless. Joan Durrington was still locked away in her own despair.

'You said the police had talked to your husband about it, and he had talked to you.' A listless nod. 'Does Donald often talk to you about his work?'

This question dragged her back to the present. 'Not very often. He doesn't talk *to* me much at all. He talks *at* me quite a lot. And he certainly finds it easier to talk about his work than about anything I might be interested in.'

'So you didn't have a medical background?'

'Why should I have?'

'It's quite common for doctors to marry nurses – or other people connected with their profession.'

'I was a schoolteacher when we met. Not a bad one, actually. Very dedicated to the cause of education. But then I had the children and Donald wanted me around, holding things together at home.' She sighed. 'Too late for me to go back to that now.'

The gulf of despair was opening up again, so Carole moved quickly on. 'You also said last Friday that Virginia Hargreaves had been in a bad state just before she disappeared . . .'

'Did I?'

'Yes. I wondered if you knew her well . . .?'

'Not very well.'

'Was she Donald's patient?'

'She was registered with him down here. I think if there was anything major, she had people in London she went to.'

'What kind of "major"?'

'I don't know. I do remember her talking about having a gynaecologist in London.'

'But she didn't say why she'd been consulting him?'

Joan Durrington shrugged. 'Usual sort of women's problems, I imagine. At least I don't have to worry about that any more.' Her glass was nearly empty. She looked at the gin bottle, calculating the moment of her next refill.

'When you said Virginia Hargreaves was in a bad state at that time, did you mean emotionally or physically?'

'Physically. I didn't know her well enough to have any idea of her emotional state.'

'So what was wrong with her?'

'She had an upset stomach. Some virus, or perhaps something she'd eaten. Donald reckoned it was the latter, because the vomiting and diarrhoea came on so quickly.'

'Did she go to the surgery?'

'No, no. Far too plebeian for her to sit in a waiting room with all the common riff-raff.' Joan Durrington's lips twisted cynically. 'Donald almost never makes house calls, but he moved remarkably quickly when Lady Virginia summoned him.'

'Was she actually called Lady Virginia? Because that would have meant that she was the daughter of a peer?'

'I don't know. That's what people called her round the town, but whether it was really her title or just a nickname . . . I've no idea.'

'So your husband went to see her . . . ?'

'Yes, and he prescribed something to stop the vomiting and diarrhoea . . .'

'Which day of the week was this?'

Joan Durrington shook her head wearily. 'I can't remember. We're talking three or four years ago.'

'Yes, but back then did he do house calls every day?'

'As I said, he tried to avoid making them at all. But he still had to do some. Normally, except in an emergency, he'd try to fit them in mid-week – Tuesday, Wednesday. Thursday he's down at an old people's home, The Elms.'

'So it was probably the Tuesday or Wednesday?'

'That would be usual, yes. But he might have made an exception for *Lady Virginia*.' The fascination the gin bottle held for the doctor's wife was increasing.

'You don't know whether she made a quick recovery, do you?'

'I would assume so. The stuff Donald had prescribed is usually pretty effective. Stops the symptoms within twenty-four hours. She might have felt washed-out for a couple of days afterwards, but should have been fine. All I do know is,' Joan Durrington went on with mounting anger at the recollection, 'that when Donald gave her the prescription, Lady Virginia said that her housekeeper was not there and would it be possible to have someone get the medicine from the chemist for her? And he said – well, I wasn't there, so I don't know the exact words, but I'll bet he said, "Oh, Joan hasn't got anything better to do. She'll collect it for you."'

'That's certainly what I ended up doing. It happens quite often, actually. Everybody in Fedborough knows that Dr Durrington has got this difficult wife, but there are some little tasks she's still capable of. When it comes to going down to the chemist to pick up a prescription, there's no one to beat her.'

As the bitterness in her words grew, Joan Durrington moved her hand unconsciously towards the gin bottle.

'Tell me . . .' Carole's words halted the hand's progress. Joan's eyes turned towards her, bleary with pain and frustration. 'Did your husband ever find out what it was that poisoned Virginia Hargreaves?'

The doctor's wife shook her head slowly. 'Well, if he did, he didn't tell me. Why do you ask?'

'I was just thinking . . . Virginia Hargreaves seems almost definitely to have been murdered the weekend after she was ill. I was wondering if the poisoning had been an earlier, unsuccessful attempt to get rid of her.'

'I suppose it's possible.'

Joan Durrington could wait no longer. Her hand reached its destination, picked up the gin bottle and upended it over her glass.

Chapter Thirty-One

'OK, give me a list of suspects,' said Jude. 'And some motives wouldn't hurt either.'

It was the Saturday morning. Her sitting room was as cluttered as ever, the original outlines of all the furniture obscured by throws, rugs and cushions. The windows were open and sunlight twinkled on the disarray of ornaments and artefacts that crowded on to every surface. From somewhere, wooden wind chimes made gentle percussion. To Carole's considerable amazement, she found the sound rather soothing.

Though it wasn't yet twelve, Jude had insisted on opening a bottle of white wine. 'Help the thought processes.' Carole wasn't sure about that. Her inbred puritan instinct told her that alcohol could only befuddle the thought processes. But it was undeniably pleasant, and there was an edge of decadence to sitting drinking wine on a Saturday morning.

'All right,' she said, 'taking as our starting point the fact that Roddy Hargreaves didn't kill his wife, let's concentrate on those motives. Who had something against Virginia Hargreaves?'

'An increasing number of people, it seems. The more we find out about her, the less flattering the picture becomes.'

Carole started itemizing on her fingers. 'Alan Burnethorpe had had an affair with her . . .'

'As had Francis Carlton. So, following the well-known principle that anyone who's had an affair immediately wants to murder the other person involved, both men are very firmly in the frame.'

'And Debbie Carlton isn't out of it. She was quite convincing in her doubts about the anonymous letter, but if she'd found out about Francis and Virginia . . .'

'Following the second well-known principle that any woman who's discovered her husband's having an affair immediately murders the other woman . . .' Jude found herself at the receiving end of an old-fashioned look. 'Sorry. Sorry. I am taking this seriously – honestly.'

'So . . . Debbie's mother's also a potential suspect, I suppose . . . for . . . for reasons going back into Fedborough's past,' Carole concluded lamely.

'So's her father. Stanley. Remember, the last sighting we've got of Virginia Hargreaves was by the Rev Trigwell in their grocery shop.'

'That's true.'

'And Jimmy Lister also went in and saw her that same afternoon.'

'Does that make him a suspect?'

'Could do. Remember, Virginia Hargreaves snubbed the dreaded Fiona.'

Carole snorted. 'I can't really see her in a Lady Macbeth role.'

'Urging her husband to murder? Don't rule it out. Also, don't let's forget . . .' As she spoke, the image of the dismembered corpse in Pelling House cellar came to her mind. 'Jimmy Lister was a butcher.'

'Yes,' said Carole thoughtfully. 'You said the torso looked as if it had been neatly dismembered, didn't you?'

Jude nodded, still subdued by the picture she had conjured up.

'You know,' said Carole, 'I think we should talk further to James about that.'

'Mm.'

'He's one of the few leads we have.'

'Yes.' Jude tapped the arm of her chair in frustration. 'There is another lead we haven't followed up, and I can't for the life of me remember what it is. There's something, someone's been mentioned who might be relevant.'

'I don't think there is,' said Carole. 'I'm sure *I'd* have remembered.'

Once the words were out, she realized they sounded a bit smug, but Jude seemed unworried. 'Then perhaps you weren't there when the person was mentioned.' The frustrated tapping was now on her chin. 'So maybe it was something someone said at the Roxbys' dinner party or . . .' The brown eyes glowed and she snapped her fingers. 'Bob Bracken!'

'Oh yes, I remember Roddy Hargreaves mentioning that name in the Coach and Horses. He'd owned the boatyards before Roddy, hadn't he? But we can't call him a lead. We don't know if he's still living round Fedborough – or even if he's still alive. And we haven't got any means of contacting him.'

'But we do. We know someone who knows him.'

'Who?'

'That's why you don't know the contact. You weren't there. I had lunch in the Crown and Anchor and Ted Crisp told me he knew Bob Bracken.'

'Oh.' Instant permafrost settled over Carole.

'He'll be worth following up,' said Jude, apparently unaware of the cold blast emanating from her neighbour. 'Bob Bracken must know a lot of background stuff about—'

The telephone interrupted her. Jude picked up the receiver. 'Hello? What? There is someone here, actually, but . . . All right, I'll take it upstairs.'

As she put the phone down, she raised her eyes to heaven. 'Harry Roxby. Playing Cold War espionage games.'

Carole sat peacefully sipping her wine, lulled by the arrhythmic clinking of the wind chimes. The front doorbell rang.

'Could you get that?' Jude's voice called from above.

It was the postman. There was a large Jiffy bag he couldn't get through the letter-box. He grinned at Carole as he handed it across with three other letters. The package was heavy, felt like books. 'Thought for a moment there I was getting my round wrong. Expect to find you next door.'

'Oh well, as you see, I was just . . .'

'Don't apologize. Wonderful thing, friendship. Wish there was more of it around. Cheerio then. Isn't anything for you today, Mrs Seddon, as it happens.'

As the postman walked cheerily away, Carole had a moment of doubt. Surely the rumour going round Fedborough hadn't had time to reach Fethering? Surely the postman didn't think that she and Jude . . . ?

Briskly she pulled herself back from the brink of speculation. She was just being paranoid.

A new thought came to her. She was holding letters addressed to Jude. There was no way they would just say 'Jude' on them. There had to be a surname. She held in her hands the means of solving one of her neighbour's enduring mysteries.

She hesitated, but only for a moment, and then she looked down. Ironically, the top letter *was* simply addressed to 'Jude'. The name and address were neatly typed on a small blue envelope. Carole might have stopped there, except that she couldn't.

She shuffled the letters. On the second was printed 'Mrs J. Metarius'.

What a peculiar name. Typical of Jude, that a revelation about her life did not resolve anything, only gave rise to more questions.

The main ones being: Who was Mr Metarius? What nationality was he, with a name like that? And where was he now?

Carole moved the top two and looked at the third letter, only to find a new obfuscation. This one was handwritten and addressed to 'Jude Nichol'. The same name was on the Jiffy bag.

So she had two names. Was the 'Nichol' her maiden name? Or was it another married name? How many times had Jude been married? How many more names were going to turn up?

Alternatively, perhaps she only had one surname. Nichol. The letter addressed to 'Mrs J. Metarius' might have been misdirected.

Carole heard footsteps from upstairs, and guiltily shoved her neighbour's post down on to the hall table. She felt soiled, as if she had done something cheap. Looking up at Jude coming down the stairs, she said awkwardly, 'Just the post.'

'Thought it would be. He's getting later and later on a Saturday.' Jude, totally unfazed by Carole's discomfiture, swept past into the sitting room. 'Don't fancy another trip into Fedborough, do you?' she called over her shoulder as she shut the windows.

'Wouldn't mind.'

'Harry's being extremely cloak-and-daggerish, but he says he's got some important information to give me about Roddy Hargreaves's death.'

'What?'

'That's what I mean about him being cloak-and-daggerish. He wouldn't say on the phone. Do you mind giving me a lift?' Jude consulted her large wristwatch as she gathered up a floppy straw basket and other belongings. 'I said I'd meet him near the bridge at one. All very mysterious and Checkpoint Charlie.'

'One o'clock's pretty soon. What would have happened if I hadn't agreed to give you a lift?'

'I'd have got a cab. But will you?'

'Of course.'

'Great.' Jude moved back to the hall and looked at the pile of post. 'Oh, those have come,' she said unhelpfully, on seeing the Jiffy bag. She gathered up the three letters and shoved them into her basket. 'Ooh, I'll take the mobile.' She picked that up too.

Carole followed her to the front door. 'I actually want to see if I can track down James Lister again. Got a few more questions to ask him.'

'You do that then, while I deal with Harry, who, needless to say, insisted that I should meet him unaccompanied. I stopped him before he told me what kind of flower I should wear in my buttonhole.'

'Fits perfectly then. Good idea, dividing the investigation between us.'

'Oh, I agree. What's more, working separately we

won't be adding any more fuel to the flames of Fedborough gossip, will we?'

And Mrs Metarius, or Miss Nichol, or whoever she happened to be, roared with laughter.

When they arrived that morning, they found Fedborough *en fête* – or as *en fête* as a middle-class English country town is capable of being. Had they had a Fedborough Festival programme, they would have known that the Saturday had been designated 'Street Theatre Day'. The result of this had been an invasion of the town by a wide variety of 'performance artists', each of whom had a personal definition of what constituted a 'performance', not to mention what constituted 'art'.

There was a predictable ration of clowns sounding hooters and scattering streamers, white-faced mimes feeling their way round the inside of invisible glass boxes, and people who apparently made their living by being sprayed gold and standing still for hours on end.

There were also more inventive displays. Huge butterflies on stilts stepped their delicate way up the steep incline of the High Street. A black-face chain-gang in striped American prison uniforms straggled along, stopping every now and then to perform tuneless spirituals. In and out of the shops, Henry VIII and his Six Wives played hide and seek for no very good reason.

The reactions of the good people of Fedborough to these antics varied. Some, particularly those with small children, stopped and marvelled at the free entertainment. Others, mostly of the older generation, got extremely English about the whole thing, resolutely pretending it wasn't happening. Elderly tweeded men and women walked past figures dressed as traffic islands and benappied adult babies without the slightest flicker of an eyebrow. They hadn't survived the worst that Hitler could throw at them to be fazed by a group of show-offs.

Jude and Carole, predictably enough, differed in their reactions to the spectacle. Jude looked around in giggling wonderment, while Carole's body language reflected her long-held dread of audience participation, fiercely resisting the notion that any of the performers might make her *do* anything.

A clown in eccentric Victorian frock coat and steeple hat urged them to pose for his ancient camera. Carole was not quick enough to walk away, and while he fiddled under a black cape before the inevitable explosion from his flash-pan, Jude grabbed her in a hug for the photograph.

With some vigour, Carole moved away. One didn't want to give any fuel to the misapprehensions of Fedborough.

Jude found this reaction terribly funny, and was still giggling after they had parted and she had set off down the High Street towards Fedborough Bridge.

The rendezvous Harry Roxby had chosen for them once again revealed him to be a rather young fifteen. Following the instructions he'd given her on the phone, Jude crossed over the bridge, away from the main part of the town. She walked along the deserted towpath. The side of the river nearer the town was the tourist route, past the old boatsheds which had proved the financial undoing of Roddy Hargreaves. In that direction people could follow the river for miles, go into the open country, even join up with the South Downs Way. The side where Jude was, the path led only to the houseboats that rode up and down on the tide along the Fether. Most of them were in such a state of dilapidation that, but for James Lister's assurances to the contrary during his Town Walk, she would have doubted whether any were still inhabited. Presumably, though, their owners were unworried by the outside appearances of their homes and lived in cosily neat interiors.

The houseboat nearest to the bridge was the only one that looked smart. The high windows of the main section were shrouded by pale cotton blinds. Behind these, rows of portholes, diminishing in size, punctuated the hull towards the back of the boat. Burnished wood gleamed; so did the spotless brass of the boat's fittings. The conversion made such a design statement that Jude didn't need to see the neat sign reading 'Alan Burnethorpe – Architect' to identify its owner.

Harry's instructions had been very specific. She was to stop before she reached the houseboats, exactly opposite the centre of the inlet dug out for Roddy's ill-fated marina. This she did with some annoyance. There was no sign of anyone. Was the boy having her on? Had he got too deeply into his role-playing espionage game? Was she part of some adolescent practical joke?

Jude decided to give him five minutes, then see if Carole had found James Lister in the Coach and Horses. She looked down at the swollen khaki of the river, at that time of day flowing resolutely, but bizarrely, upstream.

'Hello, Jude.'

Harry's voice, definitely his voice, but she had no idea where it was coming from.

'Where are you?'

He let out a little crowing giggle. 'I can see you, but

you can't see me.' The sound seemed to be emerging from the river itself.

Jude stepped forward towards the edge. Suddenly there was a rustling of grass in front of her, and she saw Harry Roxby's head.

He showed her the hiding place. A walkway had been dug down into the bank, presumably to connect with some long-vanished landing stage. There were the remains of wooden steps, but tall grass had grown over to conceal the entrance completely.

'I found it,' said Harry proudly, sounding nearer ten than fifteen. 'It's my secret hideaway. Nobody knows when I'm down here.'

Jude was in no mood to play Peter Pan games. 'You said you had something to tell me.'

'Yes. It's something that I think could have a bearing on our investigation,' he said portentously.

'Come on, Harry, get on with it.'

His expression showed he'd rather have spun the suspense out longer, but he succumbed to the strength of her will. 'The thing is, Jude, I'd never met Mr Hargreaves . . . you know, the one who's supposed to have killed his wife.'

'So?'

'So I didn't know what he looked like. Then yesterday I saw the local paper. Probably been lying round the house for days, but I never bother looking at it, because nothing interesting ever happens down here.' He still needed to maintain his pose of the uprooted and misunderstood metropolitan. 'But there was a photograph of him in it, of Mr Hargreaves, and I realized I had seen him.'

'That's not surprising,' said Jude, who was getting a little sick of Harry's conspiratorial game-playing. 'Roddy Hargreaves was quite a familiar figure around the town.'

'No, but I saw him recently. The day he died. Last Saturday. I could have been the last person to see him alive.'

He had Jude's full attention now. 'Where did you see him, Harry?'

'Exactly where you're standing.' The boy knew she was hooked, and now dared to extend his dramatic pauses. 'I was down here in my hideaway . . .'

'What time of day was this?'

'Early evening. Half-past seven, eight o'clock, maybe.'

'What were you doing here?'

'Oh, I'd had a row at home. Dad was being impossible, as ever, asking when I was going to start "making something of my life". So I came down here. I do that quite often. Nobody knows I'm here and—'

'Yes, all right. What happened?'

'Well, I heard voices. On this side of the river. Which is quite unusual, because the only people who come along here are the ones who live in the houseboats, and they come and go at different times, so you don't often hear them talking.'

'Go on!'

'I looked up through the grass. They couldn't see me . . .' Recognizing the exasperation in Jude's face, he speeded up. 'And I saw this man with a purple nose, who I now know was Roddy Hargreaves.'

'Who was he with?' murmured Jude. 'Did you recognize who he was with?'

'Yes. Someone you know too.'

'For heaven's sake!' She was unable to maintain her customary serenity. 'Who was it, Harry?'

'That man who came to dinner at our place the same night you did, the night I found the . . . the torso.'

'Which man?'

'The one who was dressed in black.'

'Alan Burnethorpe?'

'That's right,' said Harry Roxby.

Chapter Thirty-Two

Harry hadn't had a lot more to say. The only conversation he'd overheard had been the two men bemoaning the unhappy fate of their plans for Bracken's Boatyard. Interestingly, though, Roddy Hargreaves had sounded more genuine in his sadness than Alan Burnethorpe. Roddy Hargreaves had also sounded drunk. According to Harry, he had been walking very unsteadily.

Which could, Jude reflected, support the theory that his death had been accidental. It had rained on the previous Saturday – Harry said his hideaway had been very damp and uncomfortable – so the towpath would have been slippery. A drunken man, despairing at the sight of the project which had ruined him financially, totters on the muddy bank of a fast-flowing river . . . maybe the slip that landed him in the current had been half willed, half involuntary . . . ?

But, if that was the case, why had he been talking to Alan Burnethorpe?

Harry said he'd seen the two men walking back towards the town, saying something about needing a drink. Then, because he was wet and hungry, he'd gone back to Pelling House for the next round of the ongoing row with his father. And, looking at his watch a week later, he concluded he'd better do the same thing now. Mum did lunch at half-past one on a Saturday.

Jude walked back to the bridge with him, lost in thought. She waved distracted thanks and goodbye and watched him scamper off up the High Street through the rabble of performance artists. Harry Roxby'd be all right, she decided. Just going through a difficult stage of his life, which had been exacerbated by the move out of London. His real problem was the relationship with his father. If Grant could be persuaded to be less competitive, things'd be smoother. Jude knew the situation was archetypal. Grant Roxby was less secure than he appeared, aware that he was ageing, aware of the inevitable dwindling of his powers. A new rising generation would take over from him in time, and Harry represented that generation. By constantly diminishing his son's achievements, Grant was trying to extend his period of control.

Maybe, in time, Jude thought, she might be able to help the easing of that relationship. But she had two more pressing priorities at that moment. One was working out how Virginia and Roddy Hargreaves had met their ends.

The other was getting something to eat. She'd only had coffee at breakfast and the white wine had sharpened the pangs of hunger. Jude was starving.

Fortunately there was a fish and chip shop on the other side of the road. She looked at her watch. One-twenty. She had an idea of paying a return visit to Debbie Carlton's when the Art Crawl opened again at two. In the meantime, a large cod and chips, open, with lashings of salt and vinegar.

Jude ate her lunch on a bench overlooking the Fether. As she licked the last delicious fishiness off her fingers, she took another look at the large face of her watch. Only twenty-five to. Still a little time to kill.

Oh, the post she'd snatched up as she left Woodside Cottage. The post which, unbeknownst to her, had caused Carole such moral angst.

Jude looked at the three letters. She had a pretty good idea what two of them would be, but the third, the one just addressed to 'Jude', could have come from anywhere. It wasn't unusual for her to get letters like that. In the world of therapies and alternative medicine everyone knew her as simply 'Jude'. Her surnames were used only on more official communications.

Using a finger as paperknife, she opened the letter. On a small blue sheet were typed the following words:

If you think you know how Virginia Hargreaves died, meet me on the towpath opposite Bracken's Boatyard on Saturday afternoon at four o'clock.

Jude looked along the towpath. The rendezvous appointed in the letter was only yards from where she was sitting. Exactly where she had met Harry Roxby less than an hour ago. She didn't find this odd. Jude was a great believer in synchronicity. She'd seen its workings too often to have any doubts as to its authenticity. Events did not happen randomly.

This had to be Harry playing his espionage games again. The coincidence of the location was too great for any other explanation. He must've posted the letter the day before, then that morning, unable to cope with the suspense he'd created for himself, used the phone to call Jude and move the rendezvous forward. It would have been completely in character.

Jude looked at the paper. Small, blue, with matching envelope. Probably Basildon Bond or something like that. The kind of notepaper that is sold in packs by newsagents throughout the country. But not the kind of notepaper to be used by Harry's computerized generation. They'd have their printers permanently set for A4 copier sheets and print out everything on that.

She held the note up to the sunlight. Yes, definitely typed, she could see the indentation of the keys. Different quality from the smoothness produced by a laser or bubblejet printer.

On the other hand, given the enthusiasm Harry Roxby was investing into his game of espionage, he was quite capable of disguising an anonymous communication, giving it a deliberately misleading appearance.

Yes, Jude would put money on the fact that the letter came from Harry. Still, she'd probably come back to the towpath at four. Just to be sure.

The downstairs door was unlocked, but when Jude climbed up to Debbie Carlton's sitting room/gallery, the space was empty. Still, it was two o'clock sharp. Maybe Debbie had been delayed.

Jude moved across to look at the picture she owned, noting with pleasure that a couple of the other frames nearby had red dots on them. The Fedborough Festival promised to be a deservedly profitable period for Debbie Carlton.

The terracotta urn still looked wonderful, full of the warm South. It would bring a breath of Italy into Woodside Cottage. Of all the pictures on display, this remained the one Jude would have chosen.

A door opened behind her, and she turned to see a rather flustered Debbie Carlton coming into the room. She was straightening her pale blue shirt and running a tidying hand through her ash-blonde hair. 'Oh. Jude. Hi.'

'Sorry. I was in town, and I just couldn't resist having another look at my purchase.' That was the cover story she had prepared. What she really wanted to get the conversation around to was the anonymous letter sent to the police. Jude had pondered the strangeness of that a good few times. Debbie's assertion that she'd assumed the letter to be a product of Francis's paranoia had sounded genuine at the time, and yet she remained the only person with a motive for disrupting her ex-husband's life. Jude wanted to find out more.

The pretended reason for her presence was, however, one that no artist could resist. Debbie Carlton coloured prettily and said, 'It's yours. You've paid for it. You can look at it as much as you want.'

'Glad to see you've sold a few others.'

'Yes. Yes.' Debbie appeared distracted, nervous, rather as Carole had described her when Francis was on the scene. Surely he hadn't come back.

But no, it wasn't him causing her unease. The door she had come through opened again, and Alan Burnethorpe entered. He was too smooth an operator actually to look flustered, but he wasn't at his ease.

'Well,' he said, seeing Jude, 'what an art-lover you are.'

'Yes. Did you know I'd bought this one?'

'No. Debbie hadn't mentioned it. Perhaps I should be offended.'

'Why?'

'You buy art here. But from the way you were looking at them, my drawings apparently leave you cold.'

'Wouldn't you say female nudes appeal more to men?'

'Not exclusively. Some women like them a lot.' There was a slyness in his voice. Clearly Fiona Lister's slur on Jude's relationship with Carole had spread right through Fedborough. Jude felt relieved Carole wasn't present.

Alan Burnethorpe showed no signs of moving, so Jude reckoned it was her cue to beat a retreat. Maybe she'd get another chance to discuss the anonymous letter to the police.

As she opened the door at the foot of the stairs, Jude heard Debbie's tense voice whisper, 'What's she going to think?'

'Doesn't matter too much what she thinks.' Alan Burnethorpe sounded sardonically smooth as ever. 'She doesn't know many people in Fedborough. I think our secret's safe with her.'

Chapter Thirty-Three

Carole had chosen a good day to find James Lister. He was propping up the bar when she entered the Coach and Horses, because, as he soon explained with a confidential wink, 'Fiona's organizing a charity lunch and, *while the cat's away . . .*'

Carole wondered if he'd realized how apposite in the context the word 'cat' was.

In his wife's absence, James was once again all flirtatious bravado, and he was clearly very pleased when Carole agreed to have lunch with him 'in a little French place I know just round the corner'.

She was totally unworried about him making any sexual advances to her. Fiona Lister might not actually be present, but the deterrent qualities of her personality spread outwards like radiation from Chernobyl, guaranteeing her husband wouldn't – probably couldn't – do anything physical. And, in the cause of advancing her investigation, Carole was prepared to put up with any amount of clumsy verbal innuendo.

The 'little French place' seemed pretty ordinary to her, but James Lister made an elaborate routine of chatting up the owner and insisting on a table in the window, overlooking the High Street. With a wink, as he ushered Carole to her seat, he told her that 'Jean-Pierre's always got a table for me'. Since the restaurant was only a quarter full, this didn't seem such a big deal.

She was slightly annoyed, though, when James, with a sideways look at her as he edged her chair in, and another wink to the proprietor, whispered, 'Not a word to the wife, eh, Jean-Pierre?'

'Of course not,' the owner murmured back, *'you dog.'*

James Lister looked very pleased with himself as he took his seat. Oh well, thought Carole, if that's how he gets his kicks . . . If he's making the outrageous assumption that I might have any sexual interest in him, I suppose it doesn't do any harm. All I'm here for is to pick his brains, and the more relaxed and intimate we are for that, the better.

'Now what's the lovely lady going to drink? Stay with the white wine, eh? Jean-Pierre does a very fine Graves.' He pronounced it like the things found in churchyards.

'Bit sweet for me. If he's got a Chardonnay or something . . .'

'Very well Jean-Pierre, a bottle of your finest—'

'Just a glass. I've got to drive later.'

He seemed relieved. If they'd got a bottle, he'd have felt obliged to drink wine too, and he really wanted to stay with the beer. He asked for a Stella Artois. Then there was a food-ordering routine with Jean-Pierre, involving a lot of 'Do you have any of that wonderful casserole with the truffles and . . . ?'

James ended up ordering a rare steak and chips – 'or whatever the French is for French Fries.' Carole chose a mushroom omelette. Unlike Jude, she'd had an adequate breakfast. James went into the masculine knee-jerk reaction of trying to get her to order something more elaborate and expensive, but soon gave up.

Their drinks arrived. He took a long swallow, wiped the froth off his white moustache and then seemed to think he should have made a toast. 'What shall it be – to us?'

Carole wriggled out of that by saying, 'How about – to the success of the Fedborough Festival?'

Though not what he'd had in mind, as a dutiful burgher of the town he couldn't fault the worthiness of her suggestion. He raised his glass to hers. 'I'm not sure what to make of all this Street Theatre business . . .'

'It's not my idea of entertainment,' said Carole tartly. 'I take the rather old-fashioned view that the proper venue for theatre is *inside* a theatre.'

'I wouldn't disagree with that.' He seemed relieved that he wasn't lunching with a fervent advocate of the *avant garde*. 'Are you going to see any of the proper theatre in the Festival?'

'I don't think so. We—' She remembered Fedborough's view of her relationship with Jude. '*I*'ve done a bit of the Art Crawl, but nothing else. Are you seeing much?'

'Oh yes. Fiona's on various committees and is a Director of the Festival.' She would be, thought Carole. 'So we'll be doing the Mozart in All Souls on Monday, and then *The Cherry Orchard* on Wednesday.' He made it sound as though root-canal work would be a more attractive option.

'Still, enough about me.' He wiped his moustache again, roguishly this time. 'Let's talk about *you*, Carole. I hardly know anything about you. Tell me everything.'

That was the last thing Carole ever intended to do. Least of all to James Lister. She shrugged. 'I took early retirement from the Home Office.' Still sounded the wrong verb. 'I was *given* early retirement from the Home

Office' would be nearer the truth. But never mind that. 'And I'm divorced.'

'Ah.' This seemed to confirm something in his mind. 'I knew Fiona was wrong.'

'About what?'

'Oh.' He coloured. 'Oh, she was just saying . . . she just thought . . .'

Carole knew exactly what he meant. Maybe now he'd go back to his wife and tell her she'd got the wrong end of the stick about Carole and Jude's relationship. James Lister was a straightforward soul. In his scheme of things, the fact that a woman had once been married automatically excluded the possibility that she might be lesbian.

There was an edge of disappointment in his expression, though. No doubt, like a lot of men, he had been intrigued by the chance of finding out what lesbians actually *did* to each other.

'So your marriage didn't work out?' he blundered on.

'No.' Which was all Carole was prepared to say on the subject. But, slightly cheekily, she couldn't resist adding, 'Unlike yours.'

'What? Oh yes.' He cleared his throat. 'In fact, you know, Carole, what you see on the outside of a marriage can sometimes be misleading. Fiona is a wonderful woman in many ways—'

No, I can't stand it, thought Carole. Not the 'my wife doesn't understand me' routine. Anything but that. Time to move the conversation on. And he'd given her the perfect opportunity.

'You're so right,' she interrupted. 'From what I hear, Roddy and Virginia Hargreaves's marriage looked all right from the outside.'

'Ye-es, to an extent. I mean, there was a feeling round Fedborough that it was a slightly unlikely pairing.'

'Why?'

'Well, she had a title,' he said reverently. 'She was really "Lady Virginia" . . .'

'Yes, I know that.'

'And Roddy was . . . well . . .'

'From the little I saw of him, he was fairly upper-crust too. Public-school accent, and all that.'

'Yes . . .' James Lister shook his head knowingly. 'But he hadn't got a title.'

'Oh, look.' Out of the window, Carole had just seen Jude walking up the High Street, picking her way between stilted butterflies, in her customary careless ripple of drapery.

'It's your friend, yes.'

'She'll be going up to the Coach and Horses. I said I might be in there.'

'Oh. Do you want me to go out and ask her to join us?' he asked unwillingly.

'No, no, don't worry. She's probably doing some more of the Art Crawl. We've fixed to meet later. It's fine.'

James Lister relaxed visibly, drained his beer and asked Jean-Pierre for another. Then, remembering his manners, he asked if Carole would like more wine.

She agreed to another glass. The cosier they got together, the easier it might be to ask the questions she had in mind.

'Presumably,' she embarked, 'everyone in Fedborough's been talking a lot about the Hargreaves . . . ?'

'Not that much, really. I mean, all kinds of rumours were going around before, but once Roddy's body was found . . . there wasn't much room left for speculation, was there? Besides, everyone's got caught up with the Fedborough Festival starting and . . . you know, things move on.'

'Yes.' Carole warmed to her task. 'So the theory is . . . Roddy killed her that February weekend three years ago . . . Why?'

'Why?'

'Why did he kill her?'

'Well . . . We've just been saying it's difficult to see inside a marriage, that things look different on the outside . . . Presumably, he killed her because they were married.'

Not an entirely satisfactory answer, but that wasn't what Carole was there to talk about, so she moved on. 'All right. If we accept that, then we must also accept that Roddy was the one who cut up her body. And then ask the question: why would he do that?'

'To make it easier to dispose of.'

Everyone seemed to be agreed on that point. Carole nodded thoughtfully. 'Makes sense. So somehow he disposed of the arms and legs and then . . . why didn't he dispose of the torso?'

'Someone was suspicious of him? He was afraid of being seen getting rid of it? I don't think we'll ever know the full details.'

'No. And yet, aware that a large part of his wife's body was hidden in the cellar, Roddy Hargreaves then sold Pelling House to Francis and Debbie Carlton. Doesn't that seem strange behaviour to you?'

James Lister shrugged. 'Roddy was a strange chap. Pissed – sorry, pardon my French, drunk – most of the time. He'd forget things.'

Another less than satisfactory explanation. 'You said

you sold your business about three years ago . . .' He nodded acknowledgment. 'And the Frankses next door to you sold up round the same time?'

Another nod. 'Stanley had been getting very forgetful. For different reasons, we were both running our businesses down.'

'Terry Harper said the grocery was in quite a state when he bought it.'

'Yes. Our withdrawal at the butcher's was rather more orderly. Last six months we were moving stuff out of the place, cutting down the amount of goods we stocked.'

'And was Stanley Franks doing the same?'

'The effect was the same, but in his case it was because he was getting so forgetful. He really couldn't manage any more. I kept offering to help, said he could store stuff in the smokehouse, that kind of thing, but he wouldn't listen. I think he was very aware of the state he was in, but pretended it wasn't happening. He got very snappish if anyone suggested anything, offered him help, or criticized him.'

'But you used the smokehouse as a storeroom?'

'You bet. Stopped smoking our own goods more than a year before I retired. You could get the stuff from wholesalers, it saved an awful lot of palaver. And none of the people in the town seemed that bothered. Not much point in making an effort as a small shopkeeper when your customers can get a wider range at the supermarkets than anything you've got on offer . . .'

James Lister's hobby-horse was threatening to loom into view, so Carole moved quickly to a new question. 'You told me and Jude that it would be easy for a qualified butcher to dismember a human body . . .'

He chuckled knowingly. 'Dead easy.'

'What would he use – a saw?'

'No way. To do a neat job, you wouldn't need to cut through any bones. Just use a boning knife round the joints. They'd come away neat and tidy, no problem.'

'But it wouldn't be such an easy job for someone unqualified?'

He shook his head, enjoying being the fount of knowledge. 'No way. Get a real pig's breakfast once you get the amateurs involved. I'm sure they'd use saws, axes, machetes, cleavers. When it's done properly, you know, butchery's a very tidy trade.'

Their steak and omelette arrived. After some coy badinage with Jean-Pierre, James Lister guffawed. 'What a subject to be talking about over lunch, eh? When all I want to know is how a pretty little thing like you came to end up in Fethering, of all places.'

Though it went against every instinct she possessed, Carole manufactured an appropriately girlish giggle. 'Just one more thing before we eat, though . . .'

'Mm?' His steak knife was already sawing through the red meat.

'If Roddy Hargreaves had no training as a butcher, how was he able to make such a neat job of dismembering his wife?'

James Lister chuckled. He was bored with this conversation now, and wanted to move on to more intimate topics. 'I've no idea. Maybe, in an earlier part of his life, he'd trained as a butcher. You'd be amazed the people who've got butchery skills tucked away in their past . . .'

'Really?' Carole leaned closer.

He was enjoying this. Fuelled as he was by the beer, her proximity made him potentially indiscreet, even a little reckless. 'I tell you, there's one very fine upmarket lady of Fedborough who . . . you'd take your life in your hands if you mentioned it to her . . . but she used to work as a butcher.'

'Who was that then?' Carole managed to get a teasing, almost sexy, quality into her voice.

'Ooh, I don't think I should tell you.'

'Go *on* . . .' she pleaded.

'Well . . . Not a word to a soul, but I'm talking about Fiona. My wife.'

'Really?'

'Oh yes. Early days of our marriage, before the kids came along, she used to help in the shop with me and my old dad.'

'Well, well, well.'

'Bloody good butcher she was too.'

And certainly still knows how to put the knife in, thought Carole Seddon. But her only words were, 'Was she?'

Chapter Thirty-Four

Jude had done as Carole surmised, and taken in some more of the Art Crawl. She had found the quality of the art mixed. Works in one or two exhibitions she liked a lot, others she loathed. She was relieved that she saw nothing she liked better than the watercolour she had bought from Debbie Carlton.

She wanted to talk to Carole about Debbie. And the appearance of Alan Burnethorpe in her flat. Jude had no wish to succumb to the knee-jerk reactions of Fedborough's gossips, but it was hard to put an entirely innocent interpretation on his presence there. And it did open up a whole new range of interesting possibilities . . . Yes, she needed to discuss the case with Carole.

In the meantime, even where she couldn't enjoy the art, she could enjoy the private view of Fedborough's houses. The Art Crawl, as Debbie Carlton had said, was a Snoopers' Charter, and Jude enjoyed a good snoop as much as the next person.

She and Carole had made flexible arrangements for meeting up again. The most likely event was that they'd bump into each other in the town, but if that didn't happen, they'd agreed to home in on Carole's Renault, parked up near the Castle, at three o'clock, four o'clock or five o'clock.

Jude had missed the three o'clock potential rendezvous, and was contemplating being there for four, when she remembered she had another assignation at that time. So sure was she that it belonged to another of Harry Roxby's little games that she had almost forgotten about the anonymous letter.

Still, might as well turn up. There might be someone there. She might get some useful information.

Walking down the High Street, weaving her way through performance artists, Jude got out the letter once again. As she reread it, she became aware of a strangeness in the phrasing. The writer wasn't actually promising anything. *'If you think you know how Virginia Hargreaves died . . .'* The message could be asking for information, rather than offering it.

Jude crossed Fedborough Bridge, and walked along the dead-end of towpath. Exactly opposite Bracken's Boatyard, another thought struck her. She'd heard the name of Bob Bracken, the previous owner who'd sold the premises to Roddy Hargreaves, but would Harry Roxby know the name? Didn't the use of the words 'Bracken's Boatyard' suggest that the writer was someone who'd been a resident of Fedborough for quite a while?

She swept back the curtain of grass from Harry's hideaway, but there was no one there. She stared across at the boatsheds. Deserted. Though the bustle of the town in Festival time lay only across Fedborough Bridge, Jude felt very alone.

She looked along the towpath towards the bridge, now intrigued. Maybe the anonymous letter had nothing to do with Harry . . . Who else would she see walking along from the bridge towards her?

She suddenly remembered something she had overheard that lunchtime in the Crown and Anchor. Francis Carlton had been talking about why he'd come back from Florida to talk to the police. And Alan Burnethorpe had been very quick to suggest they might have been tipped off. Maybe the anonymous letter had . . .

There was a sound from behind her.

'Good afternoon, Jude. So you made it,' said a voice she recognized.

Chapter Thirty-Five

Lunch with James Lister had gone on rather longer than Carole would have wished. Towards the end, his arch flirtatiousness had given way to maudlin self-pity. Though Carole recognized this was an entirely understandable emotion from anyone married to Fiona Lister, she found it hard to be sympathetic. And she wanted to move on, find Jude and discuss her findings.

But James Lister's long-winded leave-taking of Jean-Pierre, followed by his reluctant farewell to her – including an unnecessarily slobbery kiss on the stairwell of the restaurant – meant that Carole didn't arrive back at the Renault till after four.

There was no sign of Jude. Frustrating; Carole might only just have missed her. Never mind, an hour more of the Art Crawl wouldn't come amiss.

Carole didn't see much she liked, very little that she'd give house-room to. She contemplated having another look at Debbie Carlton's work. She'd really liked those watercolours, and had almost completed the mental processes involved in reaching a decision to buy one. But perhaps going that afternoon would be too precipitate. The Art Crawl had another whole week to run, after all, Carole reassured herself with some relief.

When she got back to the Renault just before five,

there was still no Jude. Carole waited, then walked up to the small green outside the entrance to the Castle ruins, thinking her friend might be sitting there. But no sign.

She let a full half-hour elapse before giving up and driving back to Fethering. Couldn't hang about any longer. Gulliver would want feeding and walking, apart from anything else.

As she drove down towards the coast, Carole wondered whether she should invest in a mobile phone. Jude had one, and for moments such as this they must be very useful. It'd be very easy to sort out misunderstood arrangements or to explain delays if one had instant telephonic contact.

She was a little surprised at herself, contemplating two luxury purchases so close together. A watercolour by Debbie Carlton and a mobile phone. That wasn't appropriate for the Carole Seddon Carole Seddon knew and tried to love. Still, no need to rush into either extravagance, she told herself. Think about whether she really did need them.

When she had got back to High Tor and garaged the Renault, she fully expected to find a message on the answering machine to explain Jude's absence. But there wasn't one. She went next door to Woodside Cottage, thinking for some reason her neighbour might have got a cab back early from Fedborough.

There was nobody in.

Chapter Thirty-Six

'Your note,' said Jude. 'Your anonymous letter to me, perhaps I should say . . . asked if I thought I knew how Virginia Hargreaves died.'

'And do you?'

'I'm pretty sure she didn't die a natural death.' There was a silence. 'Almost equally sure she was murdered.'

'And who do you think killed her?'

'I don't think it was Roddy. In fact I know it wasn't.'

'Why?'

'He had a pretty solid alibi for the weekend she disappeared. He was in France.'

'Anyone can say they're in France.'

'But he was seen on to the ferry at Newhaven by the Rev Trigwell, and met off another ferry four days later by James Lister.'

'Ah. Of course, someone plotting to murder his wife could deliberately set up such an alibi and then catch another ferry back to England . . .'

'I agree they could, but from what you knew of Roddy Hargreaves – and the state he was in at the time – could you see him being that organized?'

'Perhaps not.'

Another silence fell between them. Not an uncomfortable one. The houseboat swayed gently as the tide of the

Fether tugged at its hull. July sunlight spilled through the windows and reflected off the highly polished surfaces of the old dark wood and the brass fittings.

'So, Jude . . . if Roddy wasn't the murderer . . . who was?'

'I haven't worked it out yet. There are quite a few options.'

'That's nice to know. Says a lot for the people of Fedborough, doesn't it?' A chuckle. 'Incidentally, I was talking to Debbie . . .'

'Hm?'

'She said you'd been enquiring about an anonymous letter sent to the police.'

'Oh yes. Sent by someone determined to push the burden of suspicion on to Francis.'

'Have you got any closer to finding out who sent that letter?'

Jude shook her head. 'Well, this morning I thought logic dictated that the person who sent the anonymous letter to me must, by definition, be the one who contacted the police. But now I see it was you who wrote to me . . .' She chuckled. 'It seems unlikely, doesn't it?'

'Yes.' There was an answering chuckle. But it didn't sound very amused. 'I've got a document that I think might interest you, Jude.'

'Oh?'

'Rather relevant to the death of Virginia Hargreaves. Would you like to see it?'

'Very much indeed.'

'It's through here.' A door was opened to the back part of the houseboat. 'After you.'

Jude stepped into the other room.

Too late she heard the door closing behind her, and the sound of a key turning in the lock.

Chapter Thirty-Seven

By seven o'clock Carole was beginning to feel a little uneasy. Where could Jude be? Then again, she'd always been a law unto herself, going off without explanation and reappearing equally unannounced.

But the niggle of anxiety didn't go away.

Then a new thought came to Carole, a thought that was almost reassuring. Jude had mentioned the one lead they had yet to follow up. Bob Bracken, the old owner of the Fedborough boatyards. Yes, Jude must've followed up on him. She was probably even now talking to the old boy.

But the surge of confidence brought on by this thought soon started to dwindle. If she had tracked down Bob Bracken, Jude was spending a very long time with him. And why hadn't she phoned to say what she was doing? Carole knew she had the mobile with her.

By eight o'clock the anxiety was becoming paranoia. Two people in Fedborough had died in suspicious circumstances. The person responsible was still probably at large in the town. If that person knew that Jude was investigating the crimes, she might well be next on the list to be silenced . . .

Carole couldn't stand the uncertainty any longer. She had to find out where Jude was.

The only pointer she had was the name of Bob Bracken.

And there was only one way she had of finding him.

She reached for the phone and dialled the number of the Crown and Anchor.

'You can't keep me here for ever,' said Jude through the door to her captor.

'I'm well aware of that.'

'People will come looking for me. People will come here to see you, anyway.'

'Yes.'

'So why not let me out now, and we'll forget this ever happened.'

'I can't do that. You know too much.'

'I don't. I hardly know anything. I certainly don't know how Virginia Hargreaves died.'

'No. But you're curious. You won't let things rest until you do know the truth.'

'Let me out,' said Jude in a reasonable voice. 'You can't keep me quiet for ever.'

'Why not? I managed to do it with Roddy Hargreaves.'

The sound of the tidal flood of the Fether was suddenly loud against the hull of the houseboat.

'Look, I've had enough of this!' Ted Crisp braked sharply, mounted the pavement and switched off the ignition.

'Enough of what?'

'You sitting there in silence.'

'I'm worried about Jude.'

'That's only part of what's happening, Carole, and you

know it. I don't mind that you've suddenly contacted me after four months of silence because you need my help. I don't mind that, on a busy Saturday night, I've had to leave the pub in the hands of two very inexperienced bar staff. But now we're together, you can at least talk to me!'

She tried to remonstrate, but he didn't give her the chance.

'OK, we both know what happened between us, and we both know it didn't work out, and we both suffered some hurt feelings over that. But now we're back in each other's company, the least we can do is to be polite to each other.'

'I'm not being impolite. I just feel embarrassed.'

'And how do you think I feel? Do you think it's easy for me, suddenly being with you again? Knowing how punctiliously you've avoided seeing me, walking the long way down to the beach so that you don't even go past the Crown and Anchor? Making me feel as though I'm some kind of infection, a plague-spot that you must keep away from at all costs? I may be clumsy and inept and a bloody *man*, but I have feelings too.'

'I've never doubted it, Ted. Just, after what happened, I—'

'And what did happen? What did bloody happen? Go on, you were there at the time. You tell me what happened.'

'Well, things didn't work out . . .'

'No. We were attracted to each other, maybe for a time we thought we'd got a relationship that'd last. Maybe we thought this was the big one, maybe we even thought it was "love".' He couldn't keep a sneer out of the word, but then he softened as he said, 'I certainly did. And then we got to know each other better and we went to bed together, and I think we both realized at the same time, no, this wasn't the big thing. Perhaps we're both too old, too set in our ways, to make the changes necessary to accommodate another person. Perhaps neither of us really wants a long-term relationship. Perhaps we're both too prickly, too afraid of being hurt . . . I don't know why, but it didn't work. We both know that.'

'Yes,' said Carole quietly.

'But that's no reason for either of us to send the other one to Coventry. We live in the same place. It's inevitable that, however elaborate the avoiding action you take, we are going to bump into each other. And I'd like to think that, when that happens, we could at least be pleasant to each other.

'All right, it didn't work out, but the only casualties were a few uncomfortable feelings and maybe a few adolescent dreams. We may both have been guilty of crass insensitivity – I'm sure I was – but we didn't deliberately try to hurt each other.'

'I know that.'

'So all I'm saying is, let's stop this stupid stand-off. We started out by liking each other. That was the basic feeling. OK, different backgrounds, different attitudes, different priorities, but we felt an attraction. That became stronger, and we perhaps misinterpreted it as love. Now we know it wasn't love, but that doesn't mean the attraction between our personalities has just disappeared.' He pushed both hands through his beard in a gesture of exasperation. 'What I want to say is probably the biggest cliché in the book, Carole. Can't we still be friends?'

He slumped back in his seat, exhausted by one of the longest speeches she had ever heard him deliver, exhausted also by the release of so much bottled-up emotion.

'Yes,' said Carole softly, 'I'd like to.'

'Thank God for that.' Brusquely, he turned the key in the ignition. 'Now let's find Jude.'

Chapter Thirty-Eight

It was near to the longest day of the year, and the light was slow to give in to night. There were no longer dappling reflections on the ceiling of her prison, but Jude could still see out through the porthole windows. They were set in polished brass and far too small to let her body through even if she could open them. Which she couldn't. She had tried, but they seemed designed to stay closed. So she couldn't call out to attract anyone's attention.

She'd seen people walking by, few on the houseboat side, a lot more on the Bracken's Boatyard side. Carefree families with dogs and picnic baskets trailing back to the car parks, then, as the light dwindled, furtive young lovers going the other way towards the openness and licence of the Downs. Pleasure boats had chugged downstream towards their moorings in Fethering, passing within inches of her. Jude had tried tapping on the porthole glass to attract attention, but her small sounds had been lost against the rush of the fast-flowing river.

Although apparently inaudible herself, she could hear tantalizing noises from outside, the hum of traffic crossing Fedborough Bridge, a raucous shout of laughter from one of the nearby pubs, distant brass music from some Fedborough Festival open-air concert, the clock of All Souls

Church delineating the quarter-hours of her incarceration.

In the first hour, she had looked around the room for a heavy object with which to smash one of the portholes, so that she could shout for help. But there was nothing in sight. The space she was in was a slice across the back of the boat, a low-ceilinged tapering room with a row of three portholes each side. All the wood had been punctiliously stripped down and varnished to a high sheen. The brass fittings also gleamed immaculately.

The space seemed to be used as some kind of office. On the far wall was a honeycomb of pigeon-holes, from which rolled-up charts neatly protruded. There was a manual typewriter and a pack of Basildon Bond notepaper, the source of the anonymous letter she had received that morning.

In the middle of the room was a large box-like structure, presumably engine-housing from the days when the vessel had been seaworthy. Either side of this were benches screwed down to the floor against inclement weather. More benches ran along the curved sides of the space. Realizing these were storage lockers, Jude had opened them with gleeful anticipation. But they were empty. No convenient blunt instruments in there. It made her wonder whether her imprisonment had been planned.

She had another surge of hope when she found the door on the end wall was not locked, but there too disappointment soon followed. The space behind, in the boat's tapered stern, had been converted to a washroom, with toilet and basin. While Jude was glad to take advantage of the facility, this room offered her no more than the other had. Two even smaller portholes either side, and nothing more substantial than a plastic lavatory brush with which to attack their thick glass.

There was no way out until her captor wanted her out. And after the reference to what had happened to Roddy Hargreaves, Jude hoped that moment lay a long way away.

Carole would realize something was wrong. Carole'd come looking for her. Pity her neighbour wasn't on speaking terms with Ted Crisp, thought Jude ruefully. He'd be invaluable in a situation like this.

After the first shouted exchanges, Jude's captor had gone silent, refusing to answer her questions and pleadings. Whether she was now alone on the boat, she didn't know. It had been a long time since she had heard any sounds from the other part of the vessel.

There was nothing she could do but sit in the office area and wait. Jude hated the sense of impotence. She was used to making her own decisions, organizing her life in her own idiosyncratic way. Now her plans – and even the life itself – were in the hands of someone else.

Before being locked in, Jude would not have thought her captor capable of murder. Now she was less sure. The need to silence her was a very compelling motive – as had been the need to silence Roddy Hargreaves. His fate gave an air of hopelessness to hers.

The July day was almost giving up its struggle against darkness when Jude heard footsteps walking along the towpath towards her prison. She pressed her face against a porthole, but because of the angle couldn't see much until the walkers were directly alongside her.

Two pairs of feet walking from Fedborough Bridge to the houseboats beyond. Male grubby sweatpants leading down to even grubbier trainers. Female leather walking shoes so sensible she recognized them instantly.

Carole and Ted. It was Carole and Ted!

Jude hammered against the glass of the porthole until her hand hurt. But the noise didn't reach them. The footsteps receded.

Never mind, thought Jude, as she sat back, nursing her bruised hand. The direction in which they were walking was a dead end. At some point they'd walk back. Somehow she'd manage to attract their attention then. It was simply a matter of waiting.

A bubble of hope rose within her.

Then she heard a banging on the door which had been locked behind her.

'We'll be moving soon,' said the voice of her captor.

Chapter Thirty-Nine

It was the furthest of the houseboats. No lights showed inside, and the rickety structure looked so uneven in the water that Carole found it hard to believe anyone lived there. But Ted Crisp stepped confidently on to the deck and knocked on the sagging half-open door.

'Suppose he's not there?' Carole whispered.

'He'll be there.'

Proving his point, a rough old voice from the gloom inside asked, 'Who's that?'

'It's me, Ted.'

'What're you doing here, you old bugger? Have you brought me some whisky?'

'Yes, of course I have,' replied Ted, who'd prudently raided the Crown and Anchor's stock before leaving Fethering.

'Then you're very welcome. Come on in.'

'I've brought a friend with me. Carole Seddon.'

She liked the ease with which he said that.

'She's welcome, and all,' said the voice, 'so long as she's a whisky drinker.'

Carole was about to say she didn't really care for spirits, but realized it wasn't the moment.

'Can we have some light?' asked Ted, as he stepped down into the interior of the boat.

'Oh yes, of course. I keep forgetting how dependent you lot are on seeing things.'

'Can I help, Bob?'

'No, no. Matter of moments.'

Carole, who was still waiting on the deck, heard the clatter of metal and glass as an oil-lamp was primed, then the scrape of a match as it was lit. A warm glow spread through the interior of the space ahead of her.

'Let me give you a hand down.' She felt Ted Crisp's strong hand around hers as he led her down the few steps into the houseboat.

What the oil-lamp revealed to her blinking eyes was a space whose side walls had been neatly boxed in with chipboard panels. But the dominant impression was not of neatness; the interior was rendered grotto-like by objects hanging from every strut and rafter. There were rowlocks and rusty tools, pieces of leather harness and lengths of chain, greenish bottles and sheep skulls, bicycle wheels and old boots. Without being told, she knew that everything she could see had been scavenged from the river. And that wasn't only because the interior of the houseboat smelt more like the Fether than the Fether itself.

The one part of the décor that didn't look as if it had been fished out of the water was a small shrine set on a table against the wall. A plaster statuette of the Madonna and Child stood sentried by white candles in brass holders. In front of it was a well-thumbed Bible.

The man at the centre of this grotto, seated by the table from which the oil-lamp glowed, was dressed, in spite of the July weather, in thick denim jacket, jeans and short gumboots. All had faded or were stained to the same colour, somewhere between navy and black, but lighter than either. The man's hair was white, tidied more often by a hand than a brush, and his sightless eyes were a cloudy blue.

Remarkably, though shabby, Bob Bracken contrived to look very clean. Though the houseboat smelt deeply of the Fether, there were no human odours.

The other thing that was obvious the minute Carole entered was that Jude wasn't there. While Ted busied himself finding glasses, she said urgently, 'We're looking for a friend of mine – of ours. We thought she might have come to see you.'

'What friend would this be?' the old man asked.

'Her name's Jude. Quite plump, blonde hair.'

'Colour of her hair wouldn't mean much to me, would it?'

'No, I'm sorry.'

'Don't worry.' He let out a genial cackle. 'I can still remember what a pretty blonde looks like. You're not a blonde, are you?'

'No,' replied Carole, taken aback by the suddenness of the question.

'I can always tell. Lot of things I see better now I can't see. There's a special intonation a woman who isn't blonde puts on the word "blonde" when she says it.' The old man cackled again.

'So have you seen Jude?' asked Ted. 'I've put your glass down there beside you.'

'I'll find that, don't you worry. My nose is a highly sophisticated whisky-seeking device.'

He reached out and, sure enough, his hand immediately circled the glass on the table. He lifted it to his lips and took a long swallow before speaking again. Carole watched him, the tension building inside her.

At last he put the glass down. 'No. No Jude. Haven't seen any Jude.'

'I was afraid of this!' Carole murmured. 'It's the only lead I had.'

'Don't worry.' Ted put a reassuring hand on her forearm. 'Bob still might have something useful to tell us.' The old man heard this and smiled knowingly, but said nothing. 'You've been in Fedborough all your life, haven't you, Bob?'

'Oh yes, born a Chub, and I'll die a Chub.'

'And there's not much happens in the town you don't know about?'

'That's true. Used to watch what went on from one side of the Fether when I had the boatyard. Now I watch what goes on from the other side of the Fether.' He laughed and then explained to Carole something he assumed Ted Crisp already knew. 'I say "watch", but of course it's a different kind of watching from what it used to be. When you're blind, you can't watch in quite the traditional way. But I still know everything. Got a lot of friends in Fedborough. They still come and tell me things.' He turned to where he thought Carole was, and one of the blue eyes winked.

'Carole and her friend Jude – the one we're looking for,' said Ted, 'have been trying to find out what actually happened to Virginia Hargreaves.'

'Ah. Yes. Popular topic that's been round the town these last few weeks.'

'The general view,' said Carole, 'seems to be that her husband killed her and, when the police got close to pinning it on him, took his own life.'

Bob Bracken snorted. 'Rubbish! Roddy'd never kill himself, however bad things were.' He gestured in the direction of the Madonna and Child. 'Good Catholic, Roddy. Like me. He wouldn't commit a mortal sin.'

'Then are you saying it must've been an accident? He just fell in the Fether?'

A shake of the head. 'He knows this river almost as well as I do. However much booze he'd got inside him, I'd be very surprised if Roddy fell in by accident.'

'So what are you saying?'

'Someone pushed him in, didn't they?'

'Who?'

'That's the big question. You want everything at once, don't you, young lady? I think you may have to wait a bit for the full story. Pains me to say it, but I don't know everything.'

'You do know something, though, Bob.' Ted Crisp leaned forward to refill the old man's whisky glass, which had unaccountably become empty. 'You know something that might be relevant to the case.'

'Yes, I think I do.' Again, playing the scene at his own pace, he instinctively found his glass, and took a long, contemplative swallow. 'Virginia Hargreaves . . .' he said thoughtfully. 'She was a right little madam. Nasty bit of work. A man should wed someone his own age, I always say. Think Miss Virginia – or Lady Virginia did she call herself – made it clear to Roddy early on that their marriage wasn't going to work.'

'Why didn't they split up?' asked Carole.

'From his point of view, he never would have done.'

'Because of his Catholicism?'

'Right. And with her, I don't know . . . Reckon she wanted to stay around him. Perhaps for financial reasons, as much as anything. She had this title, but I don't think there was much money on her side.'

'She owned a flat in London.'

'Yes, I remember her mentioning that. But Roddy had bought the place for her. He was quite well-heeled, you see, before he started pouring all his money away into the Fether.' He was silent for a moment, letting the threatening gurgle of water against the boatside provide an illustration for his words. 'Anyway, I'm not sure that Virginia had anywhere else to go, apart from the London flat. Not on speaking terms with any of her family, I believe.'

'And once Roddy had lost all his money, she lost interest in him?'

'I think that was it.' Bob Bracken drained his second glass of whisky, and Ted Crisp immediately refilled it. He recognized his role, and was happy to let Carole ask the questions. 'Roddy was in a bad way round that time,' Bob went on, 'with the booze, what have you. And he was having to cut his losses on the boatyard and sell up.'

'How long was it in his possession?'

'Less than a year. Eight, nine months.'

'Who owns it now?'

'Some property developer.' The old man spoke the words with contempt for the breed. 'He's been waiting to build a row of nice riverside town houses. Had the plans all drawn up for years . . .'

'Who did the plans? Who was the architect?'

'Local guy called Alan Burnethorpe. Got his office on the posh houseboat you must've come past.'

'Funny, he seems to get everywhere.'

'Oh, his family've been round here for ages. Always had lots of fingers in Fedborough pies, they have. Related to half the people in the town, for a start. His mother was one of the real characters of Fedborough. I remember, she always—'

But Carole had no time for folksy reminiscence. 'So when are the houses going to be built?'

'Not yet, that's for certain. Developer can't get planning permission. Still, he's not losing money, like Roddy did. Roddy spent a lot on the place. This guy's just letting it collapse slowly into the river.' The unseeing blue eyes were pained. 'Sometimes quite relieved I can't witness what's happened to the place. I can sit here and imagine how it used to be. And I won't have to see the "attractive riverside development" when it finally is put up.'

'You think it will be?'

'No doubt at all. Local planners round Fedborough . . . well, it's like everywhere else. The right politicians get their ears bent, the right palms get greased. Alan Burnethorpe's very good at all that stuff. It'll happen . . . though with a bit of luck when I'm no longer around to see it.'

You wouldn't be able to see it, anyway, thought the instinctive logician in Carole. But she knew what he meant.

'That weekend,' she began, 'the weekend Virginia Hargreaves disappeared . . .'

'Three years back we're talking . . . Februaryish?'

'That's right. Do you remember anything about it?'

'I remember I was very busy, that's all. Still had my sight back then, and I was quite fit. Spend a lifetime doing manual work, you don't get all flabby minute you stop. Anyway, that weekend I had a heavy job on.'

'What was it?'

'Told you Roddy had sold up. Well, suddenly the whole deal had gone through quick and the guy who's buying the site says he wants it cleared by the following Monday. Roddy wasn't in no state to do anything useful – and he said something about he was going away to France

– so he offers me a hundred quid to empty everything out of the sheds. "What shall I do with it all?" I says. "Just chuck it down the dump?" And he says, "Yes. But if there's anything you're not sure about, take it up to Pelling House and leave it there. But make sure it's tidy. Virginia likes things tidy."'

Bob Bracken was fully aware of the effect his words were having. Carole's pale eyes were sparkling with anticipation. Slowly he continued, 'Most of the stuff was easy. Straight down the Amenity Tip. Couple of things, though, I didn't know what they was, didn't know whether Roddy'd want them or not . . .'

Carole could not keep silent any longer. 'And one of them was a large box? A large heavy box?'

'That's right. Made of strengthened cardboard with, like, plastic corners. Kind of box bulk frozen meat gets delivered in. I didn't know what was in it, but I put it on my handcart and pushed it up to Pelling Street.'

'And put it in the cellar of Pelling House?'

Having totally captured their attention, he now didn't seem to mind having his narrative hurried. 'That's right. And there was an old bit of chipboard down there, so – remembering what Roddy said about keeping things tidy – I boarded the space up with that.' He gestured with pride around the interior he could not see. 'Nice bit of chipboard makes a big difference to how a place looks.'

'But did you board it up because you knew what was in the box?'

'No. Just so's to keep things nice and tidy.' The way he gave the answer provided a completely logical explanation for his actions.

'But I guess you know now what was in it?' said Ted

Crisp, unable to maintain his back-seat position any longer.

'I've got a pretty good idea, yes,' the old man replied.

'Then why didn't you tell anyone?' demanded Carole.

'Because no one asked me. Till now.'

'The police haven't been in contact with you?'

He shook his head. 'Not much use as a witness once you lose your sight, you know.'

'And you never had any conversation with Roddy about what you'd done?'

'Nope. He'd paid me the hundred up front. Only times I saw Roddy afterwards was in the Coach and Horses or one of the other pubs, pretty drunk, never on his own; wasn't the opportunity for conversations about the contents of his cellar. Anyway, very soon he'd got Pelling House on the market, and I assumed whatever was in that box'd been moved out.'

'Hm.' Ted Crisp scratched his beard disconsolately. 'So, Carole, we're still no closer to knowing who actually killed Virginia Hargreaves.'

'I wouldn't be so sure about that. Mind you, Roddy seems even further out of the frame than ever. If he had done it and knew the torso was in the boatsheds, there's no way he would have asked Bob to clear them out, is there?'

Ted's shaggy head shook. 'No way. So what have we got?'

'It's something to do with the people who work – or who have worked in Fedborough. I think we're back to butchery.'

'Hm?' He looked puzzled.

'We've got another detail, you see. The box the torso was in originally contained meat. And we mustn't forget how neatly the corpse was dismembered. Definitely a professional job, according to James Lister.'

'So does he become your number one suspect?'

'His wife Fiona would have had the skills to do it, too.'

'And of course,' said Bob Bracken slowly, 'they're not the only people in Fedborough who're trained butchers. There was always the Listers, but there was the Trollope family too.'

'Look, if you're going to push me in the bloody river,' Jude shouted through the locked door, 'do it! Just get on with it!'

'Not yet,' said her captor's voice, still calm, as it had been since they met that afternoon. 'Don't want any witnesses. Some people just went to visit Bob Bracken in one of the houseboats further along. I'll wait till they've gone back into town.'

The wait was not long. Jude was in the tiny washroom when she heard the thumps of two people jumping from deck to towpath. As the familiar legs walked past, she smashed the plastic lavatory brush against the tiny porthole with all her strength.

The glass was too strong to give, and too thick for the sound to penetrate.

Carole and Ted didn't hear her, and hurried on towards Fedborough Bridge.

Chapter Forty

Her customary good manners forgotten, Carole Seddon hammered hard on the door. 'I don't understand why we're here,' Ted Crisp complained behind her. 'I don't see what the reason—'

'This is the only lead we've got. We must save Jude. I'm certain she's with the person who murdered Virginia and Roddy Hargreaves.'

When the door was opened by a surprised-looking Alan Burnethorpe, Carole blurted out, 'All right, where is she?'

'Joke? She's not here.'

Pushing past him into the hall of 47 Pelling Street with uncharacteristic force, Carole announced, 'I must see her!'

'Joke's away for the weekend with the kids. In Naaldwijk with her parents. I'm on my own.'

'I wasn't talking about Joke! You've got someone else here!'

'Who's there? Is that Carole?'

It was a woman's voice, but it wasn't Jude's. Carole looked up to where the words had come from. At the top of the splendid staircase stood Debbie Carlton. Except for a towel gathered hastily round her waist, she was naked.

'Debbie, Jude's missing! She's not here, is she?'

'Good heavens, no.'

'I think she's in serious danger!'

'What the hell's going on here?' Alan Burnethorpe looked grudgingly out to an embarrassed Ted Crisp, still poised in the doorway. 'You'd better come in. We don't want all Fedborough hearing about this.'

As the door closed behind him, the landlord of the Crown and Anchor stood awkwardly in the hall, looking at anything other than Debbie Carlton's small pointed breasts.

'Now can we have some explanations?' asked Alan Burnethorpe wearily. 'Your friend isn't here. Nor's Joke. What is it you want?'

Carole was nonplussed. She had steamed up to 47 Pelling Street, convinced that she was going to find Jude there. Now she had to find some explanation for her arrival that didn't accuse her unwilling host of abduction and worse crimes.

'It's to do with the time Virginia Hargreaves disappeared . . .' she improvized desperately. 'The time she was murdered.'

'In that case, I don't want to hear about it. You have pushed your way into my house and—'

'No, Alan. I want to hear about it.' Debbie Carlton, completely unashamed – or perhaps unaware – of her nakedness, was moving slowly down the stairs. 'What is this?'

Carole's mind was moving fast. Having rejected one idea, she had stumbled on to something potentially even more promising. She pieced her thoughts together. 'The week before Virginia Hargreaves died, she was ill, confined to bed. Joke, as her housekeeper, had to look after her. I wanted to ask Joke the exact nature of her employer's illness.'

'I can tell you,' said Alan Burnethorpe curtly. 'If it means you leave my house quicker, I will tell you.'

'How do you know?'

'Let's say I was . . . in touch with Virginia Hargreaves at the time. She was suffering from food poisoning. Salmonella.'

'From something she had eaten?'

'Yes.'

'Something cooked by Joke?'

'Probably.'

As Alan Burnethorpe spoke, Carole looked at Debbie Carlton. Her face was almost as pale as her blonde hair. What had just been said contained some private pertinence for her.

'One more question,' said Carole. 'Alan, are you related to the Trollope family?'

'The butchers?'

He looked at her in bewilderment, then turned towards Debbie as she said, 'He's not, but I am. My mother was Len Trollope's daughter.'

Chapter Forty-One

Billie Franks had a boning knife in her hand. Black-handled, long, with a tapering blade, unevenly scooped-out, as though it had been honed many times on a whetstone.

Jude had been allowed back from her prison into the largest room of the houseboat. Her captor stood between her and the exit to the towpath. Behind her were large windows, which perhaps she'd have more chance of smashing through than the portholes. But they were on the side of the boat that opened on to the Fether, and escape by that route might only hasten the end that was being lined up for her.

Billie Franks stood between her and the towpath. Jude knew she could try rushing the older woman, but Billie had said she'd use the knife and Jude had no reason to disbelieve her. Better to play for time, and try the old trick of engaging her enemy in conversation.

'Why did you kill Virginia Hargreaves?' she asked.

'She was going to do our business down, ruin our reputation in Fedborough.'

'How?'

'That Friday afternoon she came in the shop and complained. Said she'd been ill, been poisoned, got salmonella from something she'd bought from Franks's grocery. I wasn't having that. Talk like that could ruin a business in a place like Fedborough. We had our reputation to consider.'

'What had she eaten? What had made her ill?'

'An egg sandwich.'

Of all the motives for murder acted on by real-life killers or invented by crime writers, an egg sandwich did seem one of the most unlikely. Even at that moment Jude could see how ridiculous the idea was.

But it wasn't funny. The steely determination in Billie Franks's eyes defused any potential humour from the situation.

'Stanley always made the egg sandwiches,' she went on. 'He always made all the sandwiches. There was nothing in that shop that he hadn't selected or prepared personally. Stanley had very high standards. It would have destroyed him to know someone claimed to have contracted salmonella from something in our shop.'

'Are you saying he didn't know?'

There was a momentary flicker of uncertainty in Billie Franks's eyes before she replied. 'No. Stanley wasn't in the shop when Lady Muck came in. It was just me and her.'

The line sounded like one from an old Western. Again, Jude could not be unaware of the incongruity of her situation. She, a woman in her fifties, was in a stand-off with an old woman the wrong side of seventy, a slightly drab, mumsy figure whose grey hair was petrified into an unchanging perm. It was ridiculous.

And yet the knife in the old woman's hand was very real. She definitely claimed to have killed one person, and had implied she'd killed a second. The danger was not fanciful.

Jude looked for madness in Billie Franks's blue eyes. Madness would somehow be reassuring, give a reason for the farcical situation. But Jude couldn't see it. Just a cold, determined rationality, which was much more chilling.

'So what happened, Billie?'

'I asked Lady Hargreaves to come with me to the office at the back of the shop, so's I could take down details of her complaint. She didn't know where the office was, and I took her through to Jimmy Lister's smokehouse. He'd let us have a key to the place. He didn't do much smoking there any more, and both shops used it for storage.' Billie Franks looked down with fascination at the knife in her hand. 'Inside the smokehouse I stabbed her.'

'With that?'

The old woman nodded, then repeated, like a mantra, 'Stanley had very high standards. He'd built up a reputation in Fedborough. Through all his working life. I couldn't allow that to be put at risk.'

'So then what?'

'I knew I had to dispose of the body. There was a lot of blood, but I cleared it up, stripped off her clothes and laid the body in the bath Jimmy used for draining and soaking meat before smoking it. And that's what gave me the idea . . .'

Appalled, Jude whispered, 'You mean, you smoked the body?'

'I knew it would be easier to deal with if it was dry. I jointed it with this knife. Very easy. Very quick, if you know what you're doing. My dad had taught me well.' Jude's terrified eyes homed in on the blade. 'I should have left it to soak longer, but I didn't have time. Most of the blood had been drained out. I hung the meat on the hooks inside the kiln and lit some oak dust under it.'

Jude was beginning to wonder about her diagnosis that the woman wasn't mad. And yet, in spite of the horrors she was describing, Billie Franks's voice remained level and unemotional.

'But weren't you afraid James Lister would notice the smokehouse was being used?'

'No. Stanley and I did occasionally have stuff to smoke, cheeses and what-have-you. Anyway, it was Friday night. Jimmy would be on duty at Fiona's precious dinner party. And I'd put the fire out before he went into the shop on the Saturday.'

'So what did you do with . . .' Jude couldn't match Billie's casual use of the word 'meat'. ' . . . the remains?'

'I packed the limbs and her clothes into empty meat boxes, and the torso into a bigger one, and hid the lot at the back of the smokehouse. That night, the Saturday, after midnight, I took them down to the Fether.'

'How? How did you carry them?'

'We'd still kept the big old pram Debbie'd had when she was a baby. I pushed them down to the river in that.'

Here was another image so incongruous as to be laughable in any other circumstances. A neat, ordinary old grocer's wife going through the streets of a nice middle-class West Sussex town, pushing a pram full of cured human body parts. Jude hoped she would survive to laugh with Carole at the picture.

But at that moment her chances didn't look very good.

'You did the limbs first, presumably?'

'Yes. They slipped into the water, no problem. The tide was going out. They'd be lost quickly somewhere in the Channel.'

'But the torso . . . ? Why didn't you get rid of the torso?'

Billie Franks let out a little, rueful laugh. 'Because of

the tide. Because of the bloody tide. The box with the torso in it was the heaviest, took a long time for me to get it on to the pram. By the time I got down to the river, the tide had gone too low. I couldn't risk the box getting stuck in the mud, so I hid it in one of the sheds in Bracken's Boatyard.'

'How did it get from there to the cellar of Pelling House?'

'I've no idea. All I know is, next night, the Sunday, I go down the boatyard to finish the job, and the box isn't there. I'm in a dreadful panic for days, weeks, months. I keep expecting the police to arrive at the house or the shop. But gradually time goes by and I start thinking . . . it's all right. There is a God. There's someone out there looking after us.'

Given the circumstances, this counted as one of the most bizarre expressions of belief Jude had ever heard.

'And then Stanley's health started to deteriorate,' Billie went on. 'Mental health, that is, not physical. He's still as strong as an ox. And I'm kept busy looking after him, and arranging care for him, and selling the house . . . and I really do, genuinely, forget about it.'

'About the torso? About Virginia Hargreaves's murder.'

'Yes.' The head was shaken very firmly, but still not a hair of the perm shifted. 'It never happened,' she said, as if that were the end of the story.

'But then the torso was discovered . . .'

Billie Franks sighed at the remembered inconvenience.

'And you realized the danger, and tried to divert suspicion towards Francis?'

'Yes. My anonymous letter.' The old woman smiled at the recollection. 'I thought it might work. And, even if it didn't, I got great pleasure from giving that slimy creep a few nasty moments. After the way he treated Debbie—'

'But once the police had identified the remains and started investigating Roddy, you knew your secret was at risk again. If his alibi could be proved, then suspicions were going to move elsewhere, weren't they?'

'Hm?' Billie Franks sounded distracted now.

'So you killed him too, did you?'

'What?' It was an effort to pull herself back from the depths of thought. 'Yes. Yes, of course. Roddy had to die too. Anything to save Stanley . . .' She corrected herself: 'Stanley's reputation.'

She looked down at the boning knife, as if surprised to find it still in her hand. 'And now, of course, it's you . . . Jude.' She savoured the unfamiliar name. 'You're the current threat to Stanley's reputation.'

'But I'm not going to tell anyone,' said Jude cosily. 'I don't believe in justice as an abstract concept.' Which was absolutely true. 'From all accounts, Virginia Hargreaves wasn't a very admirable person. Her death doesn't seem to have left the world much impoverished. Why don't we agree to forget about the whole thing?'

There was a silence. Billie Franks appeared to be considering the proposition.

Jude pushed home her advantage. 'Anyway, even if you managed to keep me quiet, I've still got friends who'll be trying to find me. I've still . . .' The words tapered away, as Jude realized what a foolish change of direction she'd taken.

The old woman shook her head, almost with regret. 'That's the argument *for* killing you, I'm afraid, Jude. You and everyone else who threatens Stanley's reputation. However many there are.'

She'd moved suddenly forward and seized Jude's wrist. The grip was surprisingly strong, considering her age. Jude tried to break free, but stopped when she felt the prick of the knifepoint in the softness under her jaw.

Billie Franks leaned against the glazed doors, which gave instantly. They'd been unlocked all the time, probably opened throughout the day to let in the July sunlight.

But now all outside was blackness. Jude could hear, rather than see, the rushing flow of the Fether, very close now.

'I'm sorry.' Billie sounded genuinely apologetic. 'I can't take the risk of you staying alive.'

She nudged Jude forward on to the sill of the doors. Encountering resistance, the point of the knife was pushed more firmly into the soft neck.

'I can swim,' said Jude desperately.

'Not in the Fether. The tide's too strong. No one survives in the Fether – particularly if they're unconscious when they go in.'

The moment Jude felt her wrist released, she saw Billie Franks's arm rising up with a bottle in its grasp. It reached the top of its arc, and she waited for the inevitable concussion.

'Mum.'

The monosyllable was spoken softly, from the doorway to the towpath. Billie Franks froze at the sound of her daughter's voice.

'Mum, put that down. And the knife. That's not going to help Dad.'

There was a stillness on the houseboat. The rushing chatter of the Fether sounded louder than ever.

Then Jude felt the easing of pressure from the knifepoint under her chin. The woman, suddenly older and more bent, turned towards her daughter. The bottle and the boning knife dropped, making loud clatters on the polished wood of the floor.

In the doorway, framing Debbie Carlton, Jude could see Carole and Ted Crisp.

Never had there been a more welcome sight.

Chapter Forty-Two

The Elms which had given the home its name were long gone. They had succumbed to Dutch Elm Disease in the seventies, and the house still looked a little exposed without them. Set back from the road that ran along the sea front in Rustington, it had been built as a substantial Victorian family home, with space for a small army of servants. Generations of children in changing fashions of swimwear, with their impedimenta of buckets, rakes and spades, must have scampered down to the garden gate, carefully crossed the road and then luxuriated in the freedom of the pebbles and the sand and the sea.

But it was a long time since any of The Elms' current inmates had been on the beach. A long time since any of them had been beyond the garden walls, or since most of them had been out through the front door.

The Sunday morning was fine, promising the continuity of summer, and there was a lot of traffic. Everyone in England seems to have an elderly relative in Angmering, East Preston or Rustington-on-Sea, and summer Sundays witness an invasion of the area by the dutiful, the concerned, the well-wishing and the will-hungry.

Carole and Jude had followed Debbie Carlton's instructions exactly. The night before, drama had soon settled into normality. To Debbie's relief, nobody had suggested calling the police for her mother. They had all realized the irrelevance in that situation of official enquiries. The problems that had been revealed required emotional, not judicial, resolution.

Soon after Jude's rescue, she and Carole had been in Ted Crisp's car on the way back to Fethering. He had insisted on driving them straight to the Crown and Anchor, where they'd indulged in a little illegal – but extremely necessary – late-night drinking.

And Debbie had stayed on the houseboat and talked to her mother. She promised to ring them at ten the next morning. Which she duly had done, asking if they could meet her at The Elms. They agreed on eleven-thirty, because Carole and Jude had to go via Fedborough. There was one more person they needed to talk to.

The interior of the home was as clean and cheerful as such a place could be, but the many vases of flowers on display could not quite smother the pervasive smells of disinfectant, urine and age. The neatly uniformed staff members were all extremely friendly and recognized Debbie as a regular visitor.

She met them at the main door, still wearing the T-shirt and sweatpants she had thrown on to cover her nakedness at Alan Burnethorpe's the night before. Her near-white hair looked yellowed, too flat, in need of shampoo, and there were arcs like bruises underneath her eyes. She hadn't slept at all since she last saw them.

She led Carole and Jude through into a large sitting room, off which a conservatory reached into the extensive, well-kept garden.

There were not many people in there. An old man, somehow contriving to look military in a blue-and-red-striped towelling dressing gown, sat up straight on the edge of an armchair, a Sunday newspaper held resolutely in front of him. But, Jude noted, the newspaper was three weeks old and his eyes did not seem to be moving across the page.

On a sofa an old woman was stacked awkwardly, like a broken deckchair. Her head lolled back, mouth open in a sleep that mimicked death and would soon be replaced by the real thing.

In a corner of the room, unwatched, a muted television flickered.

Debbie found three high-backed chairs and arranged them in a semi-circle, facing the conservatory. She did not need to point for Carole and Jude to see why she had brought them there.

Billie Franks was unaware of their arrival. She sat upright on the side of a lounger, looking with pride and infinite fondness at the man beside her.

Stanley Franks was, as she had said, 'still as strong as an ox'. Though his hair was white, under his blue checked shirt his shoulders swelled menacingly.

But there was no menace in his face. Only a vagueness, tinged by anxiety, as he looked down at his task.

On the table in front of him was a selection of children's building blocks. Plastic, in primary colours, not the kind that can be stuck together. And these the old man kept piling on top of each other, trying to make some structure of perfect symmetry.

But he was never satisfied. However carefully he placed the bricks, whatever adjustments he made to their alignment, the result always fell short of his expectations. With a shrug of annoyance, he would knock his edifice down. If some of the bricks fell on the floor, with practised ease Billie would put them back on the table. Then

Stanley Franks would start once again on his doomed building project.

'He does that all day,' said Debbie softly. 'Except when he dozes off to sleep. Then as soon as he wakes up, he starts again. Sometimes it makes him very angry that he can't get it right. The staff say he has become violent. They tried taking the bricks away, to see if that'd make things better, but he nearly went berserk then, so they gave them back to him. Still, he's usually calm when Mum's here.'

As Carole and Jude watched the scene, the same image was in both their minds. It was of a younger Stanley Franks, proud in the hygiene and efficiency of his shop, obsessively piling and repiling his grocery stock on the shelves.

Carole decided it was time for some serious talking. Though Jude had subsequently pooh-poohed the idea, she had been in real danger the night before. What had happened could not be left unexplained – or even unpunished.

'You said you talked to your mother last night, Debbie . . .'

'Yes. And how. All night. A lot was said that probably should have been said a long time ago.'

'She said a lot to me too,' murmured Jude.

'And did you believe all of it?'

'No.'

'What?' asked Carole sharply. 'I thought we'd got the explanation to everything – how Virginia Hargreaves died, how the body was disposed of . . .' She saw with some annoyance that Debbie and Jude were both shaking their heads. 'Well, then what did happen? Is there information you've been keeping from me?' she asked, in a moment of instinctive paranoia.

'No,' Jude reassured her. 'I got a feeling for the truth last night, and I'm sure it'll be confirmed by things Billie said to Debbie.'

'Yes,' Debbie agreed.

Again Carole's nose felt out of joint. Jude and Debbie hadn't been having secret conversations behind her back. They understood each other without speaking. Telepathy really did make her feel excluded.

'Your father killed Virginia Hargreaves, didn't he?' asked Jude softly.

'Yes.' Debbie Carlton's chin sank wearily on to her chest as the tension in her relaxed. 'I didn't know till last night. I didn't know any of it. First suspicion I had was when you mentioned salmonella, Carole, at Alan's, because I knew Virginia Hargreaves did most of her shopping at our shop. Suddenly I got an inkling of what might have happened. But then last night Mum told me everything.'

'So the story she gave me was all true,' asked Jude, 'if we recast your father in the role of murderer?'

'Well, they were both involved. He in the murder . . .'

'And she in the disposal of the body.'

'Yes. Dad had been getting very absent-minded the last year they were in the shop. We didn't realize, but it was the start of this . . .' She gestured towards the conservatory, which seemed to sum up all the pain of her father's illness. 'He was starting to make mistakes in the buying from his suppliers, getting details of orders wrong, and cleanliness standards were slipping because he'd forget basic hygienie measures.

'Mum tried to take some of the burden off him by

doing more in the shop, but he hated that. He'd always been a control-freak about the business, an obsessive if you like . . .' Debbie's eyes were unwillingly drawn back to the conservatory. 'What we're seeing now is only a grotesque parody of the way he always was.

'And if something did go wrong in the shop, Dad would get furiously angry. These terrible, blinding rages he had. So I think when Virginia Hargreaves came in and complained—'

'In a manner,' Carole contributed, 'that, from what one's heard about her character, wouldn't have been that sensitive.'

'No. Exactly. So he got her into the smokehouse on some pretext and . . .'

Jude nodded. 'Story as we know it, with change of murderer.'

'So did your mother come in straightaway and find Virginia dead?'

'No. That happened the next morning.'

'And then what?'

'It was Dad who did the first things to the body.' Debbie was almost shuddering. Though she tried to sound very matter-of-fact, what she was talking about was information she had only very recently received and had not had time to process emotionally. 'He stripped off the clothes, put the corpse in the bath and partially drained out the blood. And he . . .' She shook her head briskly to dispel a feeling of nausea. 'He put the body in the kiln.'

'The whole body?'

'Yes. Hung up on hooks or . . .' Another shake of the head. 'God knows how. But he lit the oak dust under it and . . . I can't imagine what was going through his mind. As I said, he was behaving very oddly round that time.'

'So the next morning . . .?'

'Mum arrived very early. Always did on a Saturday, because there were deliveries from the farms of eggs and dairy products. Anyway, first thing she sees is that the smokehouse is being used, and she thinks that's rather odd, and she goes in and discovers . . .' Debbie couldn't find the words.

'It must have been ghastly for her.'

'Yes. A half-kippered minor aristocrat,' said Debbie, in an unsuccessful attempt at humour. 'So she confronts Dad, and he says he doesn't know what she's talking about. Maybe he *doesn't* know what she's talking about. Maybe he's blanked out the whole thing. His mind was getting very odd.' Debbie Carlton briskly rubbed her hands together, as though the time had come to move on. 'So it was left to Mum to dispose of the body.'

'Which she took out of the kiln and then joined, to make the job easier.'

'Exactly.' Debbie sighed. She looked as if she was convalescing after a long illness. Turning her head once again towards the oblivious couple in the conservatory, she said in a drained voice, 'That's the story. My father's a murderer, though whether he's in a condition to be brought to trial is, I would have thought, unlikely. But my mother, on the other hand . . . Well, she's undoubtedly an accessory after the fact or whatever they call it, so I suppose if anyone thought the police should be informed . . .'

She looked pleadingly at Carole and Jude. Jude automatically deferred to her friend for the verdict.

'I don't think the police need be involved,' said Carole. 'If they find things out by their own efforts . . . well, that's fair enough. Nothing we can do about that. But I don't think we need to give them any pointers.'

'No,' Jude agreed enthusiastically. 'If they're going along with the assumption that Roddy killed his wife and then, when investigations got too close, killed himself . . . and if they're happy with that solution . . . then why upset their apple-cart?'

'Of course,' said Carole in her sensible voice, 'we don't actually know anything about what the police think. They may know the whole story and, even now, be building up their dossier incriminating your father.'

'Well, if they are . . .' A great load seemed to have been lifted from Debbie Carlton's shoulders. '. . . we'll have to face that problem when we get to it.'

'There is one detail that ought to be explained, though,' said Carole. 'Last night your mother told Jude that she had killed Roddy Hargreaves.'

The colour once again drained from the girl's cheeks.

'But it's all right,' Jude came in with compassionate speed. 'She was just saying it to frighten me.'

'Are you sure?' asked Debbie, who looked suddenly as if she couldn't take any more stress.

'We're absolutely sure,' Carole replied. 'We asked to meet you later this morning, because on our way here we paid another visit to Alan Burnethorpe.'

Debbie looked bemused.

'He was the last person to see Roddy alive. Harry Roxby told me,' said Jude. 'He saw the two of them together that Saturday evening. On the towpath opposite Bracken's Boatyard.'

'So did the boy see what happened to Roddy?'

'No, but Alan did.'

Carole took up the narrative. 'Needless to say, he

didn't want to tell us when we went round this morning. But when I threatened to tell the police about his affair with Virginia Hargreaves, he saw his marriage – amongst many other things – at risk, and so he owned up.'

'Are you saying Alan owned up to killing Roddy Hargreaves?' asked Debbie in disbelief.

'No. They'd met that evening in one of the pubs. Roddy, according to Alan, had been in maudlin mood and insisted they go down to the Fether to look at what he called "the collapse of their dreams".'

'The Bracken's Boatyard site?'

'Exactly. So Alan agreed. He said that Roddy was hardly coherent down by the river, drunk and despairing. They walked along the towpath to the end of the houseboats, then turned round and walked back. Alan said he'd got to get back into town, but Roddy wanted to stay for what he called "one last look at the boatyard where it all went wrong".'

'So he did commit suicide?'

Carole twisted her lips wryly. 'I don't think we'll ever know. Alan said he looked back from Fedborough Bridge and saw Roddy Hargreaves swaying on the towpath. Then Roddy seemed to lose his footing.'

'There are some old steps down there,' Jude contributed. 'It seems he probably fell down those.'

'Deliberately?'

'I don't think we'll ever know the answer to that, Debbie.' Carole shook her head. 'He may have slipped, he may have deliberately walked into the river. The only thing we know for certain is that nobody pushed him.'

There was a silence while Debbie Carlton took this in, another addition to the overload of disturbing information she'd received in the previous twenty-four hours. Then she asked, 'Why didn't Alan tell the police about what happened to Roddy?'

Carole shrugged. 'Come on, can you see him doing that? Stirring up more investigation, which might easily lead to his being questioned about other aspects of the case. I wouldn't put Alan Burnethorpe down as one of the most public-spirited of men. In fact, "totally selfish" is the description I'd go for. He'd do anything to keep his nicely organized little world intact.'

She sighed. 'So I'm afraid we'll never know the precise reason for Roddy Hargreaves's death. Like a lot of his life, its details will remain for ever blurred.'

They were silent, all thinking of the dead man, of the confusions in his sad existence. A wife who didn't love him, a disastrous aptitude for losing money, Catholic guilt, and the belief that the solution to all his problems lay in a bottle. A total failure. And yet none of them could think of him without affection.

Carole ended the silence by turning sternly to Debbie Carlton. 'We've established that your mother didn't murder Roddy Hargreaves . . . but the fact remains that she threatened Jude last night with—'

'It doesn't matter, Carole.' The bird's nest of blonde hair shook, as if it could erase the memory completely.

'It certainly does, Jude. You were in very real danger. Did you talk to your mother about that, Debbie?'

The girl nodded. 'She was just protecting Dad. It was totally out of character. Mum hasn't got a violent nature. I swear she'd never do anything like that again.'

'Unless there was another threat to your father's reputation.'

'I don't know.' Debbie faltered. 'I suppose . . .'

Jude tried to lighten the atmosphere. 'So all we have

to do is to see that we never again let Billie think we are putting your dad's reputation under threat.'

'Yes.' Debbie Carlton looked pleadingly towards Carole, but an implacable sternness remained in the older woman's eyes.

As ever, it was Jude who soothed away the impasse. 'Carole, what alternatives do we have? Either we take Debbie's word for her mother's future good behaviour or . . . what? We report to the police what happened last night, put an old woman under the pressures of court proceedings, possibly remove the only stable element in her husband's life . . . We can't do it.'

There was still a long moment before Carole was convinced, and during that time her eyes held Debbie's. Finally, the contact was released.

Brushing her hands against her thighs in a businesslike manner, Carole announced, 'What Jude and I were planning to do was to go and have lunch at a rather nice pub we know. The Crown and Anchor at Fethering. Would you like to join us, Debbie? It's my treat.'

'Well . . .' The girl smiled with relief. 'That sounds a very good idea indeed. I'd better just . . .'

They watched her go into the conservatory. The sun had shifted since their arrival and Stanley Franks's white hair now looked like a halo in the brightness. His daughter leaned down to kiss the old man's cheek. He showed no signs of having noticed the gesture.

'I've got to be off now, Mum. Call you later.'

'Yes, of course.' Billie Franks looked at her husband with pride. 'He's a lot better today, you know. I think he's turned the corner.'

The old woman was unaware that Carole and Jude had even been at The Elms that morning.

*

The Crown and Anchor was busy. Many of the dutiful, the concerned, the well-wishing and the will-hungry coming down to visit elderly relatives had chosen to reward themselves with a nice pub lunch. Ted Crisp and his staff were kept constantly occupied behind the bar.

It was not often Carole had seen him at work when the pub was full and she was impressed by his efficiency. The customers responded to his gruff humour and a lot of laughter rang around the bar. She felt glad that a small bridge between the two of them had been mended.

All three women had large glasses of Chilean Chardonnay and the comfortable feeling of having ordered roast beef and Yorkshire pudding, with all the trimmings.

'There is one thing I owe you an explanation about,' announced Debbie Carlton, after a silence.

She looked ill at ease. 'Never apologize, never explain,' said Jude lightly.

But Debbie didn't take the proffered chance to get off the hook. 'No, I need to, for me if not for you. I want to explain about me and Alan Burnethorpe.'

Jude looked interested. Carole looked embarrassed.

'Well, you both saw me with him, Jude at my place and then you, Carole, at—'

'Yes, yes.' Carole cleared her throat. 'There's no need anyone should know you've been, as it were . . . I mean . . .'

Debbie chuckled at her discomfiture. 'We hadn't actually been making love when you arrived, you know.'

'Oh.'

'That wasn't why I was naked. I was modelling for Alan. He was drawing me.'

'But,' said Jude slyly, 'I gather he makes a habit of drawing his mistresses.'

'Yes.' Debbie nodded, taking a deep breath before continuing. 'I'm not pretending that we haven't been having an affair – though it's not something I'm particularly proud of. It's just . . . after Francis walked out . . . I really lost all confidence in myself as a woman . . . I know what Alan's like. From when I was a child, I've always known his reputation round Fedborough. But . . . he was nice to me. He treated me . . . in a way that made me feel like a woman again. My self-esteem was so low. Does that make any sense to you?'

Jude nodded, and Carole, with surprising gentleness, said, 'Yes. It does.' Over Debbie's shoulder, she could see Ted Crisp joking with someone at the bar. He caught her eye and gave her a cheery wave. Carole felt blessed in his friendship.

'Anyway,' Debbie Carlton continued resolutely, 'that's over. Me and Alan. All that's happened this weekend . . . the things Mum said, and what you just told me about Alan witnessing Roddy's death and keeping quiet about it . . . and . . . well, everything. It's made me realize that that relationship is selfish and going nowhere . . . and actually rather demeaning to me. So may I congratulate you on being the first to know that the affair is over.'

'What about Alan himself?' asked Jude.

'Don't worry. He'll be the second to know. Well, actually, given the fact that there are two of you, he'll be the third to know. But don't lose any sleep over how he takes the news.'

'I wasn't going to,' said Carole.

'No. He'll move on to someone else.' For a moment, Debbie Carlton looked slightly wistful. 'He's just one of those men, who you know's a bastard, but . . . he is quite good to be with. Do you know the kind I mean?'

'Yes,' said Jude ruefully.

'No,' said Carole.

'Anyway, I'm going to live my own life from now on.' Debbie bunched her fists to accentuate this positive approach. 'The reaction to my paintings in the Art Crawl has really given me a lift. I have got artistic talent. I can make a living from my pictures. And that's what I'm going to concentrate on for the next bit of my life.'

'And men . . . ?' Jude let the word dangle.

Debbie looked thoughtful. 'I'm not going to go out looking for them. I suppose, if one comes along . . .' She grinned. 'He'll have to be a bloody good one, though.'

Carole made a decision. 'You say the reaction to your paintings in the Art Crawl has been good. They haven't all gone, have they?'

'No. Going fine, but still plenty left.'

'Excellent. I'll come along and choose one tomorrow.'

'Thanks. Don't feel you have to.'

'I want to,' said Carole firmly. 'And you haven't given up the interior design business, have you?'

'Good heavens, no.'

'That is good news.' Carole Seddon rubbed her hands together with confidence and satisfaction. 'Because I definitely want you to do my sitting room.'

Chapter Forty-Three

The Fedborough Festival finished, and Fedborough life continued much as before. Memories closed over Roddy Hargreaves just as effectively as the waters of the Fether had done. It was perhaps unfair that he'd gone down in the communal recollection as a murderer and dismemberer, but then Roddy had never cared that much about Fedborough opinion, and wherever he was now he could at least no longer be harmed by the town's gossip.

The memory of Virginia Hargreaves, by contrast, lived on, and her myth grew. The grisly circumstances of her death added to the attractions of the story. So, of course, did the fact that she had a title. 'The torso in the town' became a regular feature of Fedborough's Town Walks.

But after the end of that September, no more Town Walks were conducted by James Lister. He had the temerity to die of a stroke without asking his wife's permission and, with typical lack of consideration, contrived to do it in the middle of one of her Friday-night dinner parties.

All Fedborough turned out for his funeral at All Souls. The service was conducted, with his customary tentative tremulousness, by the Rev Philip Trigwell. In his address he said that everyone would remember James Lister as a good man, though not without faults. James would be remembered best as an honest local tradesman, though some people would remember him best as a generous host and pillar of Fedborough's social life. He was sure of a place in heaven, though of course some people in different denominations saw heaven in a different way from the Church of England, and there was nothing wrong with that.

For the message on James's gravestone, Fiona had chosen, with her customary unawareness of irony, the words, 'At peace at last'. She, being made of sterner – not to mention, in her view, socially superior – stuff than her husband, continued to live for many, many years, spreading her bile even-handedly amongst all the inhabitants of Fedborough.

Andrew Wragg stayed with Terry Harper. The younger man still threw tantrums, but, as middle-age coarsened his beautiful body, his threats to leave grew decreasingly credible. He started to drink a lot, with predictable effects on his waistline. His temper and his art grew worse, and Terry Harper continued to adore him.

The Burnethorpes stayed married, in apparent harmony. Nobody who knew Alan well could imagine that Joke was his only physical outlet, but he restricted his extra-mural activities to the discreet anonymity of London. He went on producing sensitive architectural conversions and accurate impersonal drawings of female nudes.

Donald Durrington continued to be respected as chief partner in the local medical practice. His wife continued to drown the misery of her marriage in drink.

And Francis and Jonelle Carlton . . . Well, nobody really cared what happened to them. They soon moved permanently to Florida, and that was miles away from Fedborough.

The town was so self-involved, you see, that people who left it virtually dropped off the map. That's what happened to the Roxbys. After a Fedborough winter, Grant decided that the family was missing the varied stimuli of London. The children needed access to theatres, cinemas and cultured people. Kim, as ever, agreed with him, so Pelling House and its history were sold yet again.

The Roxbys' girls were quite happy to return to London. They were getting to the age when ponies were becoming less interesting and clubs featured increasingly in their conversation. The only family member who objected to the move was Harry. Typical of his bloody father, he thought, to uproot him from all his Fedborough friends and imprison him in some concrete wilderness. And so Harry Roxby's adolescence continued.

Debbie Carlton's career as a painter flourished, so much so that after a few years she was able to give up her interior design work. When Stanley Franks finally died, Debbie moved her mother out of the houseboat and into the flat in Harbidge Street. She herself moved to London, which offered more opportunities for her as an artist, but she was down in Fedborough most weekends.

And Billie Franks continued as she always had. She knew everyone in Fedborough and everyone in Fedborough knew her. But nobody in Fedborough knew everything about her.

After their brief intense involvement in the affairs of the town, Carole and Jude didn't go back to Fedborough much. They lived eight miles downriver in Fethering, you see, and that was a world away.